"I didn't kill Arm...

Michelle spoke the denial with such heartfelt intensity that for an instant Philip's doubts fled. "Even if I do believe you, I've still got to run this investigation the best way I know how. You know how it works."

Her eyes hardened. "But your small, dirty mind has conjured up all sorts of juicy scenarios that have warped your objectivity."

Philip's temper spiked anew. "If we're going to work together and figure out who killed Armon, that giant-sized chip on your shoulder has got to go."

"Go to hell, Betancourt."

Surprising himself, he reached out and wiped a tear from her cheek with his thumb. "You're real tough, aren't you?"

The way she was staring at him wreaked havoc on his willpower. She looked vulnerable and tough at once, standing there with tears on her cheeks and hurt in her eyes.

Oh, how he wanted to kiss her. Wanted to devour the mouth that had lied so easily to him…

"Wow! Mega-talented Linda Castillo delivers a powerhouse punch in *Remember the Night*, a steamy tale of passion and intrigue in the Big Easy."
—bestselling author Merline Lovelace

Dear Reader,

Once again Intimate Moments is offering you six exciting and romantic reading choices, starting with *Rogue's Reform* by perennial reader favorite Marilyn Pappano. This latest title in her popular HEARTBREAK CANYON miniseries features a hero who'd spent his life courting trouble—until he found himself courting the lovely woman carrying his child after one night of unforgettable passion.

Award-winner Kathleen Creighton goes back INTO THE HEARTLAND with *The Cowboy's Hidden Agenda,* a compelling tale of secret identity and kidnapping— and an irresistible hero by the name of Johnny Bronco. Carla Cassidy's *In a Heartbeat* will have you smiling through tears. In other words, it provides a perfect emotional experience. In *Anything for Her Marriage,* Karen Templeton proves why readers look forward to her books, telling a tale of a pregnant bride, a marriage of convenience and love that knows no limits. With *Every Little Thing* Linda Winstead Jones makes a return to the line, offering a romantic and suspenseful pairing of opposites. Finally, welcome Linda Castillo, who debuts with *Remember the Night*. You'll certainly remember her and be looking forward to her return.

Enjoy—and come back next month for still more of the best and most exciting romantic reading around, available every month only in Silhouette Intimate Moments.

Yours,

Leslie J. Wainger
Executive Senior Editor

Please address questions and book requests to:
Silhouette Reader Service
U.S.: 3010 Walden Ave., P.O. Box 1325, Buffalo, NY 14269
Canadian: P.O. Box 609, Fort Erie, Ont. L2A 5X3

REMEMBER
THE NIGHT
LINDA CASTILLO

Silhouette®
INTIMATE™ MOMENTS®
Published by Silhouette Books
America's Publisher of Contemporary Romance

This book wouldn't have been possible without the love, support
and knowledge of many people, most of whom aren't named. To
Mom and Dad, who taught me to dream big. To Debbie, Jack,
Kim and Mike, for opening their homes and their hearts. To
Mami and Papi and all their children—for welcoming me into
the family with open arms. To my intrepid critique siblings—
Cathy, Diane, Jennifer and Vickie—for picking me up when I
couldn't do it on my own. And for Ernest, for loving me—
and showing me what a hero really is.

 SILHOUETTE BOOKS

ISBN 0-373-27078-X

REMEMBER THE NIGHT

Copyright © 2000 by Linda Castillo

Visit Silhouette at www.eHarlequin.com

Printed in U.S.A.

LINDA CASTILLO

knew from a very early age that she wanted to be a writer. Her dream came true the day Silhouette called her and wanted to publish *Remember the Night*.

She loves the idea of two fallible people falling in love amid danger and against their better judgment—or so they think. She doesn't hesitate to put them through the emotional wringer. She enjoys watching them struggle through their problems, realize their weaknesses and strengths along the way and, ultimately, fall head over heels in love.

Linda spins her tales of love and intrigue from her home in Dallas, Texas, where she lives with her husband and three dogs. She'd love to hear from you at P.O. Box 670501, Dallas, Texas, 75367-0501.

IT'S OUR 20th ANNIVERSARY!
We'll be celebrating all year,
Continuing with these fabulous titles,
On sale in May 2000.

Romance

#1444 Mercenary's Woman
Diana Palmer

#1445 Too Hard To Handle
Rita Rainville

 #1446 A Royal Mission
Elizabeth August

#1447 Tall, Strong & Cool Under Fire
Marie Ferrarella

 #1448 Hannah Gets a Husband
Julianna Morris

#1449 Her Sister's Child
Lilian Darcy

Desire

 #1291 Dr. Irresistible
Elizabeth Bevarly

 #1292 Expecting His Child
Leanne Banks

#1293 In His Loving Arms
Cindy Gerard

#1294 Sheikh's Honor
Alexandra Sellers

#1295 The Baby Bonus
Metsy Hingle

#1296 Did You Say Married?!
Kathie DeNosky

Intimate Moments

 #1003 Rogue's Reform
Marilyn Pappano

 #1004 The Cowboy's Hidden Agenda
Kathleen Creighton

#1005 In a Heartbeat
Carla Cassidy

 #1006 Anything for Her Marriage
Karen Templeton

#1007 Every Little Thing
Linda Winstead Jones

 #1008 Remember the Night
Linda Castillo

Special Edition

 #1321 The Kincaid Bride
Jackie Merritt

 #1322 The Millionaire She Married
Christine Rimmer

#1323 Warrior's Embrace
Peggy Webb

 #1324 The Sheik's Arranged Marriage
Susan Mallery

#1325 Sullivan's Child
Gail Link

#1326 Wild Mustang
Jane Toombs

Chapter 1

Philip Betancourt parked his unmarked cruiser on the street and watched the swarm of blue uniforms converge on the old Victorian, wondering what he'd find inside besides a dead body. Not far from the French Quarter, the house stood among century-old live oaks, tumbling wrought-iron fences and vacant lots, in a neighborhood that had been on the decline since his academy days a decade ago.

He got out of the car and shivered as cold January rain crept down the collar of his trench coat. *Hell of a night for murder,* he thought, and started for the house.

There were enough flashing lights to land a 747 right there on the street. A patrolman stretched yellow crime-scene tape around the front porch. A paramedic unloaded a gurney from an ambulance parked curbside. Curiosity seekers crowded the sidewalk and spilled into the street.

Philip had seen a lot in the five years he'd worked homicide, but had yet to figure out why people found murder so damn interesting.

Flashing his badge at the patrolman, he ducked beneath the tape and ascended the steps to the porch. The house was divided into four apartments. Philip made a mental note to question the other tenants as soon as possible. He believed firmly in the forty-eight hour rule. If a homicide wasn't solved in those first crucial hours, the trail ran cold. Nothing bothered him more than the thought of someone getting away with murder. Except, perhaps, the thought of a murderer outwitting him.

On the porch, a uniformed cop took a statement from a black woman wearing a colorful sarong and headdress. Straight ahead, the front door stood open and a corpse lay in the foyer. The body was draped, but Philip could tell by the protruding wing tips the victim was male. A rather affluent male, judging by the label on the sole of the shoes. A crimson stain the size of a saucer stood out starkly on the light blue cover. Bending, Philip pulled the cloth aside and looked into the pale, staring eyes, wondering who had seen fit to put a bullet in the man's chest.

"About time you showed up, Betancourt."

Dropping the cover, Philip straightened and smiled at the short black man sporting a double-breasted suit and garish tie. Cory Sanderson had been his partner for the last year, and despite his outlandish fashion sense and gigolo grin, there wasn't a man on the force Philip trusted or respected more.

"Hell of a way to start the new year," Philip said, scanning the room. The apartment was meticulously clean and smelled faintly of coffee. A vase filled with grocery-store flowers sat in the center of a scarred coffee table. Opposite, a yellow-and-green-striped sofa with a homemade patch on the center cushion was piled high with pillows. He knew immediately the apartment belonged to a woman.

"What do we have?" he asked, as the initial jab of excitement scuttled through him. It was a sort of dark anticipation that had little to do with the actual loss of a human life—and everything to do with the challenge of solving the crime.

"Male Caucasian. Late fifties. Looks like he took a slug in the chest. We've got one witness. Female Caucasian. Mid-twenties. No sign of forced entry. No sign of a struggle. No visible marks on the woman."

"Whose apartment is this?" Philip asked.

"The female witness." Cory responded with the calm professionalism Philip admired despite the fact that his partner was still considered a rookie within the department. "Came in on a 911 call about an hour ago. Patrolman secured the scene. Medical examiner's on the way along with the lab techs and photographer."

Philip nodded, pleased by his partner's thoroughness.

"Neighbor claims to have seen a man dressed in black running down the alley," Cory said.

"Patrolman check it out?"

"Yeah. Nothing."

They were standing in a large living room with worn cypress floors and high ceilings spotted with rust stains. An old-fashioned bay window shrouded with lace faced the street. Farther back, Philip saw a kitchen adorned with antiquated cabinets, peeling linoleum and appliances from the fifties. Whoever lived here had somehow managed to transform shoddy into quaint.

He walked into the kitchen and looked out the rear window. A wooden staircase descended to a narrow courtyard where barren clay pots lined crumbling brick walls.

"How'd your date with Chrissy go?"

Philip winced at his partner's question, wondering if it was worth the trouble to make something up or just tell the plain ugly truth. Hell, it wasn't the first time a man had been left in the lurch by a woman. In his case, it probably wouldn't be the last.

"Let's just say we didn't hit it off." Since Philip's divorce a year ago, Cory had taken it upon himself to set him up with every available female south of Lake Pontchartrain.

Cory shot him a surprised look. "Don't tell me you blew it with Chrissy."

Trying to make small talk with a woman who spent her days selling herbs and little bottles of scented oil guaranteed to cure everything from irregularity to impotence had been no easy task. But, determined to succeed in the ever-baffling world of dating in the nineties, Philip had tried. He'd even been arrogant enough to believe he'd somehow managed to pull off mission impossible—until she'd excused herself to use the powder room and never returned. He couldn't remember ever feeling so foolish. He'd sat at the table in his dinner jacket and tie in one of Vieux Carré's best restaurants for nearly half an hour before realizing she wasn't coming back. The hell of it was he didn't even know why she'd left.

"Next time you get the urge to play matchmaker, my friend, remind me to schedule a root canal." At thirty-seven years of age, Philip was old enough to know when he was out of his element. He was probably one of the few men on earth who was more comfortable at a murder scene than at a table making small talk with a woman.

Cory grinned. "I thought you had this dating thing down."

"Yeah, I thought I had the marriage thing down, too." Philip hadn't intended to sound angry. He certainly hadn't intended to sound bitter. To his disgust, he accomplished both.

"You know what your problem is, Betancourt?"

"I have the feeling you're going to tell me."

"You don't know how to treat a woman."

A laugh squeezed from Philip's throat. "Good thing I have the veritable expert as a partner."

"I'm serious, my man. You're obsessed with the job.

You're about as fun as a rock. No wonder Whitney left you for that lawyer.''

The last thing Philip wanted to talk about was his ex-wife. Either of them. "Don't you have a murder to solve, Cory?''

"Last lady I fixed you up with told me all you talked about was the job, man.'' Cory rolled his eyes. "Number one rule—don't talk about dead folks over étouffée. Turns women off.''

"Yeah, Cory, all I ever think about is murder. Hell of a thing to do in our line of work.'' Not wanting to discuss the tattered remains of his personal life, Philip wandered into the hall. He'd sworn off women the day his divorce was final, and had yet to regret the decision.

At the end of the hall, he peered into the bedroom. His gaze skimmed over an old brass headboard and threadbare quilt. The sight of the woman standing at the window halted him dead in his tracks.

For a split second he stopped being a cop and simply admired the view from a purely male perspective. She wasn't beautiful in the classic sense. Sun-streaked brown hair that hadn't seen a decent cut in some time fell in unruly tendrils to her shoulders. Thick lashes fringed eyes dark against a pale complexion. She looked distinctly French with her imperfectly shaped mouth and exotic eyes.

Philip heard Cory behind him, but he didn't look away from the woman, wasn't sure if he could. "Who is she?''

"Michelle Pelletier. She's the one who called 911.''

Philip's eyes continued their perusal. A pair of denim shorts revealed runner's legs, straight and strong with just enough flesh to intrigue. Her thighs tapered to shapely calves and delicate ankles. The small red spot on her left knee could have been a rug burn. He made a mental note to have one of the lab techs get a photo of it later. In the back of his mind he wondered if she was a witness—or the killer.

Easing his gaze away from those long, distracting legs, he looked at Cory. "Do we have a name on the vic?"

"No positive ID yet, but the witness says his name is Armon Landsteiner," Cory said. "We're checking it out."

"The name sounds familiar."

"It should. If the body in the foyer belongs to the Landsteiner I'm thinking of, his son is the lawyer who got the Rosetti case thrown out last year."

Philip's stomach tightened at the mention of the Rosetti case. He'd spent eight arduous months working a protection money racket that had left one Algiers shopkeeper dead and two others so scared they wouldn't talk to police. He'd worked the case with a vengeance, going by the book down to the letter—until the day he'd followed Rosetti into that warehouse without a warrant. Philip had called it hot pursuit, but the judge had called the evidence inadmissible. Thanks to hot young defense attorney Baldwin Landsteiner, Philip hadn't gotten a conviction.

"If that were Baldwin Landsteiner lying there, I might just change my philosophy about there being justice in the world," Philip said.

"It gets worse. If that's *the* Armon Landsteiner, his wife, who died several years back, was the sister of Victor Desjardins."

"Damn, you're just a fountain of pleasant information tonight, Cory. You got any *bad* news?" Philip didn't like hearing the district attorney's name mentioned in the same breath as the word *homicide*.

"Desjardins is going to get his briefs in a wad over this one," Cory said.

"Yeah, then he's going to make our lives a living hell." Philip despised high profile cases. It wasn't so much the public scrutiny that bothered him—he was more than confident in his abilities as a homicide investigator—but the politics. He'd never been good at making people happy. In fact, he was pretty adept at keeping most people in a constant state of righteous indignation. The only good thing about that was they usually left him alone to do his job.

"Do we have a weapon?" he asked.

Cory flipped a page on his notepad. "Patrolman found a nine millimeter Beretta next to the body. It's been bagged and tagged."

Philip contemplated the woman and realized he'd been putting off asking about her. Something about her nagged at him, like the beginnings of a headache. She wasn't wearing shoes. Odd for January, he thought, and wondered if there'd been some hanky-panky going on before the murder. "Do we have any details on the woman?"

"Twenty-seven years old. Says she worked for Landsteiner as an intern at his law firm. She's a student at Tulane." Cory hit Philip with a lopsided grin. "At this point we're not sure how helpful she's going to be."

The woman turned from the window. From the hall, Philip made eye contact. Her gaze was level, wary and unmistakably intelligent. The word *lush* came to mind and lingered. At the same time something dark and hot and completely unexpected stirred low in his gut.

Shaken by his response, he broke eye contact and stepped back. "What do you mean?" he asked Cory.

"She says she doesn't remember the shooting."

That stopped him. Philip swung his gaze to his partner, not missing the flash of amusement behind the chocolate-brown eyes. "If I heard you right, that isn't even remotely funny."

Cory raised his hands in defense. "I haven't questioned her. Patrolman talked to her while his partner secured the scene. Just preliminary stuff."

Philip swore. The humor of the situation eluded him, especially knowing the D.A. might have a personal stake in the case. "Lapse of memory due to alcohol or drugs?"

"Doesn't appear that way. Patrolman said she was hysterical when they arrived."

"Pretty damn convenient," Philip muttered under his breath. The last thing they needed was a complication, especially a complication with legs that could stop traffic on a superhighway. "I'm going to go talk to her. Call in a female patrol, will you?"

"Sure thing." Cory started down the hall, then turned and grinned at Philip. "Remember your sensitivity training, Betancourt. I have a feeling you're going to need it on this one."

"Tell that to the corpse."

Philip entered the room to find the woman sitting on the bed with her face in her hands. Slender shoulders slumped forward as if the weight of the world rested on them. It could have been a posture of anguish or perhaps grief, but he refrained from making judgments based on body language alone. First impressions could be fatal if misunderstood.

The moment he stepped through the door, her head snapped up. Praline-brown eyes swept to his, and the world seemed to stop. She was the most striking woman he'd ever laid eyes on. She reminded him of a rough-cut diamond, unpolished and hopelessly flawed, but with a definite sparkle just beneath the surface.

An oversize Tulane sweatshirt fell over a pair of frayed denim shorts that reached modestly to midthigh. No makeup. No jewelry. Once again the shorts bothered him, not only because her legs were distracting, but because it was January. Philip wondered why she wasn't crying. Most women cried when they were faced with something as terrible as death. Despite his efforts not to allow it, his eyes traveled the length of her until he found himself staring at toenails painted an intriguing shade of burgundy.

"He's dead, isn't he?"

The deep, smoky drawl took him aback. The voice didn't

fit her, seeming too rich and much too provocative for the tousled waif sitting on the bed. It was a voice one might expect from R & B singers in shady Bourbon Street jazz clubs. The kind of women he'd spent his years in vice busting for improprieties.

"I'm afraid so," he said.

"Oh, God. I can't believe it."

Only when she spoke a second time did he notice the small gap between her front teeth. Another imperfection that only added to one of the most intriguing faces he'd ever seen.

"I'm Detective Betancourt. You're Michelle Pelletier?" Even though he used the proper French pronunciation, his voice sounded coarse and unrefined in comparison to hers.

"That's right."

He pulled the notepad from his jacket. "Can you tell me what happened, Miss Pelletier?"

Her shoulders tensed, a minute gesture that told him the question struck a nerve. "I remember dialing 911. Seeing...Armon lying on the floor. But everything else...I don't know." She looked at Philip through dark, cautious eyes. "Things are...foggy."

He stared back, trying to get a handle on her frame of mind. "Take your time."

"Armon didn't come over often. Never without calling first." A sad smile tugged at the corner of her mouth. "He was always such a gentleman."

Philip watched her carefully, concentrating on her body language as much as her words. She was trembling, he noticed, but that could come from any number of emotions, so once again he refrained from drawing conclusions.

"I don't remember opening the door. I can't even remember seeing his face. Everything...seems distorted. The memory, I mean. Just when an image seems close, it fades away.'' Her hands stilled. "My God, I can't remember. How can that be?"

"You're doing fine. Try to concentrate. Take a deep breath…." His voice trailed off when he spotted her right hand. It was clenched so tightly her knuckles were white. A drop of blood seeped from between her fingers. Moving forward, he reached for her hand, brought it to him palm up. Her fingers opened.

"What the…" A diamond cuff link glimmered in the light. She'd been holding it so tightly the post had cut her palm.

She blinked as if the sight of the cuff link stunned her. "I didn't realize… It…belongs to Armon."

Extracting a small evidence bag from his coat, Philip used it to scoop up the cuff link. "Where did you get this?"

"I—I'm not sure."

He dropped the bag into his pocket for later analysis, then looked at her palm. The cut wasn't deep, but it was still bleeding. Without thinking, he pulled his handkerchief from his pocket and pressed it into her palm. "Hold on to that."

Startled eyes latched on to his.

He stared back, acutely aware of how small her wrist felt locked in his grasp. Her pulse fluttered beneath his fingertips. Another wave of unexpected heat rolled through him.

Releasing her, he stepped back. "Did you touch the body?"

Her thin, delicately arched brows furrowed. "I—I don't know. I must have, but I'm not sure. When I try to remember, it's like I'm…looking through fog."

The cop in him didn't buy it. Impatient, he rubbed a hand over his five o'clock shadow. "Go on."

Silence thickened the air around them for a full minute, then she released a frustrated sigh. "This isn't helping you. I'm sorry. I don't know what's wrong with me."

Either she was stalling for time to get her story straight

or she was truly in a state of shock. "Nothing's wrong with you. You're shaken up. Take another deep breath."

Together, they slowly inhaled.

"Good girl," he said. "Try again."

She pressed her fingertips to her temples. Another minute passed. She fidgeted. "Things just keep getting jumbled in my mind."

"Were you hurt in any way? Did someone hit you?"

She shook her head. "No, that's not it."

Another jab of impatience rippled through him, but he held it in check. He tried not to think about the body cooling in the foyer or the minutes ticking away. Forty-eight hours went by pretty fast when you were working around the clock.

"Try to concentrate on what happened," he said.

"I was going to study. I'd fixed coffee." Propping her hands together, she pressed her fingertips against her mouth. "I remember a tap on the door. Armon never used the doorbell. He had this big diamond ring he used to tap on the glass." Her voice cracked with the last word.

"Was there anyone with him?"

"I don't know," she said slowly.

"Did you have a fight?"

"No."

Something inside Philip quickened at the direct answer. If she was trying to lead him to believe that she couldn't remember, she'd just screwed up. "So you *do* remember?"

"No...we..." she stammered. "He was a very kind man. We were friends. In all the years I knew him, we never fought."

That could be checked, he thought, and scribbled a note on the pad. He had yet to meet a woman and man who didn't fight occasionally. Personal experience told him it happened more often than most people were willing to admit. "What happened after you answered the door?"

"I—I'm not sure."

"Did you invite him in?"

"Yes. I mean, probably. I wouldn't leave him standing on the porch."

"What happened next?"

"I...don't...know."

Exasperation inched through Philip. "Is there some reason why you can't talk to me? If you're...uncomfortable, there's a female officer on the way. Sometimes that makes things easier."

The woman's eyes flicked to his. Philip found himself holding his breath in the moments before she spoke. He wasn't sure if it was in anticipation of her response or of hearing that sultry voice.

"No, that's not the problem."

As annoyed with himself as he was with her, he frowned. "Maybe you should enlighten me as to what the problem is."

Her lips parted. The movement drew his eyes to a soft, interesting mouth. Her lips were full and nicely shaped. The space between her front teeth was once more visible. Odd, but the tiny flaw added a great deal of appeal. More appeal than it should have, and he slapped the thought away.

"The problem is I...don't remember." She rubbed her forehead with her fingertips. "It's like a nightmare. The kind that terrifies you, but you can't recall what it was about."

Either she was an award-winning actress or this woman truly couldn't remember. Philip wasn't sure which scenario was worse.

"There's a body in your foyer and you're telling me you have no idea how it got there? You expect me to believe that?"

"I just need a few minutes to pull myself together—"

"Time is the one thing I don't have right now," he snapped.

A wounded look flashed across her face, but she quickly masked it with a toughness he'd seen lots of times on the street. Times when someone had gotten in over his or her head and didn't quite know how to swim. Philip wondered if she knew how to swim.

Her chin went up. "I'm doing my best, Detective."

"You're going to have to do better." He knew he was being hard on her, but he didn't care. A man was dead and this woman was all but holding a smoking gun. In the back of his mind, he wondered if her prints would turn up on the Beretta.

"Do you own a gun, Miss Pelletier?"

He saw the answer in her eyes even before she spoke—a mixture of guilt and fear tempered with a measure of defiance that told him she wasn't necessarily sorry for it. The anticipation inside him stirred, sharpened. In that instant, gut instinct told him she knew more than she was letting on.

"That's not against the law, is it, Detective?"

"Only if you use it to kill someone."

Anger flickered in her eyes. "If you've got something to say, I suggest you get it out in the open."

"I think you're the one who has something to say, Miss Pelletier. I'd like the truth. All of it. Now."

She visibly swallowed, but didn't look away. "Armon was my friend. I'd never...hurt him. Never. That's the only thing I know for certain right now."

Philip didn't miss the anguish in her voice. Nor did he miss the pain in her eyes. He half expected her to break down and cry, but she didn't. Judging from the stubborn set of her jaw, she probably wouldn't, either. He wondered what it would take to cut through that tough facade and find the truth.

"Did you kill Armon Landsteiner?" he asked harshly.

Renewed temper flared in her eyes. She slid off the bed and approached him. "No!"

Philip's gut tightened as he took in the length of her. She was taller than he'd first imagined. Just a few inches short of his six-foot frame. Even through the baggy sweatshirt he could see the subtle outline of curves he had no business noticing while acting in an official capacity. What the hell was the matter with him tonight?

"I'm merely trying to find out what happened, Miss Pelletier. Your inability to remember is making my job difficult." His voice worked. That was good. Giving himself a quick mental shake, Philip glanced toward the door. Where was that female patrol?

He couldn't remember the last time he'd felt awkward with a female suspect. He told himself it was because of all the sexual harassment charges flooding the system. Hell, it wasn't safe for a male cop to be alone with a female witness or suspect. But, closer to the truth, Philip knew it was because this particular suspect appealed to him in a way that was as dangerous as the pistol that was on its way to the lab.

She blinked at him as if suddenly realizing they might still be on the same side. "I'm sorry you don't believe me."

Rather than debate the point, he switched tactics. Maybe some background information would help him fill in the blanks. "What kind of relationship did you have with Armon Landsteiner?"

"I'm an intern at his law firm, Landsteiner & Associates. He hired me through the work program at Tulane."

Not the answer Philip was looking for, but he let it slide, making a mental note to look into the relationship later. "You're in law school?"

She squared her shoulders. "I graduate in June."

Philip bit back the antilawyer remark teetering on the tip of his tongue. He smiled instead, hoping to get her to relax. Witnesses were more likely to open up if a measure of trust existed between them and their interrogator. "How long have you worked for Landsteiner?"

"About four years. Armon hired me as an undergrad."

"Where did you work before that?"

She folded her arms around herself and eyed him warily. "I was a waitress at Terrebonne's."

"In Vieux Carré?" He used the French pronunciation for the French Quarter.

She nodded, looking at him as if she were a cornered fox about to be mauled by an approaching hound.

So much for putting her at ease. "What about before that?"

"I didn't work."

Philip made a note to delve more deeply into her past should the need arise. "What time did Landsteiner arrive at your apartment this evening, Miss Pelletier?"

She opened her mouth, then clamped it shut. Her gaze swept to the alarm clock beside the bed. "I'm not sure. I usually arrive home from class around nine o'clock. Sometime after that."

"You don't remember." Philip couldn't keep the sarcasm out of his voice.

"No."

"Did you have any alcohol to drink tonight?"

Indignation flared in her eyes. "I don't drink."

For a crazy instant, Philip couldn't look away. Despite his growing suspicions about her, another tug of attraction struck him squarely in the gut. Reminding himself she was an inch away from standing on the wrong side of the law, he forced his gaze to his notepad.

"Tell me about your relationship with Landsteiner," he said.

"I've already told you."

He glared at her. "We can do this downtown if you prefer."

She flinched. "Armon and I were friends—"

"How close?"

"Very close."

"Were you romantically involved?"

"I resent the implication behind your line of questioning, Detective."

His patience slipped, putting an edge in his voice. "I realize these questions might not be to your liking, Miss Pelletier, but I intend to do my job thoroughly in spite of whether or not I offend you."

He wasn't sure if he was irritated with her for making his job more difficult, or with himself for letting her get to him in a way that was not only unprofessional, but went against his personal code of honor. Just because he spent most of his time alone these days didn't mean it was okay to go off the deep end over a pair of big brown eyes.

Turning away, she paced to the opposite side of the room. She moved with graceful self-assurance, but to the perceptive eye, an underlying lack of confidence belied her cool exterior.

Philip swore he wouldn't let his gaze drop, but his eyes drifted down her rigid spine to the soft curve of her backside. He couldn't remember the last time he'd been so mesmerized by the sight of a woman's behind. What was he thinking, letting his libido get away from him in the middle of an interrogation?

"I'm sorry," she said, staring through the window. "I'm just…frustrated that I can't remember. It scares me."

He stared at her, letting the silence work.

"Armon and I were friends. I worked for him. Nothing more. We were never lovers." She turned to face Philip. "And I didn't kill him."

The anguish in her eyes stopped him cold, and for a single, wild instant Philip believed her. Disgusted with himself, he plowed his hand through his hair and let out a sigh of frustration. "If you have nothing to hide, why don't you just make this easy for both of us and level with me?"

"I am leveling with you. I've told you everything I remember."

"Then we've got a problem."

Taking a step back, she looked toward the door as if expecting someone to walk in and arrest her. "I know this must sound crazy to you, because it sounds crazy to me, but I can't remember what happened." The words hung between them like a lead weight. "I can't remember anything that happened after I walked into my apartment after class and before I made that 911 call."

Skepticism tumbled over him. He didn't believe her. Not about her memory loss. Not about her relationship with the deceased. Philip hadn't yet decided if she'd actually pulled the trigger, but he'd know more after questioning her thoroughly. Somehow, she was involved in this mess up to that pretty little chin of hers. If she was the killer, he was going to nail her to the wall.

He gestured in the general direction of the corpse. "This isn't helping your friend, Miss Pelletier."

She reacted as if he'd struck her. "You're not going to find the real killer by badgering me."

"A man was murdered in your house tonight. My gut tells me you know what happened. I'm not going to walk away and hope you'll remember something important while I go bark up another tree. That's not how I do my job."

"Armon was my friend. I want to know what happened to him as badly as you do."

"Then cooperate with this investigation."

A sound of disbelief escaped her. "You think I've chosen not to cooperate? That I'm lying? That I shot a man in my own apartment, then called the police and claimed to have amnesia? That's insane!"

Philip had been around too many years to believe in anything as melodramatic—or convenient—as amnesia. It never ceased to amaze him the lengths people would go to keep themselves out of jail. "All I know is that you're not answering my questions."

"And while you're standing here blasting me with questions, the real killer is getting away. Has that possibility occurred to you, Detective?"

He hadn't expected her to challenge him; she didn't look like the kind of woman to give a cop a hard time. But he supposed most murderers didn't look like murderers, either. Well, if she wanted to play hardball, he could throw a curve with the best of them.

"It also occurred to me that you could be lying."

"I didn't kill Armon, damn you."

"How did that bloodstain get on your shirt?" Despite his efforts to control it, temper resonated in his voice.

She looked down the front of her shirt. Her face blanched. "I…oh, God, I don't know. I just…don't know."

Guilt seeped through his anger when her eyes filled. She'd been so strong until now that something inside him twisted at the thought of breaking her. But she didn't cry. She stood silently with her arms wrapped around herself, looking as fragile as porcelain, as if another harsh word would shatter her into a thousand pieces.

The urge to comfort her surged through Philip with surprising force. For an instant he imagined what it might feel like to wrap his arms around her….

Eradicating the idea before it fully materialized, he took a mental step back, regrouped.

She stared at the stain on her shirt. "I'd like to change clothes."

"Not now. We're going to finish this interview downtown."

Her gaze snapped to his. "That's not necessary."

"I'm afraid it is."

"I know my rights." Her voice quavered with the last word.

"Then you know I'm well within mine to take you downtown for questioning. As a witness." *For now,* a little voice added. "I want to get to the bottom of what happened tonight, and you appear to be the key."

"I don't want to go downtown."

"You don't have a choice." Philip knew he didn't have a choice, either. He had a murder to solve, and he'd be damned if he was going to let himself be swayed by a smoky voice and a body designed by the devil himself.

"Are you arresting me?" Incredulity rang in her voice.

"No. But I suggest you start cooperating, or you might find yourself needing a lawyer before the night is through."

Chapter 2

Michelle stared at the detective, disbelief warring with all-out panic. He stared back, his expression as cold and emotionless as carved granite. His eyes were more gray than blue and reminded her of a storm. The kind that was violent and unpredictable and wreaked havoc on everything in its path. Thick, black brows rode low over intense, all-seeing eyes. Laugh lines bracketed a mouth that looked as if it didn't smile easily or often. A five o'clock shadow darkened an arrogantly cut jaw.

Under different circumstances he might have been attractive, at least on some primitive level that had more to do with hormones than intellect. Good thing ego-driven, alpha males had never appealed to her.

Michelle struggled to calm her frazzled nerves. Having worked in the legal profession for the last four years, she knew police procedure. She told herself that just because she was being taken downtown for questioning didn't mean she was a suspect. It certainly didn't mean she was guilty. After all, even suspects were innocent until proven guilty.

She wondered if that hackneyed phrase included her kind of people.

Betancourt stepped closer. "A female officer will drive you downtown. You can call your attorney from there."

Her breath stopped in her throat when his eyes flashed down the front of her. Suddenly it struck her that she wasn't wearing a bra beneath the oversize sweatshirt. Unnerved, Michelle folded her arms across her chest.

As if realizing he needed to justify his roaming gaze, he said, "The female patrol will need to bag that sweatshirt. It's procedure to ID the stains. We'll also test the fabric for powder burns."

Michelle repressed the subtle physical awareness that swept through her. "If you'll get out of my bedroom, I'll change clothes."

"I'd prefer you to wait until the female officer arrives."

"What do you think I'm going to do, Detective, hide the evidence under my pillow?"

"Or else take that sweatshirt into the bathroom and flush it down the toilet." His gaze burned into hers.

She stared back, aware she was breathing too fast. "I have nothing to hide."

"Then talk to me, dammit."

The sincerity in his voice surprised her. But she knew better than to trust a man like Betancourt. She'd learned that lesson the hard way a lifetime ago. The experience had cost her a piece of herself that could never be replaced.

"I wish I could," she said quietly. "I wish it were that simple."

Abruptly, the thought hit her that she needed a lawyer. Her heart stopped as the repercussions rumbled through her. The only lawyers she knew well enough to call upon were Armon's two sons and daughter. She didn't even know if they'd been told about their father's death. They would be devastated....

Pain speared her. Suddenly, she wasn't nearly as worried

about herself as she was about the three people with whom she'd worked for the last four years. They'd been her family, her only friends since she'd come to New Orleans. Michelle accepted the responsibility of being the one to break the terrible news. Better they hear it from her than from the unfeeling cop with the cold eyes.

Turning away, she started for the door. "I've got to make a phone call."

"Wait a minute."

She heard Betancourt behind her, but she didn't stop. Leaving the bedroom, she started down the hall. Ahead, a woman wearing a red jacket brushed silver fingerprint powder onto the phone. In the foyer, a well-dressed black man knelt next to the body. A sense of surrealism swooped down on her when she realized it was Armon Landsteiner lying there dead.

"Miss Pelletier?"

Michelle vaguely heard the detective's voice. She felt dizzy, disoriented, overwhelmed by the bizarreness of the scene around her. The body of her dear friend lay in the foyer. Her apartment had been taken over by police who suspected her of a horrendous crime. It was as if she'd stepped onto the set of a horror movie in which she was the star and the players were more real than any nightmare.

Just before she reached the phone, a pair of strong hands closed around her upper arms from behind. "The phone is being dusted for prints." Authority laced Betancourt's voice.

Twisting within his grip, she spun around. "I've got to call Armon's family. They don't know yet. They deserve to know." Only after she'd spoken did she realize she was crying. Damn. The last thing she wanted to do was break down in front of this cold-hearted cop. But her emotions had taken all the bashing they could handle.

"I'll notify the next of kin," he said.

A wrenching sense of despair settled over her. She closed her eyes and felt the tears squeeze between her lashes. She couldn't stop thinking about Armon. Such a kind man, such a good friend. God, how was she going to tell his children he was dead? How would they react, knowing it had happened in her apartment?

"No," she said. "I'd rather they hear it from me. I work with them. They're my friends."

"It's my job," he said firmly. "The best way for you to help is to come downtown and answer some questions."

Horrified that her emotions were spiraling out of control, Michelle brushed furiously at the tears on her cheeks. "I didn't kill him, Detective. I don't remember what happened, but I know I didn't kill him."

For the first time, he looked uncomfortable. "If that's the truth, you have nothing to worry about."

His voice drifted over her like a warm bayou breeze. Not at all unpleasant considering the circumstances, and Michelle found herself starkly aware of his hands against her biceps. But as much as she needed comforting, she certainly didn't need it from a cop. Especially this cop with his hard, suspicious eyes.

"Let go of me."

"This is a crime scene. You can't touch anything." His hands slipped from her arms. "You got yourself under control?"

Her flesh felt warm where his fingers had pressed. Not sure she trusted her voice, Michelle nodded jerkily, knowing it didn't matter if she had herself under control or not. He suspected her of a terrible crime. And he was going to take her downtown whether she agreed to go or not.

A stout policewoman in an ill-fitting uniform approached them. Michelle didn't miss the look that passed between her and Betancourt. Michelle had seen that look before, and dread swelled inside her. Even if she wasn't being arrested, she knew what she faced in the coming hours. Interrogations, especially if a serious crime was involved, were lengthy and exhausting. The name of the game was to wear down suspects until they slipped up or spilled their guts.

Of course, if she lived in a nicer neighborhood or if her clothes had a designer label, perhaps Detective Betancourt wouldn't be so quick to haul her downtown. Michelle tried to staunch the bitterness that rose inside her, but it came anyway, as thick and stinking as the muddy bayou town from whence she sprang.

It took every ounce of strength she possessed to walk into her bedroom and remove her sweatshirt while the female officer looked on. Michelle watched the woman stuff the sweatshirt into an evidence bag. Numbly, she pulled on an oversize shirt, then stepped into her sneakers.

They didn't handcuff her, but she was no longer a free woman. If they saw fit to arrest her and incarcerate her for murder, there wasn't a thing she could do about it. Her only hope was to get her memory back. If she couldn't do that, her only other alternative was to find out for herself who had killed Armon Landsteiner.

The interrogation room was everything Michelle feared it would be, only worse. Located on the third floor of the Broad Street Police Station, it was windowless, cold, and stank of old furniture and cigarettes. An ugly, institutional gray paint covered the walls. A coffeepot containing what looked like engine sludge sat in the center of a rectangular wood table.

Michelle sat alone in one of three chairs, trying to ignore the crude words carved into the scarred surface of the table. Where was Betancourt, anyway? She didn't wear a watch, but knew she'd been sitting in the dank room at least twenty minutes. It galled her that he hadn't bothered to show up yet.

Though she was entitled by law to an attorney, she hadn't been able to bring herself to call any of the Landsteiners in an official capacity. They'd lost their father to a brutal crime.

The last thing they needed was to spend the night at the police station. Of course, after the initial shock wore off, she knew that, as attorneys and friends, they would want to be actively involved with the investigation.

Foremost in her mind was the knowledge that she'd lost her best friend tonight. She couldn't seem to grasp the fact that Armon was dead. The information registered; she'd seen the body lying in her foyer. She'd seen the blood and the pale, staring eyes. But, somehow, she just couldn't believe he was gone. It only doubled her pain knowing he'd been taken by an act of violence—and that she was inches away from being accused of the crime.

If it hadn't been for Armon, she wouldn't have survived those first months in New Orleans. In the four years she'd known him, he'd become the father she'd never had. Armon Landsteiner had been a generous, compassionate man who loved life fiercely. A brilliant attorney, he'd been respected by his colleagues and loved by friends and family alike. He was the only person who had ever cared enough about Michelle to reach out and make a difference in her life. His kindness and generosity had saved her when her future was bleak and she'd been sliding down that slippery slope into the pit of hopelessness that had plagued her mother.

And she swore she'd never be like Blanche Pelletier.

Shoving thoughts of the past to the back of her mind, Michelle took a deep breath and ordered herself to concentrate on the problem at hand. Somehow, she had to get her memory back. She didn't know anything about amnesia, but figured she was good enough at research to give herself a quick education—as soon as she got out of here.

She wondered what could have caused her memory loss. Had she seen something so terrible that her mind simply blocked it? Or had she done something unspeakable? Her heart bucked hard in her chest at the thought, but Michelle quickly calmed herself. She knew for a fact that she wasn't capable of hurting Armon. Still, just knowing there might be some vital information locked away in her mind made her feel somehow responsible. That responsibility weighed heavily on her shoulders.

How could she convince Betancourt she was telling the truth when the notion of amnesia sounded crazy even to her? Couldn't he see she wanted to cooperate? Was there some kind of psychological test she could take that would prove her amnesia was real?

No, a cynical little voice answered. Betancourt had tried and convicted her the moment he'd laid eyes on her. What would he think when he found out what had happened all those years ago in Bayou Lafourche?

The thought sent a quiver through her.

Too restless to sit, she rose and began to pace. Since she was obviously stuck here for a while, she supposed the most productive thing to do was work on her memory. After pouring herself a cup of coffee, she went back to the table and sat down. Closing her eyes, she eased her thoughts back to the morning to retrace her day. It seemed like an eternity since she'd risen and dressed. She couldn't afford to live in the Quarter, so every morning she walked the two blocks to a coffee shop near Jackson Square for a beignet and coffee. Then she hopped on the streetcar to her office at the Whitney Bank Building. Such a typical day, she thought with a shudder. How could it have ended in tragedy?

Her workday had been uneventful, as had her class afterward. A creature of habit, Michelle always came straight home after school. If she'd followed the same routine tonight, she would have arrived at her apartment at least an hour before she'd made that call to 911. What had happened during that hour? As far as she knew, she could have walked into her apartment and found Armon's body. But that didn't explain who had let him in or what he was doing there in the first place.

The interrogation room door swung open.

Michelle started, inadvertently knocking over her coffee.

Betancourt sauntered into the room, taking her in with a single swoop of his lethal gaze. ''I see you found the coffee.''

She looked into those stormy gray eyes and her pulse kicked. She'd worked with all levels of law enforcement, street cops as well as detectives, but none of them unnerved her as completely as this man. He had the most penetrating stare she'd ever endured.

His charcoal suit was nicely cut, but not overly expensive. Beneath, a starched white shirt was beginning to wrinkle. He'd unfastened the top button of the collar at some point in the last hour. A conservative tie hung askew.

Slipping off his jacket, he draped it over the back of a chair. His gaze fell to her spilled coffee. ''Let me get that before it eats a hole in the table.'' He strode to the coffee station and returned with a handful of napkins. One by one he spread them over the spill. ''Stuff looks lethal.''

''Why is it that cops always make the worst coffee?'' She looked down at her cup, wondering why they were talking about coffee when her entire world was coming apart at the seams.

''Since I made it more than six hours ago, I won't take offense.'' He filled a cup and sat across from her. ''Feeling better?''

Her head throbbed, but she wasn't going to tell him that. ''I feel fine. But that's not what you really want to ask me, is it, Detective?''

''No. What I really want to know is what happened tonight at your apartment.''

Michelle's heart bumped against her ribs. She told herself the reaction was unwarranted. She hadn't done anything wrong; she didn't have anything to hide. She tried to convince herself Betancourt wasn't concerned with her past, but she knew better.

People were always interested in her past.

The door opened, and a short black man entered and went directly to the coffeepot. "Is this fresh?"

Betancourt's mouth curved. He looked at Michelle as if they now shared a secret. "Yeah."

She hadn't expected him to smile, and the transformation amazed her. The hard lines about his mouth vanished. Even the sharp-edged suspicion in his eyes softened. For a split second he looked almost…handsome.

"Miss Pelletier, this is Detective Sanderson."

Her attention snapped to the man who'd just entered. She wondered what etiquette called for when meeting a homicide detective during an interrogation when you were the suspect. Miss Manners wouldn't have a clue, Michelle decided.

"I guess I should tell you before we begin that I still don't remember what happened," she said.

The two men exchanged dubious glances.

Sanderson took his cup and leaned against the wall behind her. She imagined they were going to try the good cop–bad cop routine, and repressed the hysterical laugh building in her throat.

"Since it's late and we're all tired," Betancourt began, "let's work on figuring out how much you *do* remember, okay?" He withdrew a tape recorder from his jacket pocket. "I'm required by law to tell you this interview is being recorded."

Interesting that he'd used the word *interview*. Michelle felt as if she were about to walk into a massacre unarmed. "Then we'll both have to be on our best behavior, won't we, Detective?"

"By the book. We're not here to cause you problems."

"You already have by dragging me down here when I've already told you everything I possibly can. I'm as baffled and frustrated as you are that I can't remember what happened."

"I'm doing my job, Miss Pelletier. I'm trying to solve a

murder. To do that I need information. Details. Anything you can tell me that might help us find who did this.''

Did he really want the same thing she wanted? Or was he the enemy, more interested in making an easy arrest than finding the truth? Experience told her he was the last man on earth she should trust.

''Do you want a lawyer present?'' he asked.

''I'm a year away from taking the bar, Detective. I haven't done anything wrong. According to you, we both want the same thing. As long as you refrain from harassing me, I can handle you and your questions.''

His gaze burned into hers. ''You sure about that?''

She met his gaze levelly. ''Positive.''

His baritone voice cut through the air like a lance as he recited the date, time and a short introduction into the recorder. ''Miss Pelletier, tell me what happened this evening after Armon Landsteiner arrived at your apartment.''

She stared at him, starkly aware that whatever she said would be a matter of record. ''As I said before, Detective, I can't remember anything that happened between the time I arrived home after class and before I dialed 911. I know it's important, and I want to help. But…I can't remember.''

''Did you go to your office at Landsteiner & Associates today?''

''Yes.''

''What time did you leave for the day?''

''Around five o'clock. Then I went to class.''

''What time did you leave the university?''

''My class is over at nine o'clock. I took the streetcar to Jackson Square, then I walked home.''

''What did you do after that?''

''I…this is where things get…foggy. I'm sure I went home. I mean, that's my usual routine.''

''Was Armon Landsteiner already there? Or did you let him in?''

Her heart pounded in perfect rhythm with the headache

grinding behind her eyes. She reached deep for the memory, struggled desperately to find something, anything to give her solid mental footing, but came up blank. "I...don't know. I remember his tap on the door, then I just don't know. I'm sorry. My God, when I try to remember, it's like there's nothing there."

Betancourt looked skeptical. "That leaves us with a big problem."

"Of course it does. I want to get to the bottom of this as badly as you do. Probably more, considering I have a personal stake."

"How did you get the blood on your sweatshirt?"

"I—I don't know. Maybe I tried to help him."

"How did you get the abrasion on your knee?"

She hadn't noticed the small wound until the police photographer had taken a snapshot of it at Betancourt's prompting. "I don't remember."

Raking his hand through his hair, he punched the off button on the recorder, frustration plainly visible on his face. "Right."

Her temper spiked. "I'm telling the truth, damn you."

"You're withholding information in an official investigation."

Michelle felt as if she were under siege, not by his questions, but by those intense, knowing eyes. "I'm cooperating to the best of my ability."

He turned on the recorder. "How did you meet Landsteiner?"

"I was a waitress at Terrebonne's. He was a customer. He came in for dinner regularly."

Betancourt's gaze cut to his partner, then went back to Michelle. "You were never romantically involved?"

"Never."

"How did you come to work for him?"

"I'd just enrolled in law school. I needed experience and a mentor. He was one of the best attorneys in the city. I registered for the work program at Tulane. He hired me through the program. It's all in the school's records.''

"What brought you to New Orleans?''

"A scholarship." The scholarship was the single most important achievement in her life, a one-way ticket out of Bayou Lafourche. She wouldn't let anyone take it away from her. Not fate. Not Betancourt.

She held her breath, praying he didn't ask any more questions about her past. Having spent the last four years putting the nightmare behind her, she'd be damned if she'd let him dredge it up now. What had happened in that dank little town wasn't relative to what had happened to Armon Landsteiner.

"You can bet we'll check it out," Philip said.

"I have nothing to hide."

"We all have something to hide."

She gave him the best go-to-hell look she could manage and lied. "I don't.''

Michelle lost track of time and place as the interrogation continued. Betancourt questioned her relentlessly, asking her the same questions a dozen different ways until she thought she would scream in frustration.

At 2:00 a.m. he blew out a sigh and plowed his hands through his dark hair. "In light of the circumstances, I'm going to ask you to agree to a psychological evaluation by the department psychiatrist.''

All the strength drained out of her as she realized how little had been accomplished in the time they'd been locked away. For the first time in a long time, she felt utterly and completely vulnerable.

"I'll agree as long as my attorney doesn't have a problem with it." She didn't have an attorney, but Betancourt didn't know it.

"I'll set it up." He switched off the recorder and stood.

Feeling exhaustion press into her, Michelle rose. She wasn't sure if they were finished, but she didn't care. She wanted out of there. "I'll do everything in my power to cooperate, Detective. Let me know when the evaluation is, and I'll make myself available."

He looked as if he wanted to say her schedule no longer mattered, but he didn't. Instead, he approached her and extended his hand.

Michelle couldn't have been more surprised if he'd pulled an alligator out of his pocket. She wiped her damp palm on her jeans and reached out. Their hands met. His eyes darkened, intensified as his fingers curled around hers. The contact went through her like an electric shock. His grip was warm and firm, his hand covering hers completely. For a startling moment, she almost forgot he was the enemy.

"Where in Lafourche Parish are you from?" he asked.

His question jerked her back to reality. Michelle stiffened, starkly aware that he still gripped her hand. She knew Betancourt was too discerning a man not to have felt her reaction. Belatedly, she realized he'd run a cursory background check on her as she waited.

Unnerved, she extracted her hand. Her gaze swept to Detective Sanderson, then back to Betancourt. She considered not answering his question; she even considered lying, but knew he'd eventually find out. Better to tell the truth than get caught in a lie. After a while, lies just got all tangled up anyway. "I'm from Bayou Lafourche, Detective."

"I'm not sure where that is."

"Most people aren't. It's a small town." She wasn't about to elaborate.

A smile quirked one side of his mouth. If she hadn't been so angry, she might have admired the way it softened the hard lines of his face. He was a good-looking man, and knew it. Too bad he wasn't smart enough to realize she was immune.

The door to the interrogation room swung open, and a

uniformed cop poked his head in. ''There's a lawyer by the name of Baldwin Landsteiner here who says he's going to personally contact the deputy superintendent if Miss Pelletier isn't released in the next thirty seconds.''

Chapter 3

Philip leaned his hip against the table and watched Baldwin Landsteiner burst through the door like a doctor into an emergency room. Wearing his trademark Italian suit and expensive tie, he epitomized everything Philip hated about lawyers. He was brilliant. Ruthless. With a complete disregard for the truth.

"Michelle." Landsteiner's eyes fastened on the pale young woman standing at the table. "Are you all right?"

She took a tentative step toward him. "Baldwin. My God, what are you doing here?"

With self-righteous indignation etched into his boyish features, Baldwin approached her. "The cops came to the house and told me…about Dad."

She blinked rapidly. "I'm so sorry—"

"I came to get you the hell out of here." His icy gaze swept to Philip. "I'll have your badge for this, Betancourt. You know better than to haul someone in for questioning without the benefit of counsel."

"It's good to see you again, too, Landsteiner. How's

tricks?'' Philip smiled despite the anger rippling through him. He didn't like the man and knew the sentiment ran both ways.

The lawyer's pale green eyes glittered with contempt. ''I'll bury you this time.''

''I look forward to it.''

Rounding the table, Michelle reached for Baldwin's hands and gripped them in hers. ''It's all right. Please, just take me home.''

Baldwin turned his attention to Michelle, then looked down at their clasped hands. ''Why didn't you call me? I would have been here sooner. I couldn't believe it when they told me you were being questioned.''

''You had enough to deal with. How are Danielle and Derek holding up?''

''I spoke with Derek on the phone. He's handling this better than Danielle. She isn't dealing with this well at all.''

Philip watched the exchange with interest, wondering about the relationship. Michelle Pelletier wasn't the kind of woman the high-profile lawyer typically surrounded himself with. Landsteiner preferred society women with diamonds the size of chicken eggs and a wardrobe befitting a queen. With her denim jacket and faded jeans, Michelle didn't fit his criteria by a long shot.

Philip studied her face for clues as to how she felt about Landsteiner, but saw only grief. Few people could fake such a powerful emotion. Still, he had worked plenty of cases where the murderer was close to the victim and actually *had* mourned his or her passing. The irony never ceased to amaze him.

''How about you, Baldwin? Are you all right?'' she asked.

''Still in shock, I think. But I'm dealing with it. I just hope they find the bastard responsible.''

An uncomfortable twinge went through Philip when Baldwin embraced her. Almost against his will, he watched their bodies come together. Before he could identify the source of his discomfort, he ruthlessly shoved the twinge away.

She pressed her cheek against Baldwin's shoulder. "Thank you for coming. This is a mess."

Landsteiner's gaze landed on Philip. "What the hell is she doing in your dungeon, Betancourt? Is she the best suspect you could come up with?" A sharp, humorless laugh escaped him. "You must be desperate."

"She's a witness in a murder case," Philip said. "I think you know the routine."

"You're the one who doesn't seem to grasp the routine. There are laws in this country against the police questioning a suspect without a lawyer present."

"There are also laws against murder and racketeering, but that didn't keep you from defending scum like Rosetti." Philip shouldn't have said it. He knew better than to dredge up another case at a time like this. But men like Baldwin Landsteiner didn't bring out the best in him—and he didn't necessarily give a damn.

Amusement sparked behind the lawyer's gaze. "Still sore about that one, huh? I can't blame you, considering it was your shoddy police work that got the case tossed. I merely pointed it out to the judge."

Anger punched through Philip. He left the table and advanced on Baldwin. "There are plenty of scum in this town and even more scum-sucking lawyers to defend them. But your card will come up again."

"Next time I'll make sure you get your badge yanked for good. Shouldn't be too hard to do with your record." Baldwin's gaze slipped to Michelle. "Let's go." He guided her toward the door, then stopped and looked back. "You'll be off this case in twenty-four hours, Betancourt. I guarantee it."

Philip stared, his heart drumming. Two strides and he would be on top of Landsteiner. He pictured his fingers closing around the other man's neck. Fury-fueled adrenaline burst into his muscles.

Cory laid a firm hand on his forearm. "Easy, my man. He's just trying to rile you."

Cursing, Philip let out a breath and shoved his hands into his pockets. He should have known that was coming, should have expected it. He told himself the Rosetti case didn't matter. That shopkeeper had died over a year ago; Philip had been cleared of wrongdoing. Still, people had long memories when it came to mistakes. As much as Philip didn't want to admit it, the fact that it had been *his* mistake still cut him to the quick.

He watched Michelle walk to the door. "Miss Pelletier?"

Turning, she met his gaze levelly. "Yes?"

She looked pale and shaken, but her expression told him she was anything but weak. He'd seen that look before, and it revealed plenty about what she was made of. Not exactly steel, but some alloy that was just as strong.

"I'll schedule that psychological evaluation as soon as possible," he said.

Landsteiner's eyes narrowed on Michelle. "What evaluation?"

She ignored him, her gaze never leaving Philip. "I'll cooperate fully, Detective."

"I'd appreciate it if you didn't take any trips in the coming days. I have more questions." Philip steeled himself against the force of her gaze, telling himself those sultry eyes were the last thing he should be thinking about when there was a murder to be solved—and she was the prime suspect.

"Of course. I'll be available."

Landsteiner's protest elicited a smile from Philip. Watching them walk out the door of the interview room, he wondered how the illustrious Baldwin Landsteiner would feel after learning his client was claiming amnesia about his father's murder.

"Shakespeare had the right idea when he said we should

kill all the lawyers." Cory's voice severed the remaining tension.

Philip accepted the coffee being offered. "Thanks."

"You took it easy on her."

Is that what he'd done? Not quite sure how to respond, he sipped the coffee, grimacing at the bitterness.

Cory studied him. "You could have arrested her."

"I know."

"Ten to one her prints show up on the Beretta."

"Probably."

"My gut tells me that lady is guilty as sin."

Philip didn't want to think of her in relation to sin. "Maybe. Guilty of something."

"You think she did it?" Cory asked.

"I think she's knows something. I'm not convinced she pulled the trigger."

"An older, affluent man with lots of flash and money. An attractive young woman looking for security works her way into his will or life insurance policy. It's been done before."

Philip nodded, hating it that he didn't trust his gut on this one. He'd known Michelle Pelletier for just a few hours and already she was wreaking havoc on his judgment. "I want a thorough background check on her. Finances. Family. I want to know everything there is to know about her all the way down to her favorite color. See if Landsteiner had life insurance policies." He downed the coffee, knowing he was going to need the caffeine before morning. "Check to see if he filed a will."

"Where are you going?"

"I'm going to see what the lab turned up and go over the witness reports and the 911 tape." He fished the cuff link out of his pocket and held it up. "I'm taking this to the lab."

Cory raised his brows. "Where'd you find it?"

Philip grimaced, and told Cory about Michelle gripping it

so tightly she'd cut herself. "She didn't even realize she was bleeding."

"She could have been playing you."

"I don't think so." Philip looked at his watch and frowned. "First light I'm going to pay the Landsteiner clan a visit."

"Sort of like walking into a wolf's den unarmed, isn't it?"

"Yeah, only I'm not Little Red Riding Hood."

Cory gave him a sober look. "You can't let him get to you like that, man."

Philip rubbed his hand over his bristly face, wishing he had the time for a shower and shave. "Let it go, Cory."

"He's pushing your buttons, and you're letting him."

"Tell it to the people who have suffered because of the creeps he puts back on the street. Or else keep it to yourself."

His partner's eyes hardened. "I'm on your side, Betancourt, but I've never see you so close to losing it. Don't let Landsteiner rattle you. The man's on a mission and you're his target."

As much as Philip didn't want to admit it, he knew his partner was right. But anger still pumped through him from Landsteiner's remark about the Rosetti case. Thanks to Landsteiner, Philip hadn't gotten a conviction, and Rosetti had been put back on the street. Two days later, the only witness had been shot down on the sidewalk outside his shop. Philip had taken that one personally. How could he not when an innocent man had died because of him?

"I'll keep that in mind." He dropped his coffee cup in the trash. "Let's work this case."

The hum of the Lexus's tires on the wet street seemed unnaturally loud in the tense silence inside the car. Michelle gazed through the passenger window, barely noticing the rain or the darkened storefronts along Canal Street. She knew Baldwin had questions, but she just couldn't face any more right now. She felt exhausted and battered, as if every question Betancourt asked had been a physical blow. Closing her eyes, she rested her head against the seat.

"What happened to my father?"

The question jerked her nerves taut. She looked at Baldwin, wishing she had an answer. She wanted answers so badly she could taste it. "I don't know."

He glanced away from his driving, his gaze meeting hers with a sharpness that made her want to look away. "Why did Betancourt drag you downtown like some kind of criminal?"

Unable to hold his gaze, she focused on the darkness beyond the window. "I found...Armon's body. I made the call to 911. I may have seen what happened." A hysterical laugh hovered in her throat. "But I can't remember any of it. For whatever reason, my mind has completely blanked out the memory. Other than what I've just told you...I have no idea what happened."

"You don't remember? Were you there when it happened? My God, if you were there, you had to have seen something." He stopped at a red light and gave her his full attention. "What the hell's going on, Michelle?"

Oncoming headlights illuminated his features. A patrician nose dominated his face. His mouth was sculpted and oddly feminine. Golden blond hair tumbled onto a forehead that was high and sloped. Most women considered him almost godlike in his masculine beauty. Michelle had never seen him that way. In the four years she'd known him, he'd been like a brother to her, and she'd worked hard to maintain that balance.

She forced her gaze to his. "I'm trying to tell you I have some kind of amnesia." Even as she said the words, disbelief welled inside her. Amnesia didn't happen to people like her. She hadn't received a blow to the head or physical trauma of any kind. Why couldn't she remember?

"Are you serious?" Incredulity resounded in his voice.

"That's why Betancourt wants me to agree to a psychological evaluation."

"Betancourt won't be a problem."

"He's just doing his job." Why was she defending him? Baldwin didn't speak again until he parked the Lexus curbside in front of the Pontchartrain Hotel.

"Why did you bring me here?" She couldn't imagine walking into New Orleans's plushest hotel after what she'd been through. She felt dirty. Exhausted. She wanted to be alone. In her own apartment where she could grieve, where she could fall apart in privacy.

"I reserved a room for you. The cops are at your place. You can't go home tonight." He shut down the engine, then turned to her and regarded her through pale green eyes. "Is there anything else you want to tell me, Michelle?"

What did he expect from her? "I've told you everything I remember."

He looked through the window at the bellman approaching the car. "It's nearly 3:00 a.m. Maybe we're both too tired to talk."

He was right. She felt numb with exhaustion and the remnants of shock. On impulse, she covered his hand with hers and squeezed. "I'm sorry, Baldwin."

"Me, too," he said. "Will you be all right?"

Pain quivered in her stomach, but she quickly squelched it. She'd survived all those years in Bayou Lafourche—she would survive this. "I'll be fine. How about you?"

"I'm going over to Danielle's penthouse. She's a wreck."

"She was close to him."

"So were you."

The bellman opened the door and uttered something ridiculously cheerful. Blinking back tears, Michelle got out of the car. "I'll see you tomorrow."

The full force of everything that had happened hit her the moment the car door slammed. She felt as if she were being sucked down into a deep, dark vortex of suspicion. Betancourt had made it clear he didn't believe her. She knew he would do everything in his power to crucify her. Even Baldwin had seemed to doubt her. She didn't want to think about how Danielle would react.

If only she could remember!

The bellman swung open the front door of the hotel for her. The lights of the plush lobby assaulted her eyes. Michelle tried to smile, feeling suddenly conspicuous in her faded jeans and denim jacket among the opulent lobby furnishings. She strode to the front desk, picked up her room key, then went directly to the elevator. She felt sick inside as she rode the elevator to the third floor. When the doors slid open, she rushed down the hall, searching frantically for her room. Relief flooded her when she spotted the number. She unlocked the door and stepped inside, barely noticing the scent of eucalyptus or the antiques strewn about. The room was as silent and cold as a tomb.

The emotional dam shattered with a violence that left her weak and shaking. Pain clenched her so tightly she could barely breathe. The tears followed with a vengeance. She stumbled into the bathroom, fell to her knees at the commode and vomited. She felt cold inside and out, shivering uncontrollably, as if ice flowed through her veins. After shedding her clothes, she turned on the shower and stepped beneath the spray. The reality that she would never again see Armon struck her like a punch to the stomach. Pain stabbed through her. A sob tore from her throat, choking her. Bowing her head, she dropped to her knees.

"No!" She slammed her fist against tile, hating the unfairness of it.

Water sluiced over her, drowning out her sounds of grief, washing away tears she would never cry again.

Michelle was at the office by eight o'clock the next morning. She hadn't slept and felt the fatigue all the way down to her bones. Last night, after Baldwin had dropped her off at the hotel, she'd taken a cab back to her apartment. The officer in charge had let her pack an overnight bag and some clothes. Once back in her room, she'd wrangled a computer with Internet access from the hotel concierge and researched the phenomena of amnesia until the wee hours of morning.

Finding information on the rare disorder had not been an easy task. There were several different types, but the most common—referred to as localized dissociative amnesia by psychologists—was usually brought on by a traumatic event. Michelle wondered if she'd seen something so traumatic that her subconscious had blocked it from her mind.

The notion made her shiver.

"I wasn't expecting you so early this morning."

Michelle jumped at the sound of Baldwin's voice. She stood abruptly, stunned to see him standing at the door of her office. "I thought you'd be with Danielle," she said.

His expression seemed strained. "Danielle and Derek are here."

"Here?" She came around the desk, but sensed something in the way he looked at her and stopped. "What's going on?"

"We'd like a word with you." His voice rang cold and hard in the silence of the suite. "In the conference room."

"Of course." Dread compressed her chest. Michelle didn't know what was about to happen, but her instincts screamed it wasn't good. She followed Baldwin past the reception desk to the formal conference room. Without speaking he took his seat at the head of the glossy, rosewood table. Michelle stood frozen at the door, her gaze skimming the room's occupants. Danielle sat against the far wall, looking like a ghost, her green eyes swollen and unmistakably hostile. Derek sat next to Danielle, his shoulders slumped, staring into his untouched coffee.

"Sit down, Michelle." Baldwin's voice snapped through tension-laden air like a whip.

Numb, Michelle forced herself to the chair nearest the door. "What's this all about?"

Derek cleared his throat noisily. Michelle studied him, hoping she didn't look as uneasy as she felt. His eyes were bright green behind his wire-rimmed glasses and held an emotion she couldn't put her finger on. "We had a meeting last night," he said. "Under the circumstances, namely our father's death, we've unanimously decided to terminate your employment with Landsteiner & Associates."

The words registered like the business end of a baseball bat. Disbelief and a stark sense of betrayal pierced her. "I didn't do anything wrong."

Baldwin folded his hands on the desk in front of him. "We didn't say you did. We just think things are better this way."

"Better for whom?" Michelle stared at him, shocked that they would do this to her. She desperately needed her job. As a part-time law student, she still had bills to pay. And her work had always been a big part of who she was, not to mention the sole source of the security she craved.

"We've put together a generous severance package—"

"I don't care about severance pay."

"We'll take care of any legalities with the work program at Tulane—"

"I don't care about that, either." She rose and looked helplessly at the three people she loved like family. "I know you're hurting. I know you must have doubts about me. But I swear I didn't have anything to do with Armon's death. Please. Don't do this." She'd known they would be grief stricken. She'd expected questions. Perhaps even suspicion. But she hadn't expected this.

Danielle pushed away from the table and approached Michelle. "You had your claws in him from the day he found you working in that restaurant. You took advantage of his kindness and compassion. You used him, you little swamp rat."

Michelle couldn't believe her ears. Danielle had always been aloof, but Michelle considered her a friend nonetheless. "That's not true."

The other woman's eyes flashed contempt. She looked like a sleek predator about to deliver a fatal swipe with her claws. "Did you sleep with him? Is that how you controlled him?"

Michelle stepped back, shaken and appalled. "I'm not going to justify that with an answer."

"Danielle, that's enough," Baldwin warned. "This isn't helping matters."

Danielle ignored him, her lips pulled into a snarl. "My father was found murdered in your apartment. You won't tell the police who did it. Instead you've made up some wild story about amnesia." Her high-pitched laugh echoed through the room. "Who are you trying to protect, Michelle? Your boyfriend? Did you plan it together? Or was it a crime of passion?"

"You're wrong about me," Michelle choked out.

"Did he deny you something?" Danielle pressed a perfectly manicured hand against her breast. "Oh, no, my father never denied you anything, did he? Poor little poor girl from the wrong side of the tracks. You had him wrapped around your little finger, didn't you? He gave you everything. Money. Security. What happened, Michelle? Did you get greedy?"

The words hurt, made her feel sick and dirty. Vaguely, Michelle was aware of the roar of blood through her veins. "I'm telling the truth. I would never hurt Armon. I loved him—"

Danielle's hand shot out. Michelle didn't see the blow coming. Pain zinged along her cheekbone. Her head snapped back.

"You don't have the right to love a man like my father!" Danielle spat.

Michelle stumbled backward, but a pair of strong hands caught her from behind.

"Easy does it."

She hadn't heard the conference room door open, but she damn well knew that voice. Dazed, she tested her balance, then turned and came face-to-face with Philip Betancourt.

Dark, stormy gray eyes assessed her. "You got your feet under you?"

Speechless, she nodded.

"Do you want to press assault charges against Ms. Landsteiner?"

He was so close, she could smell the woodsy scent of his cologne. His fingers pressed gently into her biceps. Warm. Strong. Foolishly reassuring. "No." Michelle stepped back.

Releasing her, he swept his narrowed gaze over Danielle. "You seem to have a penchant for violence, Ms. Landsteiner. Where were *you* last night at 10:00 p.m.?"

Danielle's face reddened. Crimson lips peeled back into a snarl. "How dare you!" A strand of blond hair fell into her face. She shoved it back, then thrust a red-tipped finger at Michelle. "I want that woman arrested."

Betancourt arched a brow. "I didn't see her assault anyone."

"Not for assault! For murder! She was sleeping with him, for God's sake! My father was killed in her apartment! All she's ever wanted was his money."

Michelle felt as if she'd just gone over the edge of a cliff and fallen into a place she could only liken to hell. Her best friend was dead. The people she'd considered family for four years had turned on her like wolves on fallen prey. Now this detective with the hard eyes was probably going to arrest her for a crime she hadn't committed.

Danielle looked like a lioness about to leap. "If you don't do your job, Betancourt, we'll find someone who will."

The detective shot Baldwin a warning look. "I suggest

you get her under control before she does something we'll all be sorry for.''

Baldwin shoved away from the desk. ''Danielle.''

Without warning, she launched herself at Michelle. ''You have some nerve coming here! Gold digger! Murderer!''

Baldwin moved swiftly, but Betancourt was quicker. He placed himself solidly between Danielle and Michelle. ''You touch her and you're going to jail,'' he told Danielle in a quietly dangerous voice.

Danielle's gaze never left Michelle, animosity glittering in its depths. ''Don't come back. You're not welcome here. You never were.''

Michelle turned away, hurt slicing her clean through. At the door, she risked a glance at Betancourt, only to find his eyes already on her, gauging her, burning into her with an intensity that made her feel emotionally stripped bare, as if he had the ability to peel away her outer shell and see the pain twisting inside her.

Her only thought as she headed toward her office was that she wouldn't let them take her dignity. It was the last thing she had that was truly hers, the only thing that couldn't be taken from her. No matter what, she wouldn't give it up.

Chapter 4

It took Philip all of five minutes to realize the Landsteiners weren't going to cooperate. Whether it was because of Philip's history with Baldwin, or perhaps, because they felt themselves above suspicion in regard to their father's death, they didn't want a cop treading on their territory.

Damn, he hated lawyers.

After twenty minutes of frustration, he decided to switch tactics and question each Landsteiner separately—in the privacy of the interview room downtown. He knew fully the value of atmosphere, just as he knew what a little one-on-one did for a witness's sense of cooperation.

He didn't expect to find Michelle in her office, especially after the ugly scene in the conference room. A person of lesser character would have made a beeline for the door after a trouncing like the one Danielle had doled out. He had to admit Michelle Pelletier had grit. Not the in-your-face kind he saw so often in his line of work, but a quiet strength balanced with a subtle toughness that inspired his admiration, even when it shouldn't have. Still, he hadn't missed the flash of hurt in her eyes when Danielle had tossed out the term "swamp rat." He hadn't known animosity existed between Michelle and the Landsteiners. Interesting development.

He stood at the door to her office without notice, watching her. She moved with brusque precision as she stacked volumes, files and personal items into a cardboard box. Her hair was pulled back into a rebellious ponytail and secured with a bow at her nape. To the untrained eye, she might have looked composed and chic. But Philip saw through the carefully fashioned veneer. From her board-stiff spine to the tight set of her jaw, he knew Danielle's words had hurt her more than she was letting on. Dark smudges of fatigue beneath her eyes revealed she hadn't slept. Her hands shook as she shuffled through papers and files.

The brown jacket and skirt fit her nicely, but lacked the crispness of a brand-new, store-bought suit. Her pumps were expensive, but scuffed beneath a carefully-applied layer of polish. Her only visible jewelry consisted of a single strand of pearls at her throat. She didn't spend a lot of money on clothes. If she'd been sleeping with old man Landsteiner, why hadn't he showered her with an expensive wardrobe?

Philip's gaze swept over the set of her shoulders, then lower. Even with the jacket, he could see that she was full breasted. The slender-fitting skirt hugged a narrow waist and the subtle flare of her hips, then fell conservatively to her knees. He told himself he wasn't ogling, that a figure like hers would draw the attention of any red-blooded male, but he knew better.

"Are you here to arrest me, Detective? Or are you just going to stare at me until I confess? Is that your usual modus operandi?"

Her voice jerked him from his musings. *Busted,* he thought, and wondered how long she'd been aware of his examination of her. Shifting his weight from one foot to the other to accommodate the tightness in his groin, he reminded himself he had a job to do. Dammit, he was a cop and this woman was a suspect in a murder case that already had his commander breathing down his neck. What the hell was wrong with him, getting caught up in the way that suit swept over curves he was better off not noticing?

"Or maybe you just needed a little entertainment to start your day. Danielle's good at that sort of thing. Did you enjoy the show?"

He cleared his throat. "I didn't enjoy that scene any more than you did."

"You deliberately provoked her."

"I asked a legitimate question. I can't help it if she's got a temper. Not to mention a hell of a right hook." He frowned, remembering the way Michelle's head had snapped back when Danielle slapped her. "How's the jaw?"

She touched her left cheekbone. "I think a little bruise is the least of my worries."

From three feet away, Philip noticed the bruise forming beneath delicate skin. The urge to reach out and touch her was strong, but he resisted. He knew better than to play with fire.

"You should have pressed charges," he said.

"No, I think you would have enjoyed that too much."

He smiled at her perceptivity. "You bet." One day she would probably be a damn good lawyer—if she didn't end up in jail first. "I stopped by to see if there was anything you wanted to add to your statement."

"I haven't remembered what happened, if that's what you're asking."

"I've got more questions."

"I figured you did." She picked up a volume and set it in the box. "I may have remembered…some details. About last night."

His pulse jumped at the thought of new information. He didn't have squat in the way of evidence, save for the Beretta and her blood-smeared sweatshirt. The remaining lab reports were due back this morning. "Talk to me," he said.

Her praline-brown eyes swept to the door. She shook her head. "Not here. I'm not sure how much of that scene you witnessed, but I'm not up to another one."

The emotion in her voice made Philip uncomfortable. He didn't want to think of her on an emotional level. He didn't want to think of her as vulnerable, either. But just beneath that tough facade, both lay side by side. "I'm sorry about your job."

Snapping the box closed, she bent to lift it. "We both know you're not here to offer condolences, though, don't we?"

He looked down at the box in her arms and realized belatedly it looked too heavy for her. "I could use some caffeine. Why don't you give me that box, and we'll go get a cup of coffee and talk about last night?"

Her expression told him she was capable of carrying the box whether it was too heavy or not. But after a moment she conceded. "Since you're the cop, and I seem to be your number one suspect, I guess you're calling the shots."

Derek met them at the door as Michelle and Philip walked through the reception area to leave. "I'm sorry it worked out this way," Derek said, handing her a sealed envelope that probably contained her last paycheck.

Squaring her shoulders, Michelle met the other man's gaze levelly. "So am I," she said, accepting the offered envelope.

Philip shot Derek a crisp smile. "Don't take any trips, Landsteiner," he said, and they left the office without looking back.

Philip chose Café Ruby because it was quiet and the owner, a reed-thin Cajun woman with hair like Spanish moss, served the strongest French roast in town. He ordered his coffee black; Michelle ordered café au lait.

When the mugs were on the table between them, Philip

breached the silence with the question that had been eating at him since they'd left the office. "What kind of details did you remember?"

She looked embarrassed. "I wasn't sure if I should even bother you with this. I don't know how important it is, or if it's even relevant at this point, but...I had a dream last night. About the murder."

Disappointment rippled through him. He'd hoped for something concrete. Dreams were anything but concrete. "Tell me about it."

"I don't normally remember my dreams. This one was vivid. I thought maybe it was my memory trying to resurface." She took a deep breath. "Anyway, in this dream, I saw a man...dressed in black. He was in my apartment with a gun. I saw him murder Armon."

Philip's interest flared. The neighbor had claimed to see a black-clad man running from the scene. "Did you see the man's face? Did he look familiar?"

A tendril of brown hair escaped her ponytail when she shook her head. "He wore some type of mask, so I didn't see his face."

"Did he say anything?"

"No. But I got the feeling he wanted to hurt me."

"How so?"

"I don't know. But it was more than just the gun. I felt...threatened. Like it was...personal, maybe."

Philip pretended not to notice when she shivered, and he damn well ignored the sudden urge to reach out and take her hands in his to keep them from trembling.

"Do you think this dream is a memory? Something you actually saw and for whatever reason blocked?" He was suspicious by nature and the entire scenario seemed unlikely. Unfortunately, he didn't have anything more solid to go on at the moment.

"Maybe. I don't know, but I thought I should tell you. I thought it might be important." She looked down at her coffee. "I was scared out of my wits when I woke up. And I don't scare easily, Detective."

After the way she'd held her ground at the office, he didn't doubt it. Still, he wasn't sure how much weight to put in a dream. He wondered what the department shrink would have to say. "We're still checking suspicious persons reports in the area. Maybe we'll come up with something." Her neighborhood was chock-full of suspicious characters, a fact neither of them mentioned.

Wrapping her hands around the mug, she sipped some of the coffee. "Thank you."

"For what?"

"For believing me."

"To be perfectly honest with you, Miss Pelletier, I haven't decided yet whether or not I believe you."

"You believe me enough to check out my story."

"That's my job. That's how homicides are solved. We check out leads one at a time until we get a break." Finishing his coffee, he set it on the edge of the table to be refilled. He chose his next words carefully. "I spoke with Danielle Landsteiner this morning. She's under the impression you were sleeping with her father."

Indignation heated Michelle's gaze. "Danielle's wrong."

"I understand why you might not want something like that to become public knowledge, why you might want to protect Landsteiner's reputation—or your own, for that matter—but this is a murder investigation. It could be important—"

"You can say it all you want, Detective. And you can think it until hell freezes over. But my relationship with Armon was based on platonic love and respect and nothing more. I refuse to defend the relationship to you or anyone else." Slinging her purse over her shoulder, she rose. "I have to go."

Surprise flitted through him, followed by a jab of irritation. "We're not finished."

"I am." She turned away.

Philip stood abruptly. Before he could stop himself, he reached out and grasped her forearm. "We can do this the easy way, or we can do it downtown, Miss Pelletier. It's your call."

She glared at him over her shoulder, then looked down to where his fingers dug into her arm. "Don't threaten me."

"That's not a threat. It's police procedure. I'm merely giving you a choice as to where you want to answer my questions." He let his hand fall away.

An emotion he couldn't identify flickered behind her eyes. "Why didn't you threaten to take Danielle or Baldwin or Derek downtown?" She'd lowered her voice, but he didn't miss the smoldering anger behind it.

"What makes you think I didn't?"

"Maybe your reluctance to inconvenience them has more to do with status. Are you afraid to ruffle wealthy feathers, Detective? No telling who they know in the superintendent's office."

His temper stirred. "Your apartment was the scene of a murder last night, Miss Pelletier. You were there. Your gun was on the floor next to the corpse of a man you knew personally. Ten to one it's the murder weapon—"

"I didn't kill him!"

"You're not giving me the answers I need!"

The café fell silent. Annoyed, Philip looked around and realized they'd made a scene. Damn, he couldn't remember the last time he'd lost his temper in public, certainly not in the course of an investigation. Not only was such conduct unprofessional, it was counterproductive. What was it about this tough little waif that had him acting like a fresh-faced rookie?

"Sit down," he growled.

She gave him a killing look. Then, tightening her lips, she lowered herself into the bistro chair. "You can bully me all you like—"

"If you want to clear yourself, you're going to have to cooperate."

"I am cooperating. You just can't seem to accept the idea that I'm telling the truth."

"If you can't remember the shooting, how can you be so sure you didn't pull the trigger?"

Her quick intake of breath told him the question had hit home. "I know what I'm capable of," she snapped. "Armon was like a father to me. I could never hurt him. Never."

"What about self-defense?"

"That's ridiculous."

He had to hand it to her; she was consistent. Most liars weren't, and got caught because their stories varied or their motivations didn't add up. Philip didn't want to make a decision this early in the game as to whether or not Michelle was lying. He wasn't finished putting things together. The amnesia didn't sit well with his sensibilities. But when he tried to envision this woman pulling the trigger and letting the old man die in her foyer, he just couldn't do it.

As if on cue, the owner came over to refill Philip's cup. "Stop harassing my customers, Betancourt, or I'll have to call a cop." Her voice grated like sandpaper.

Philip smiled despite the fact that his temper was still pumping. "Has anyone told you that you make the best coffee in town, Ruby?"

The woman wasn't buying it. "Pretty words will get you nowhere with me. *T'es trop brute.*" Her gaze landed on Michelle. *"Gette-le."*

Philip didn't understand Cajun French, but he could tell by Michelle's amused expression that she did. "I'm not even going to ask you what she said," he grumbled after the owner left.

"You must be a regular. She seems to know you pretty well."

He arched a brow. "Really?"

"She says you're a brute and that I should keep an eye on you."

"Probably not bad advice." Guilt over losing his temper nagged at him. "I shouldn't have lost my temper."

"Is that your idea of an apology?"

He held her gaze. "That's as good as it gets."

A smile played at the corner of her mouth. "Can I ask you a question?"

"Ask away."

"Am I your only suspect?"

"At this point everyone who knew or had dealings with Landsteiner is a suspect."

"Do you have any leads?"

"You mean other than all the circumstantial stuff we found at your apartment?"

She blew out a sigh.

"You know I can't discuss the details with you." Rubbing his hand over his chin, he felt the beginnings of stubble, and realized he was working on thirty-six hours without sleep. Maybe that was why his brain was operating at the speed of slow-rising dough. "Did Landsteiner have any enemies?"

She shook her head. "I can't imagine that he did. Everyone liked Armon. He was a very kind, generous man."

"Someone didn't think so. Lawyers make enemies sometimes."

"If he did, I didn't know about it."

"Did any of the Landsteiners have a reason to want him dead?"

"You mean his family?"

"Any arguments between them? Differences of opinion? About the firm, maybe?"

"None that I'm aware of."

"Why do they have so much animosity toward you?"

She winced. It was a minute reaction, but for a split second, the veneer of toughness slipped to reveal the hurt and mistrust buried in the depths of her eyes. He wondered about its roots, thought it might be interesting to find out what made her tick.

"Do you have any brothers or sisters, Detective?"

Where was she going with this? "A sister. She lives in Florida with a half-dozen kids. Why?"

"You're familiar with the term sibling rivalry?"

"You aren't a sibling."

"Not by blood, but the rivalry was there. This may sound odd, but I think Armon's children were jealous of my relationship with their father. They didn't understand it, therefore they condemned it. Not openly, of course. They tolerated me because Armon...cared for me." Her hands twisted on the table in front of her. She looked down, stilled them. "I didn't realize the extent of that jealousy until this morning."

"Why did Landsteiner fixate on you?"

"He didn't fixate on me."

"Okay. Why did he help you?"

Her eyes met his, darkened. "I can't answer for him."

More secrets, Philip thought, and his curiosity stirred.

"Armon loved his family very much, but he didn't share the same closeness with his children as he did with me. I'd sensed resentment in the past, especially from Danielle, but I always shrugged it off. I didn't think I'd ever have to deal with it."

"What about Derek and Baldwin? Any jealousy there? Did either of them ever approach you in a sexual way? Or do anything that led you to believe they wanted a relationship?"

She shook her head. "Never."

Philip nodded, but he wasn't satisfied. Not by a long shot. When he looked at Michelle Pelletier, he saw secrets. Some buried, others so close to the surface he could *feel* them. He'd sensed all along she was hiding something. For the life of him he couldn't figure out what—or why.

"I did some research on amnesia last night," she said. "Over the Internet."

He'd intended to do the same, but hadn't had the time. Trying to ignore the exhaustion pressing into him, he sighed. "I'm sure as hell not an expert. What did you find?"

"Data is sketchy because amnesia is rare. But I was able to find out that some forms of memory loss can be caused by a traumatic emotional event. Psychogenic amnesia is the term the shrinks use. I also found out that there are tests and drugs available to physicians to recapture lost memories."

She looked…hopeful. It surprised the hell out of him that she was actually looking forward to being tested. Like that added up. Why should it? Nothing else did when it came to Michelle Pelletier.

"Your psychological evaluation is scheduled for seven o'clock this evening. I'll brief Dr. Witt. He's a good man." Philip had considered paying him a visit after that Algiers shopkeeper had been killed, but he'd always managed to talk himself out of it.

"I'll be there," she said.

"You should probably bring your lawyer."

A hard laugh broke from her throat. "I think you know I don't have a lawyer."

"Your choice."

"I'm counting on this evaluation to clear me, Detective."

He wanted to be skeptical, would have if she hadn't been looking at him as if her life depended on that evaluation. He supposed, in a way, it did. "With or without your memory, I'll find who did it."

Her eyes were clear and bottomless and so mesmerizing that for a moment Philip felt as if he might tumble headlong into their depths. He tried to blame his distraction on fatigue—he was getting too damn old to work around the clock—but he knew it had more to do with the woman sitting across from him than his lack of sleep. The realization wasn't a comforting one.

Pulling out a business card, he eased himself to his feet and laid a ten dollar bill on the table. "If you remember anything before the evaluation this evening, give me a call." He handed her the card. "My pager number's on the back."

"Thank you."

He noticed the box sitting on the chair next to her. "Can I drop you back at your car?"

"Well…no. I'm fine." She scooted back from the table and rose.

"Let me get that box for you."

"I can get it—"

He leaned forward to lift the box. She did the same and their heads came together with a quiet thud.

Not hard enough to cause pain, but he definitely felt it. Philip straightened, feeling awkward. Their gazes met. A chuckle escaped him when she rubbed the top of her head. Laughter bubbled out of her. Throaty. Soft. As lyrical as the final notes of a saxophone. And so damn sexy he reconsidered the wisdom of offering to take her to her car.

His gaze dropped to her mouth, and he quickly regretted it. It was the first time he'd seen her smile, and the sight affected him, reached into him, touched something warm and needy he didn't want to acknowledge. Not now. Not with this woman. He felt as if he'd ventured too close to a dangerous cliff. One more step and he'd fall over the edge.

It was a stupid moment, one that couldn't go on, one he shouldn't have let happen. He was a cop, for God's sake. She was a suspect. He didn't want to think of her laughter when he looked at her. Or that her eyes held secrets as dark and mysterious as the bayou. He didn't want to think of the way that suit swept over her body. Dammit, he didn't want to think of her at all.

"Actually, uh, I don't have a car. I mean, I usually take the streetcar…or the bus."

The fact that she was flustered pleased him. "In that case, I'll just drop you at your apartment on my way to the precinct.'' Huskiness roughened his voice. Ignoring it, and its source, he picked up the box.

"I'm not staying at my apartment. I haven't…gone back there yet. I'm staying at the Pontchartrain." She must have noticed the question in his gaze, because she attempted to explain. "Baldwin paid for a couple of nights."

"I'll drop you at the hotel, then." Philip didn't look at her as he made his way to the door. He wasn't even sure she'd followed until he heard her footfalls on the tile. He felt off-kilter. His heart beat just a little too fast. The room felt stuffy, and he resisted the urge to loosen his tie. Worst of all, he was thinking about his number one suspect in terms of the way she smelled as opposed to motive, means and opportunity.

He should go home and grab a couple hours of sleep to clear his head—fatigue was messing with his brain—but he knew he couldn't sleep. Not when lab reports and witness statements waited for him at the precinct. He couldn't afford to get distracted. Not by fatigue. Certainly not by this woman. Another mistake would cost him not only his peace of mind, but his career.

Philip acknowledged that he had broken one of his cardinal rules. He'd let himself feel something for a suspect. Worse, he'd allowed himself to connect with her. Not as a cop, but as a man. Even as he swore it wouldn't happen again, he knew he was vulnerable, and he damn well didn't like it. He couldn't think of a worse fate for a man who prided himself on objectivity and gut instinct. He'd have to be careful in the coming days. He'd keep his distance from her and concentrate on the case. And if the evidence warranted it, he'd bust Michelle Pelletier without hesitation and no matter what the cost.

Michelle couldn't think of a way to avoid Betancourt's offer to drive her to the hotel. She wasn't exactly sure what had happened at the café, but she didn't like it. In the span of a millisecond, an uncomfortable awareness had bloomed between them. An awareness that had nothing to do with his status as a cop or hers as a suspect. For an instant as she'd stared into those cool, gray eyes, he'd reacted to her as a man. And as much as she didn't want to admit it, she'd responded as a woman.

Tense silence filled the car as they passed the narrow storefronts and ivy-shrouded balconies along Chartres Street and headed toward the hotel. Betancourt scowled at the traffic. When a red light stopped them at Esplanade a few blocks from her apartment, he cast a stony look in her direction.

"This isn't the greatest neighborhood for you to be walking in," he said.

The words surprised her. Not because it wasn't true—the neighborhood *had* seen better days—but because he sounded concerned. "When I first moved to New Orleans, it was all I could afford. My landlord hasn't raised the rent, so I stayed. Besides, I'm careful about my personal safety. I take precautions."

The truth of the matter was she couldn't afford to live anywhere else and still have transportation to Tulane and her job at Landsteiner & Associates…. The thought of the job she'd lost sent a stab of pain through her middle. She'd loved her work, the routine, the predictability, just as she'd loved the people with whom she'd worked. Armon had gone out of his way to give her new responsibilities so she could learn as much as possible about the legal profession. She didn't want to think about the opportunity that had been ripped from her grasp.

Michelle sighed, realizing she would miss class tonight because of the psychological evaluation. She wondered if that was how dreams slipped away, one setback, one stone, one hurdle at a time. She wondered if that was how it had been with her mother. Had Blanche Pelletier had dreams? Had she watched them slip away over the years until she convinced herself none of them were possible?

Shifting uncomfortably in her seat, Michelle looked out the window. She'd promised herself a long time ago she would never be like her mother. She'd never lose hope, or give up on her dreams no matter how many roadblocks were thrown in her path. She'd already overcome so much. Glancing at Betancourt, she pondered the question of how long it would take him to find out about her past. How deep would he dig?

Fear quivered through her when she realized the truth would eventually come out. Would he use it against her? Would he destroy her dreams? The part of her that had become cynical over the years said yes. Not because it was personal, of course, but because a man like Philip Betancourt did his job no matter who got hurt.

"Nice place."

Michelle started at the sound of his voice. She hadn't realized he'd parked the unmarked cruiser in front of the hotel.

Betancourt eyed her. "You looked like you were a million miles away."

No, she thought dully, she'd been fifty miles to the southwest in the muddy little town of Bayou Lafourche. But she wouldn't tell him that. If he wanted to know about her past, he was going to have to find out on his own. She wasn't going to dig her own grave.

"Thanks for the ride." She reached for the door latch.

"Anytime." He got out of the car and lifted the box from the trunk, handed it to a waiting bellman along with a couple of bills.

She risked a glance at Betancourt. He stared back at her with such intensity that it was difficult for her to hold his gaze. His face was set in a scowl. His mouth was thin and unyielding. Turbulent gray eyes she couldn't begin to read assessed her. He was standing so close she could smell his aftershave, a clean woodsy scent that made her feel like she'd just stepped off a roller coaster.

Turning, she started toward the hotel.

"Michelle?"

It was the first time he'd used her first name. She looked at him over her shoulder, refusing to admit she liked the sound.

"Call me if you remember something," he said. "Even if you don't think it's important."

Without another word, he got into the car and pulled onto the street. Michelle stared after him. Her knees were shaking. In the backwaters of her mind, she acknowledged her attraction to him. The insaneness of it made her want to laugh—or cry. She was attracted to a man, a cop no less, who was about to ruin her life.

A sense of déjà vu engulfed her, along with the bitter taste of a betrayal she'd long since buried. She hadn't forgotten the lessons the past had taught her. No matter how far she traveled or how fast she ran, the secrets she'd left in that little town followed, clinging to her like a bad smell. Michelle knew she couldn't trust Betancourt, or risk making herself vulnerable. She'd vowed years ago never to make herself vulnerable to another man, especially another cop.

Chapter 5

Twenty minutes later Philip strode through the double glass doors of the Broad Street Station and headed for the homicide division. "Get your feet off my desk, Sanderson."

Cory jumped, then lowered his feet to the floor. "I thought you'd be home sleeping, Betancourt."

"Maybe in my next life." Philip's voice was clipped. "What have you got for me?"

"Plenty if you like Alfred Hitchcock." Cory slid a manila folder in front of him.

Arching a brow at his partner's cryptic answer, Philip reached for the folder. "I always preferred cops and robbers over mysteries."

"Then you're not going to like this one."

The first sheet of paper contained the medical examiner's report. Philip quickly scanned it, his eyes cutting directly to the cause of death. Armon Landsteiner had died of a single gunshot wound that pierced his heart's left ventricle. He'd died instantly.

"What a way to go." Philip set the folder on his desk for

later, preferring to hear Cory's take on the ballistics and lab reports before reading them himself. "What about the slug?"

"Nine millimeter."

"From the Beretta?"

"Yeah."

"Her prints on the gun?"

"All over it."

"Blood from her sweatshirt match the vic's?"

"Yep."

Dammit, he didn't want to arrest Michelle. "What about powder burns?"

"That's where old Alfred comes in." Cory frowned. "There were no powder burns on her shirt or her hands."

"So she didn't fire the gun."

"If she did, she would have had to wear gloves, dispose of them, then change shirts before we got there."

"Then she would have had to touch the body to get the blood on her shirt."

Cory sighed. "Yeah. Doesn't fit, does it?"

"Seems unlikely."

"But not impossible."

That was what bothered Philip the most. "Anything else?"

"Oh, yeah." Cory grinned. "It seems old man Landsteiner provided for Miss Pelletier with a nice little life insurance policy to the tune of $100,000."

The information broadsided Philip with the force of a speeding truck. Another nail in her proverbial coffin. "He was worth a lot more."

"A couple of million. I'm still looking for the will."

"He's got to have one. Anyone worth that much has a damn will. The man has assets. Did he have a lawyer?"

"He used a firm over in Metairie. I'm waiting for a call back to see if the lawyer drew up a will."

"I went to see the Landsteiners, but they stonewalled

me." Philip looked at his watch. "I'm going to question them separately, starting with Baldwin."

"That ought to be fun." Cory laughed. "What about the suspect? Has she, uh, remembered anything?"

Tension crept into Philip's shoulders at the mention of Michelle. All the way back to the station, he'd been aware of her scent in the car. "She claims she had a dream about a man in black."

"You think she's in cahoots with her neighbor?"

"It's possible, but I don't think so."

His partner's eyes narrowed. "Why not?"

Because every time Philip looked at her he couldn't think of anything except those bottomless brown eyes. Or the way that suit swept over a body that heated his blood and damn the consequences....

Irritated with the direction his thoughts had taken, Philip expunged them. "I spoke with the neighbor again. She substantiates the claim. Says she saw a man in black running through the courtyard a few minutes before the police arrived."

"So their stories match. They could have corroborated."

"What would the neighbor have to gain?"

"Part of the insurance money."

"That's a stretch, Cory."

"Just throwing out possibilities, my man."

Philip opened the manila folder again and scanned the ballistics report. "So if she's sleeping with the old man, why isn't she living high on the hog? Why is she living in a bad neighborhood and wearing secondhand suits?"

"Maybe he was cheap." Clasping his hands behind his head, Cory leaned back in his chair. "On the other hand why would a high roller like Landsteiner leave that kind of money to a woman he wasn't intimate with?"

Philip hated it when things didn't add up. Nothing added up when it came to Michelle Pelletier. "Did the background check reveal anything interesting?"

"Real interesting." Cory leaned forward and reached for a legal pad on his desk. "She was born in Bayou Lafourche—"

"Where is that?"

"I checked the map. It's a small town in bayou country, about fifty miles southwest of here. Mother's name was Blanche Pelletier. Her father wasn't named on her birth certificate." Cory looked at Philip and frowned. "Her mother worked at the Fortrex Chemical Plant. Died of cancer when our suspect was seventeen. Then Miss Pelletier went to work at the plant, spent five years there. Good work record. Went to the community college and earned some kind of a scholarship to Tulane."

"Lucky break."

"I'll say. I haven't met many folks who grew up poorer than me, but this one did. I haven't been able to dig up the details yet on that scholarship."

Philip listened, fascinated and strangely touched by Michelle's past. One thing was obvious. She hadn't had an easy life. He knew what the working conditions were like in some of the plants in south Louisiana. Hot. Dirty. Backbreaking. Most would keep the Occupational Safety and Health Administration busy for decades. Yet she'd endured. What kind of woman survived those kinds of odds and ended up at Tulane with a job at one of the most prestigious law firms in the city?

"She's got a brother," Cory continued. "Nicolas. Convicted of murder ten years ago. Just released from Angola Prison."

"I'll be damned."

"This is where it gets interesting. She's got a record."

Philip went perfectly still as a thick wave of disappointment washed over him. Muttering a curse, he rubbed his hand over his jaw. His eyes felt gritty. He needed coffee. Dammit, he needed a break in this case. One that didn't point to Michelle. "What charge?"

"Not sure yet. It's a juvenile offense, so the records are sealed. We can get a subpoena, but it'll take some time."

"Get the damn subpoena." Anger that Michelle hadn't bothered to mention her record rumbled through Philip. He wondered what else she was hiding.

"She didn't tell you about it, huh?"

Philip scowled at his partner. "Would you?"

Cory grinned. "If I was in her shoes I definitely wouldn't tell *you.* Now, I might tell *me,* since it's common knowledge I've got a heart."

Despite his efforts to control it, Philip's temper simmered. Stuffing the reports into his briefcase, he started for the door. "I'm going to go talk to the Landsteiners, then try to grab a couple hours of sleep. I'll be back in time for the psych evaluation. You going to be here?"

Cory leaned back in his chair, then put his feet back up on Philip's desk. "I'll be here later. Right now, I'm going over to Metairie to see about the will, then I've got a dinner date. You should try it some time, Betancourt. Might improve your outlook on life."

"Not likely." Philip reached the door and turned. "And keep your damn feet off my desk."

Michelle's leather pumps clicked smartly against the tile floor as she left the elevator and headed toward interview room 3 of the Broad Street Police Station. Knowing she would need every ounce of confidence she could muster in the coming hours, she'd spent a few extra minutes primping. Her suit, albeit not brand-new, was made by her favorite designer and fit her well. Hibiscus-colored lipstick slicked her lips. Her hair curved into a conservative chignon at her nape. She'd gone to the extra trouble, figuring that even if she didn't feel put together, at least she would look it.

But, damn, she didn't want to be here. An inherent mistrust of doctors had kept her away from them over the years. Her mistrust of cops in general made the situation doubly worse. Just because Betancourt had been civil to her over coffee didn't mean he cared about the truth—or the outcome of this evaluation. Michelle knew he wouldn't stop until he'd made an arrest. If that meant sacrificing her in the process, no doubt he'd do it. He was like a predator waiting to pounce. He wanted one thing, and that was to nail her for Armon's murder. She'd be wise to remember what had happened the last time she'd trusted a cop.

It didn't matter that his smile had touched her for a brief moment this morning. Or that his eyes reminded her of a gulf storm that was as breathtaking as it was treacherous.

Michelle shoved the thoughts aside. She couldn't think of Betancourt in those terms now. Regardless of the kindness he'd shown her, regardless of how his gaze affected her, she couldn't let her guard down. Betancourt would stop at nothing to solve his case. He would use her, then he would destroy her—just as Deputy Frank Blanchard had all those years ago.

Only Michelle wasn't the girl she'd been back in Bayou Lafourche. She was a woman now. Stronger. Smarter. She damn well knew how to fight back. The past had immunized her to Betancourt's unique brand of charm. She would deal with him just as she'd dealt with all the other problems that had cropped up in endless supply in her life. Identify and eliminate. Simple.

Trying to ignore the butterflies in her stomach, Michelle stopped outside the interview room door. ''You can do this.'' Her voice sounded high and tight in the silence of the corridor. Anxiety pumped through her with every beat of her heart. Taking a deep, shaky breath, she forced her hand to the knob and opened the door.

Betancourt's powerful presence immediately drew her gaze. Facing the single window, he stood with his back to her, his hands in his pockets. When she stepped into the room, he turned and hit her with a look that stopped her heart dead in her chest. His expression wasn't friendly.

Michelle held her breath as that lethal gaze skimmed down the front of her. She wasn't accustomed to being scrutinized, and the act unnerved her, despite her best efforts to stay calm. She returned the stare, hoping he couldn't hear the pounding of her heart as clearly as she did.

He'd shaved since she had last seen him, but he didn't look clean-cut. The word *predator* came to mind, but she quickly shoved it aside. She didn't want to think of predators when she was feeling so damn vulnerable.

He'd changed into a black suit. The color agreed with him, she thought, enhancing eyes that were nearly as dark and every bit as forbidding. She wanted to say something to let him know she didn't appreciate the scrutiny, but her voice failed her.

"Ah, you must be Miss Pelletier. Thank you for coming."

The words jump-started her brain. Michelle tore her gaze from Betancourt. A balding man with friendly blue eyes approached her with his hand outstretched. "I'm Dr. Lomas Witt. Detective Betancourt and I were just discussing the case. How are you feeling?"

She wondered if Betancourt had filled the good doctor's head with suspicion. "Much better." She extended her hand.

"Good." He motioned toward the sofa. "Please, have a seat."

Michelle felt Betancourt's gaze as she crossed the room and lowered herself onto it.

The interview room was larger and not nearly as unpleasant as the one she'd been detained in the night before. An arrangement of silk flowers sat atop an oblong table in the center of the room. To her left, a tarnished brass lamp on an end table cast yellow light in a circular pattern on the floor.

Betancourt moved from his place by the window. "Hello, Miss Pelletier."

Was she imagining it, or did he look angry? "Detective."

"I'm bound by law to inform you that this session is being recorded," he said.

"I'm familiar with the routine."

Removing a small tape recorder from his jacket pocket, he placed it on the table, then punched a button. His gaze latched on to hers. "You've chosen not to have your lawyer present during this interview?"

"That's correct." Her voice seemed small and inconsequential compared to his.

Dr. Witt cleared his throat. "Detective Betancourt briefed me on the situation, Miss Pelletier. He also told me about the nightmare you suffered. Have you had any glimpses or flashbacks of memory since last night?"

Michelle shook her head. "No. Just the nightmare."

"What we're going to do today," the doctor said, "is attempt to induce hypnosis to help you remember what happened on the night of Monday, January 10. Are you familiar with hypnosis?"

"No."

"Unlike television's depiction, true hypnosis is basically a state of complete relaxation where you, the subject, can focus fully on what is being said and 'let go,' so to speak, of your repressed memories if, indeed, you've suffered some type of memory loss."

"What can I expect?"

Dr. Witt smiled reassuringly. "Some of my clients have mild feelings of floating, sinking, anesthesia, or separation from their body, but their personal experiences vary widely. You will remain aware of what's going on. All of your senses will remain intact. It always makes my patients feel better when I tell them they can stop anytime they wish."

Michelle looked from Dr. Witt to Betancourt. "Will it help me remember what happened?"

Leaning his hip against the table, Betancourt folded his arms over his chest and returned her gaze with an unsettling intensity.

"I can't guarantee it," Witt said. "But many times hypnosis does help restore lost memories. In most cases people who seek hypnosis want to remember something so they can deal with a personal issue. Your case, Miss Pelletier, is different. We may be able to break through your memory barriers with just one session, or it could take a dozen. About twenty-five percent of the population are resistant to hypnosis, and can't be hypnotized at all. Only four out of ten people are good subjects."

"Hopefully, I'm one of those four in ten."

"You're going in with the right attitude." Rising, Dr. Witt pulled a chair closer to the sofa. "Are you ready to begin?"

Michelle swallowed to ease her tight throat. "Yes."

"Would you prefer to lie down?"

"No."

"All right." He opened a file on his lap and paged through several sheets of paper. "Are you comfortable?"

Michelle almost laughed at the absurdity of the question. No, she wasn't comfortable. Cops trying to nail her for a murder she hadn't committed made her nervous as hell. "I'm fine."

"I want you to try to relax, Michelle. You're nervous, aren't you?"

The observation made her feel transparent, as if the emotions roiling inside her had been bared for the world to see. "A little."

"Set your bag on the floor. Relax your hands."

Michelle did as she was told, resting her hands easily in her lap.

"That's good. Now, I want you to lean back against the sofa cushion. Take a deep breath and close your eyes."

She didn't want to close her eyes. Not being able to see would only make her feel more vulnerable. Relaxation seemed next to impossible at this point. Still, she had to try.

If she wanted to find out what had happened to Armon, she had to go through with this.

She closed her eyes.

"Very good. Now, take a deep breath and let it out slowly. Concentrate first on relaxing your hands. Imagine all the tension in your body leaving you through your fingertips."

Even with her eyes closed, Michelle was starkly aware of Betancourt's presence. Was he watching her? Judging her? Wondering if she'd murdered a man in cold blood?

"Now, I'm going to take you into a state of total relaxation. I want you to clear your mind. Focus on my voice. Are you with me?"

Not sure if she was supposed to speak, she nodded.

"All right. That's good. The tension is draining from your body. Your eyes are tired. So tired you can't open them. You feel warm. Safe. Sleepy. Relaxed. Your body feels heavy. So heavy you can't move."

The doctor's singsong voice lapped over her like gentle waves over sand. Michelle focused solely on his words. For Armon, she thought. She was doing this for him.

She concentrated on the tension leaving her body through her fingertips. Slowly, her churning thoughts eased. She *was* tired, she realized, but then she hadn't slept more than an hour or so the night before.

"Are you comfortable, Michelle?"

"Yes." She hadn't realized she was going to answer until she heard her own voice.

"I'm going to ask you some questions now. Can you answer some questions for me?"

"Yes." Odd to hear her own voice when she hadn't intended to answer. It was as if someone else was answering. What if he asked her about Bayou Lafourche? Would she tell the truth?

"All right. I want you to think back to January 10. It was

a Monday. Rainy and cold, I think. Do you remember what you were doing that day?''

"Yes."

"Tell me about it."

Michelle relayed a condensed version of her day, ending with her leaving Tulane for home.

"I want you to stay relaxed, Michelle. I want you to concentrate on the tension flowing out of your fingertips. The tension has left you. You are relaxed. You feel warm and safe. Can you feel how heavy your arms are?''

"Yes." She was tired, on the verge of sleep, and felt as if she were floating inside a cloud.

"Where did you go after you left campus, Michelle?''

"I went home."

"Did you have a visitor that night?''

"Yes. Armon came over. I knew it the instant he knocked on the door. He had this special knock he always used. I was happy to see him.''

"Did you let him in?''

"Yes, of course." A shadow invaded her consciousness. A dark flash. Like the shadow of a thunderhead on a sunny day. "He seemed upset."

"How so?" Betancourt's voice cut in, deep and impatient.

"Armon was...acting strangely. He seemed edgy. Distracted. I was worried about him.''

"Did he tell you why he was upset?''

"I asked, but he just laughed. He wouldn't say.''

"What happened next?''

Dark images hovered at the edges of her consciousness. Shadowy figures. Voices. Anger and fear. She wanted to know the truth, but the darkness terrified her. She knew the truth lay in the darkness, but the part of her that was afraid didn't want to bridge the gap. "He asked for coffee. But I got the impression he was stalling. I went to the kitchen, to give him some time.''

"You made coffee?''

"Yes." The image of Armon's smiling face came to her so clearly that she almost raised her hand to touch him. "He was quite the coffee connoisseur. He liked it strong, with chicory."

"What happened after you made coffee?" Betancourt asked.

Her chest tightened, making it difficult to breathe. Armon's image flickered, darkened. "Something's wrong." Fear encroached, creeping over her, like quicksand, sucking her down.

"Michelle? What's happening?"

"I don't know." Vaguely, she was aware of her breaths coming too quickly, but she couldn't seem to get enough air into her lungs.

"Easy, Michelle." It was Dr. Witt's voice, steady and reassuring. "You're calm and relaxed, remember? You're safe here. Your limbs are heavy. Your eyes are closed. Can you take a deep breath for me?"

A breath shuddered out of her.

"Yes, that's good—"

"What happened after you made coffee?" Betancourt pressed.

"I walked back to the living room." The scene flashed like a strobe in her mind's eye. Vivid. Terrifying.

"What do you see?"

Adrenaline cut through her belly. "I...don't know."

"Tell us what you see, Michelle."

The barrel of a gun. Her gun. Her heart beat wildly in her chest. Part of her didn't want to know what had happened, didn't want to step into the darkness and relive the horror.

"What happened?" Betancourt's voice. Angry now. She pictured him leaning toward her. Too close. Too aggressive.

"Lieutenant, please." The doctor's voice almost broke her focus, but she got it back.

"Armon. Standing in the foyer." A sob rose from deep in her chest, but she choked it down. "He sees me, but he doesn't let on. He doesn't want the man at the door to see me." She couldn't breathe, couldn't move. Could only watch in frozen terror as the man in black raised the gun.

"What man? Who is it?"

The blast deafened her.

A high-pitched mewl broke from her throat. Then she was running. To Armon. Kneeling at his side. She smelled gunpowder, the coppery scent of blood. Horror pooled in the back of her throat.

"Dammit, what do you see?"

The barrel coming up, pointing at her. Blood on her hands.

Her concentration shattered, the images scattering like a glass thrown violently to the floor.

"Oh, God, no!" Her eyes snapped open. She blinked, focused on the two men standing over her. Dr. Witt in his white coat and baggy pants. Detective Betancourt staring at her as if he wanted to shake the information out of her.

She looked down at her hands, expecting to see blood. None there, but she could still smell it. Warm and sickly sweet. Nausea seesawed in her stomach. "I think I'm going to be sick."

"I'll get you some water." Dr. Witt made for the cooler against the wall.

Stomach clenching like a fist, Michelle rose abruptly. The room darkened, swayed. "Where's the ladies' room?"

"Easy. Just take it easy." Betancourt reached out to steady her. One arm went around her shoulders. The other hand circled her left biceps.

His touch was amazingly gentle for a man who didn't seem to know the meaning of the word. A contradiction to everything Michelle knew about the hard-nosed detective. For an insane instant, she wanted to melt into his arms and just let him hold her for a while. It seemed like an eternity since anyone had held her, since a man had held her. But

Betancourt was not only a man, she reminded herself, but a cop with a job to do.

"You're shaking."

She had to get out of there. The walls were closing in. Claustrophobia threatened. She wanted to wash her hands even though she could plainly see there was no blood on them.

Easily, she broke from his grip and stumbled to the door. By the time she reached the hall she was running. She heard someone call her name, but she didn't stop.

Betancourt followed her to the end of the hall and watched her disappear into the ladies' rest room. Frustration coupled with another emotion he didn't want to acknowledge sent him to the door, where he knocked hard enough to hurt his knuckles.

"Michelle? Are you all right?"

There was no answer. Not that he'd expected one. "We need to talk," he said to the door.

"Go away, Betancourt."

He looked down at his shoes and smiled despite the frustration flaring through him. He couldn't count the number of times he'd talked to a woman while staring at the exterior of a closed door. What the hell was it about women and doors? "We made some headway, Michelle. We need to talk about it while this is fresh in your mind."

No answer.

"I'm not going to go away until we talk."

No answer.

He wanted to punch the door. "Michelle? Are—"

A female dispatcher opened the door, then shoved past him with a glare. "Men's room is down the hall on the right, Betancourt."

Chagrined, Philip stepped back, cleared his throat. "She's a witness in a case. Is there anyone else in there?"

The woman shook her head, then continued down the hall.

Without preamble, he opened the door and peered inside. Michelle faced the sink, watching him in the mirror with dark, wary eyes. She looked as fragile as porcelain standing there gripping the edge of the counter with white-knuckled hands. Dampened tendrils of hair framed her shock-paled cheeks. Most of her makeup was gone, washed away by the water she'd splashed on her face. But rather than detract from her appearance, the dewy skin and rose-petal mouth added a great deal of appeal.

Philip stepped into the room and let the door close behind him. "Why didn't you tell me you had a brother who went to prison?"

She stiffened. "My brother isn't relevant to any of this."

"Everything is relevant when there's an unsolved murder."

"Get out, Betancourt, or I'll have *you* arrested."

He stepped toward her, anger pumping through him with every beat of his heart. "What else haven't you told me?"

"I've told you everything that matters."

A fresh burst of temper ripped through him. "I'll be the judge of what matters and what doesn't." He crossed to her, stopping an arm's length away, knowing he was too furious to get any closer.

"You've been yanking my chain," he growled. "Letting me beat my brains out trying to get to the truth, when all the while you're keeping secrets. I damn well don't appreciate it."

Her suit jacket lay in a heap on the counter. Through her silk blouse, Philip saw the outline of a lacy bra and the swell of her full breasts. Hell of a time to notice she was built just the way he liked.

Steeling himself against her, he raised his eyes to hers. "Was that a performance in there a moment ago, too?"

Color rose high in her cheeks. "You're a jerk."

"Tell me something I don't already know."

"That wasn't easy for me, damn you!"

A sliver of satisfaction that he'd managed to rile her temper slid through him. "The truth, Michelle. That's all I want."

"I haven't lied to you."

"You've lied by omission. Don't spew semantics at me. That really ticks me off."

Defiance burned in her eyes. "Maybe you can't handle the truth. Maybe you're not smart enough to see through all the irrelevant stuff, Betancourt. Maybe I don't trust you to do the right thing if you know too much."

What the hell was *that* supposed to mean? Philip's temper spiked another notch. "I know about your record, Michelle. About your arrest as a teenager." He was fishing; he didn't know for certain she had a record, only that she'd been arrested.

Turning from the mirror, she faced him, the quick rise and fall of her chest revealing he'd hit a nerve. "I don't know what you're talking about."

"What was the charge? You want to share that with me?"

"I don't have a record," she said hollowly.

"State of Louisiana archives don't lie."

"They don't always tell the whole story, either."

"What story? Talk to me…"

Frustration billowed through Philip when she stared silently back at him. He didn't want to push her too hard, not after what she'd just been through. He didn't want her to pull away just when she was beginning to trust him. But, dammit, she was keeping things from him; she'd lied to him. The hell of it was he didn't think she was lying about Landsteiner.

"All right." Philip rubbed his hand over his face, mentally changed gears. "What happened in there a few minutes ago? Did you see who murdered Landsteiner?"

Her gaze remained level on his. "I saw…someone. A man. The murderer, I think."

"Who?"

"I don't know. I didn't see his face. He wore some type of mask. A ski mask...maybe. I'm not sure."

Philip cursed—he'd wanted something solid, a name or description. "Think you can give me a physical description?"

"Maybe. I'll try." Turning, she punched soap from the dispenser into her hands and began scrubbing them. "Whoever it was, he wanted to kill me."

The urge to protect rose inside him with surprising force. "How do you know that?"

"The gun. He pointed it at me." Her voice quavered, and she closed her eyes. "I thought he was going to kill me. He could have. I don't understand why he didn't."

"Maybe he knew you wouldn't be able to identify him. Maybe you weren't his target. Maybe Armon was."

She choked out a humorless laugh. "I just stood there. Frozen. I watched him gun down Armon and did nothing. Oh, God." Turning to the sink, she bent and splashed water on her face once more.

Philip watched, feeling more for her than was prudent. "Do you think you can come back in and answer some more questions?"

"Don't make me do that. I can't handle it right now."

"It's important, Michelle."

With her hands against the counter, she leaned forward and let the water drip from her face into the basin. Pain shone in her eyes when her gaze met his in the mirror. "I watched him gun down Armon, and I didn't do anything to help. Armon might have lived had I...done something to help him." She closed her eyes. Giant tears squeezed through her lashes.

Philip didn't want to believe her. Dammit, he didn't want to *feel* anything for her. Her story didn't add up. There was something amiss. But despite all the evidence denoting guilt, he didn't think this woman was capable of cold-blooded murder.

''If that's how it happened, then it wasn't your fault,'' he said quietly.

''No, maybe it wasn't my fault. After all, I didn't pull the trigger. But I didn't stop the killer. I didn't help Armon. Maybe that's why I blocked the memory. Maybe I froze while he lay on the floor bleeding to death.''

''Armon was killed instantly. You couldn't have helped.''

''Maybe I ran—''

''I don't think you ran.''

''Then why the hell can't I remember?''

''We all have protective mechanisms, Michelle. Human beings are amazingly resilient when it comes to ugliness and violence.'' Philip wasn't so sure about himself. He hadn't been very resilient in the aftermath of the Rosetti case. He sure as hell hadn't enacted any kind of protective mechanism. Maybe that was why the death of that Algiers shopkeeper ate at him like acid.

Michelle yanked a paper towel from the dispenser and blotted her face. ''Do you think I killed him?''

''You're a suspect. You had motive, means and opportunity. There's too much evidence against you for you not to be a suspect.'' He didn't like the way the words felt coming off his tongue. Oddly, they no longer rang true. ''Any other cop would have—'' Philip stopped dead. What was he thinking? He shouldn't be discussing this with her.

''Would have what, Detective? Arrested me?''

Damning himself for the mistake, he remained silent, watched the emotions scroll across her face.

''You're wrong about me.'' Her hand trembled when she shoved a stray strand of hair away from her face.

''I don't think so.'' Philip wanted to touch her. Just to stop the shaking. He couldn't stand there and do nothing while she came apart right before his eyes. ''Tell me what you know, Michelle. Level with me. Tell me what you're hiding.''

His eyes never leaving hers, he placed his hands on her

shoulders. She was soft. Warm. He felt the tremors ripping through her, and he wanted to stop them, only he didn't know how. Her scent drifted lazily through his brain, an intriguing mix of baby powder laced with the heady scent of woman. Lord, he'd known better than to touch her. But logic fled the moment he'd looked into her eyes and seen the kind of pain no one should have to deal with alone.

She turned to face him. "I didn't kill Armon."

She uttered the denial with such heartfelt intensity that, for an instant, Philip's doubts fled. "Even if I do believe you, I've still got to run this investigation the best way I know how. I've got to do my job, Michelle. That means leaving no stone unturned. You know how it works."

Her eyes hardened. "Oh, I think I've gotten the gist of it, Detective." She used his formal title with a hefty dose of sarcasm. "You don't believe that a woman from a poor background can have a wealthy man for a friend. Your small, dirty mind has conjured up all sorts of juicy scenarios that have warped your objectivity."

Philip's temper spiked anew. "If we're going to work together and figure out who killed Landsteiner, that giant-size chip on your shoulder has to go."

"Go to hell, Betancourt."

Her previous statement had hit home, extinguishing Philip's temper. Surprising himself, he reached out and wiped a tear from her cheek with his thumb. "You're real tough, aren't you?"

Another tear slipped free. "I hate you."

"This is a hell of a place to discuss this."

The way she was staring at him wreaked havoc on his willpower. She looked vulnerable and tough at once, standing there with tears on her cheeks and hurt in her eyes.

He wanted to kiss her. Wanted to devour the mouth that had lied so easily to him. The realization came out of nowhere, startling him and sending a rush of blood to his groin where arousal flared hot and deep. He tried to shake it off, but his body refused. He felt himself tumbling forward, closer to her, until her scent surrounded him, drugging him with the kind of need that could drive a man insane.

Damning the consequences, Philip lowered his mouth to hers.

The intimate contact went through Michelle like an electrical storm, sending sparks from her brain to her toes and every nerve ending in between. His mouth was warm and softly demanding against hers. Surprise melded with heat, and before she fully realized the dangers, she responded, lifting her arms to broad shoulders where rock-hard muscle corded with tension.

His breath quickened at her response, warm and sweet against her cheek. When he used his tongue, she opened to him. He explored her mouth brazenly. Slow heat wound through her. Her breasts grew heavy. Her nipples beaded, though he hadn't touched her there. Gentle hands skimmed down her sides, pausing at her hips. He held her in place against him, just close enough so that she could feel his arousal against her cleft.

Michelle knew better than to respond to a man like Betancourt. But the inner warning came too late for common sense to save her. The moment his lips touched hers, her judgment fled, along with the last vestiges of her sense of self-preservation.

The gentleness of the kiss devastated her. Physically. Emotionally. She hadn't expected him to be gentle—he wasn't a gentle man—but his mouth…oh, mercy, his mouth. The man knew how to kiss, how to make a woman forget. Even a smart woman, Michelle thought. Somewhere in the back of her mind she knew he was the enemy, but at the moment his mouth was making her forget that, too.

Two thunderous knocks sounded. The door swung open.

Betancourt stiffened, cursing exorbitantly. Michelle gasped as he shoved her quickly back. She looked up in time to see Detective Sanderson standing in the doorway, staring at them as if he'd just seen the one-armed man.

Chapter 6

Cory glared at Philip across the span of the gray metal desk. "Are you *crazy?*"

Philip wasn't in the mood for a lecture. He didn't have an explanation; he certainly couldn't defend what he'd done, so he focused on the file in front of him and brooded. Hell, maybe he *was* crazy. What the hell had he been thinking, kissing her like that?

"I don't even want to know what was going on in there," Cory said.

"Nothing was going on."

"Sure looked like something to me, Romeo. You had your mouth all over that woman."

"Keep your voice down." Philip looked uneasily over his shoulder, irked that he felt the need to do so. It was late; most of the cold case division had already left for the day. Still, he didn't want it to get around that he'd acted inappropriately with a suspect.

He'd left Michelle with nothing more than a lame apology about the aftereffects of intensity and adrenaline. She'd adamantly agreed. He suspected they both knew it was a line of bull.

"What the hell were you thinking, Betancourt?"

Had the situation not been so dire, Philip might have laughed at its absurdity. "She was upset. I was trying to…" What the hell had he been trying to do? Make her stop crying? That sounded ridiculous.

"Looked to me like you were trying to give her a tonsillectomy with your tongue."

"Look, Cory, I'm not going to deny what happened was…inappropriate. It happened. It was a mistake. I'll deal with it."

"The only way you can deal with this fiasco is to hand this case over to another homicide team."

"No." Another homicide team coming in blind wouldn't know what Philip knew in his gut about Michelle. God, what *did* he feel in his gut? Lust? What the hell did lust have to do with guilt or innocence?

"Look, my man, it's not like we have a shortage of murders in this city."

"I want this case, Cory."

"Just the case?"

Philip glared at him.

"You're too involved, Betancourt, and you know it. First your relationship with Landsteiner's son, now this…suspect. If Landsteiner gets wind of what happened today, he'll bury you."

"I can handle Landsteiner."

"It's not Landsteiner I'm worried about."

Philip rubbed his hand over his face and tried not to remember the heat that had blasted through him when he'd kissed Michelle. "She's not going to tell Landsteiner a damn thing."

"How do you know? What would you do if you were facing a murder charge? Be polite? Play by the rules? Even if she was enjoying the hell out of whatever you were doing, a lawyer can twist it around, get her off on a technicality, even sue the city.'' A laugh of disbelief escaped Cory. ''Betancourt, you're the last cop I expected to do something so damn stupid.''

A tinge of anger went through Philip. ''You want to bail out of this investigation, Cory? If you do, just say the word. I'll put in for another partner.''

Cory shook his head, but he didn't look happy. ''Thanks for the offer, but I don't operate that way. I'll go down with the ship. But we both know your butt's in a major sling.''

Philip sent him a dark look. ''Thanks for reminding me.''

Silence reigned for several minutes while Cory pretended to read witness statements. Philip gave the lab reports his halfhearted attention, while his mind churned with the implications of what he'd done. He wasn't sure what he was going to do about Michelle. The kiss had been a mistake. A bad one that could affect not only the case, but his career. He should pass the case to another team. But Philip knew another team, coming in cold, might take the evidence at face value. They might not look beyond the obvious. He couldn't do that to Michelle. Any cop would see immediately that she had motive, means and opportunity to murder Armon Landsteiner.

The bottom line was that Philip no longer believed she'd done it. The realization made the situation even worse. He trusted his gut, and it rarely steered him wrong. He knew she was hiding something, but he didn't think that something was a murder confession.

''So what do we do now?'' Cory asked.

Philip looked up to see his partner frowning at him. ''We work the case, Cory, and we work it hard. I want you to canvas the neighborhood. See if anyone else saw the man in black. Talk to the neighbor again, see if you can get a description. While you're there, I want you to go back to the murder scene and have Michelle take you through it again.''

"Yeah, better you stay away from her for a while." Cory's tone was bone dry.

Philip ignored the jab. "I'm going back to Landsteiner's mansion to go through his things again and check for anything that might be pertinent. Safety deposit box receipts. Other life insurance policies. Letters. Anything that might point us in the right direction."

He also planned to do a more thorough background check on Michelle, but he didn't say as much. Breaking the rules was nothing new to Philip—he was a natural when it came to bucking authority—but he refused to involve Cory any more than he already had. Philip had crossed the line this time, venturing beyond the point of no return. He'd broken not only the department's code of conduct, but his own set of staunch rules. The hell of it was, he couldn't stop, didn't want to stop. Michelle Pelletier, with her haunting eyes and mysterious past, had gotten under his skin. She'd invaded his sleep, destroyed his peace of mind. Until he unraveled her mystery, Philip knew he couldn't stay away from her. He only hoped it didn't cost him more than he bargained for.

Michelle didn't want to think about Philip Betancourt. Not today, when her heart was raw and the grief spiked through her like barbed wire. She had to get through Armon's funeral first; she had to function, deal with the hostility sure to greet her. Then she'd handle Betancourt.

The slate sky broke open, and cold winter rain fell in sheets. Fog rolled in from the gulf, enveloping the city in a gray, swirling mist. *Fitting,* Michelle thought grimly as she exited the bus at Esplanade. Hoisting her umbrella against the downpour, she started toward St. Louis Cemetery at a brisk clip. She was so preoccupied she barely noticed the mist curling like spindly fingers around the ancient oaks along the boulevard. As she crossed through the wrought-iron gates and the above-ground tombs loomed into view, she understood fully why people referred to this cemetery as the City of the Dead.

Even the angels were weeping today, she thought.

Stopping twenty yards from the crowd, she stood alone among the trees and surveyed the scene. It was late afternoon and pretty soon darkness would descend upon the cemetery. Mercedes, Jaguars and two sleek black limousines crowded the narrow roadway. Beyond, an ocean of black clad mourners gathered beneath the maroon-and-white-striped awning. A strip of plush red carpet dissected a dozen rows of neatly arranged folding chairs. Bloodred roses blanketed a closed casket where Armon Landsteiner had been laid to rest.

Michelle had known this would be difficult. She'd almost convinced herself not to come, but she desperately needed this final goodbye. It didn't matter that the Landsteiners didn't want her here. She couldn't stay away. Armon had been her friend. She had every right to attend his funeral.

As the mourners converged, her thoughts drifted to the steely eyed Detective Betancourt. He'd invaded her mind on more than one occasion since the incident in the ladies' rest room—and she still didn't know what to do about it. She wasn't impulsive. She certainly wasn't the kind of woman to succumb to hormonal urges, no matter how powerful. Michelle had no room in her life for hormones or urges. She'd learned the cost of such weaknesses a lifetime ago and vowed never to fall victim again.

Betancourt had attributed the kiss to the intensity of the moment, blaming it on adrenaline, rather than animal attraction. Michelle had agreed wholeheartedly in the awkward minutes that followed. In the two days since, she'd tried hard to believe that adrenaline theory. It was better than believing she might be susceptible to something as banal as lust. But as hard as she tried, she couldn't deny that something powerful had clicked between them.

Michelle couldn't put aside the way her heart had stumbled around in her chest when his mouth had been pressed against hers. She'd been as close to melting as she'd ever been in her life. She tried to blame her reaction on nerves, even temper, but she was honest enough to recognize simple lust when she felt it. A response she'd just as soon not deal with at the moment, but she no longer had that option. When he looked at her with those turbulent gray eyes, her common sense scattered into a thousand pieces. How on earth could she be thinking of him in terms of physical attraction when he wanted to destroy her?

"I owe you an apology."

Michelle spun, nearly dropping her umbrella at the sound of Betancourt's voice. He was standing ten feet away, watching her, holding a wood-handled umbrella. The bottom of his trench coat was wet. She wondered how long he'd been there.

"You've already apologized, Detective. I think it would be best for both of us if we just forgot…it ever happened." Squaring her shoulders, she tightened her grip on the umbrella, determined to keep her hands steady.

He didn't look satisfied. "I'm going to continue investigating this case. If that bothers you, tell me now, and I'll pass it on to another homicide team."

"I'm your number one suspect. What do you expect me to say?"

"I was out of line the other day. It's your prerogative to tell me if you've got a problem with my…conduct."

The kiss *was* a problem, she thought, but not in the way he meant. She didn't want him to know her knees had gone weak, that her blood had pumped heat to every nerve ending in her body the instant he'd touched his lips to hers.

"Would your passing this case to another team slow down the progression of the investigation?" she asked.

Broad shoulders rose and fell. "I think I have a good feel for this case. I think we've made some headway."

She considered the words, realized with some dismay

she'd rather have Betancourt on the case than another cop who might be looking for an easy arrest. "I want this case solved, Detective. I want to know who murdered Armon, and why. The truth will exonerate me."

His gaze traveled to the crowd amassed beneath the awning. "I also wanted to tell you that you were wrong about what you said."

"I don't know what you mean."

He turned his gaze on her. "You said I wasn't capable of believing that a young woman from a poor background could be friends with an older, affluent man. You're wrong. I wanted to tell you that."

The statement touched her more deeply than it should have. She wanted to shrug it off, just as she wanted to shrug off the emotions that followed. Gratitude, relief—there wasn't room in her life for those kinds of feelings.

A weary sigh escaped her. "I'm tired of defending my relationship with Armon."

"You shouldn't have to."

"I didn't kill him."

His gaze burned into hers. "I know."

The words hit her like a burst of air to oxygen-starved lungs. She heard a sound, her own gasp, and pressed a hand to her mouth. Her vision blurred, and she realized she was going to cry. Unable to speak, blinking back those wretched tears, she tore her gaze from Betancourt and focused on the priest at the podium. Around them, the tempo of the rain increased.

"We're getting wet, Michelle. You're shivering. Let's get under the canopy."

She hadn't realized she was shivering. She felt oddly numb to the elements. There were too many emotions banging around inside her to be concerned with the weather. "No."

"You have a right to be here."

His perceptivity surprised her. "I don't want a scene. Not here. Not today."

"I'm a cop, remember? No one's going to start a scene with me around." A smile played at the corners of his mouth. "Come on. I'll walk with you."

With the temperature hovering near the forty-degree mark, Michelle knew he was right. It was too cold to be standing in the rain and getting soaked. "Just keep your billy club handy, will you?"

Philip grinned, then patted his coat. "Got it right here."

Michelle felt the stares burning into her as she approached. Scanning the sea of people, she saw disdain in their gazes, heard disgust in their not-so-subtle whispers. *They think I murdered Armon.* The realization sent choppy waves of outrage slicing through her.

The cloying scent of roses thickened the damp air as she stepped under the canopy. Michelle had sent a spray of flowers anonymously, but the arrangement was modest, and had probably been shoved aside in lieu of a larger, more dramatic one. She spotted the Landsteiners in the front row. Danielle wore a sleek black suit with a fur collar. A netted veil shrouded her face. Derek, as pale and rigid as a mannequin, looked directly at Michelle when she approached. Other than a quick word to his sister, he barely acknowledged Michelle's presence.

The chairs had been filled, so Michelle and Betancourt stood in the rear next to a table holding a vase of long-stemmed roses. At the podium, a berobed priest recited the Twenty-third Psalm. Michelle listened, trying to take comfort in the words. Grief washed over her. She held off the tears, but the pain in her chest was so sharp she could barely breathe. Through it all, she was aware of Betancourt's presence. Solid. Powerful. Oddly comforting in light of the circumstances. He was unquestionably there for her in a way no one else could be. And she felt sure he had no idea how much she needed that.

Baldwin delivered his father's eulogy with the flare of a dramatic actor. Afterward, Michelle was so caught up in her own grief that she didn't see Danielle and Derek approach until it was too late.

Dread congealed in her stomach. "This is what I wanted to avoid," she whispered to Betancourt.

"Easy." Betancourt watched them approach through narrowed eyes, his voice quietly dangerous. "If she lifts a finger in your direction, I'll haul her downtown so fast she'll get whiplash."

"Michelle, darling, I'm so very glad you came."

Danielle's syrupy tone put Michelle on full alert. Raising her chin, she gazed coolly at the other woman, her pulse spiking. "Hello, Danielle."

Lifting her netted veil with a pale hand, Danielle swept her cat-green eyes from Michelle to Betancourt. "Detective. You must be here scoping out suspects. Do you have any leads on who killed my father?"

"Yes, as a matter of fact, my partner and I have some leads we're following up on."

"Anyone I know?" Her eyes flicked to Michelle, then back to Betancourt.

"I'm afraid I'm not at liberty to discuss the details of the case with you, Miss Landsteiner."

Her eyes cooled several degrees, then she cocked her head and looked at Michelle through her lashes. One side of her elegant, painted mouth twisted into a half smile. "Michelle, I wanted to apologize for what happened the other day at the office. I was distraught. I *do* hope you can find it in your heart to forgive me."

Michelle's stomach turned. "All of us were upset, Danielle."

"You know, I might even be able to get Baldwin to hire you back. I always thought you were such a good little worker. I know you need the money—"

"Actually, I'm looking into other opportunities."

"Oh, well, I'm sure Terrebonne's will hire you back. I hope you're not angry. I behaved badly. I know you cared for my father. And I've done some thinking, Michelle. I've decided it doesn't matter what kind of relationship you had with him. My father was a grown man. He knew what he was doing."

"Armon and I were friends, Danielle. Nothing more."

"If he wanted to have a relationship with…someone like you…well, more power to him. I mean, he was a man. Men have needs." Her eyes flicked down the front of Michelle, pausing on her breasts. "He always had a weakness for…women like you."

Michelle felt the words all the way to the pit of her stomach, where they churned like shards of glass. She choked back the pain, telling herself it didn't matter. "I don't think you knew your father at all."

"Certainly not like you did." Danielle's green gaze spat fire for an instant, then she smiled slyly at Betancourt. "You see, Detective, after Mother died, my father was a very lonely man. Michelle was a waitress at Terrebonne's when he met her. You know, the restaurant over on Royal where the waitresses wear those short little red skirts? Michelle looked so cute. I remember the first time I saw her. No makeup. Looked like she'd cut her hair with a hedge trimmer. All she ever wore were hand-me-down jeans and cheap T-shirts. Oh, and that little red skirt. I'll just bet those legs of yours got you a lot of tips, didn't they, Michelle?"

Michelle felt Betancourt's hand on her arm, trying to ease her back, but she jerked away. "You're pathetic, Danielle. If I didn't dislike you so intensely, I might feel sorry for you."

Danielle put a red-tipped finger to her mouth. "You know, Michelle, that dress you're wearing doesn't look half-bad on you. Of course, it looked better on me, but I didn't care for the cut. Have you tried on the Ellen Tracy I gave you last year? No, on second thought, I really think that one's too sophisticated for a little...backwater girl like you.''

The words went through Michelle with the precision of a surgeon's scalpel. She'd forgotten the dress she was wearing had once been Danielle's. "This isn't the place for a scene.''

"Who's making a scene? I'm merely saying what needs to be said, ending something that should never have started.''

Vaguely, Michelle was aware that several people had gathered, their eyes alight with excitement at the prospect of a fight.

"You're not going to get a penny of his money, Michelle. So you can put the little grief-stricken act to rest.''

Michelle's temper exploded. Her vision tunneled on Danielle. Dropping her umbrella, she snatched up the crystal vase of roses on the table next to her and dumped the contents over Danielle's head.

Danielle's mouth opened. Water streamed down her face. A birdlike sound escaped her. "You *wench!*''

Michelle dropped the vase and staggered back, appalled by what she'd done. As if in slow motion, Derek moved to Danielle, pulled a long-stemmed rose from her sodden hair. Betancourt turned to Michelle, snapped something in a low voice, but she couldn't make out the words over the rush of blood through her veins.

She knew running was the cowardly way out. But there were too many people standing too close, pressing in on her. Too much grief and anger for her to deal with. She'd fallen victim to her own temper and made a scene. She'd allowed Danielle to get the best of her. Dignity forgotten, she turned on her heel and fled into the pouring rain.

Philip would have missed her if it hadn't been for the streetlamp. Huddled against the rain, Michelle moved down Esplanade with long purposeful strides, seemingly oblivious to the fact that she was soaked to the skin. She'd removed her high heels at some point, and they dangled from her right hand. Her black dress and jacket clung to her body like wet silk.

Slowing the vehicle, he pulled alongside her and rolled down the passenger side window. "Hell of an afternoon for a walk."

She shot him a glare over her shoulder. "No, Betancourt, it's just a hell of an afternoon."

"Get in. I'll drive you home."

Her stride quickened.

He nudged the car forward, pacing her. "You're soaked to the skin, Michelle. The hotel's two miles away. Get in the car."

"Leave me alone."

Her teeth were chattering. That bothered him. He could tell by the way her voice shook that she was hurting. Her jerky movements told him she was angry. No, he amended, not just angry. Furious. Not necessarily at him, but at the world in general, though he knew he would probably absorb the brunt of it if he stuck around. She'd been hurt and humiliated by people she'd once trusted. He supposed he could identify.

"Michelle, this is crazy." His car continued alongside her, the tires hissing on the wet pavement.

When she picked up speed and attempted to change direction, he gunned the engine, pulled ahead of her and parked curbside. Ignoring the rain, he got out of the car and approached her.

"Oh, that was a really terrific cop move, Betancourt," she snapped. "I'll just bet you're a whiz in a car chase. Maybe you should pull your weapon and shout 'halt!'"

"I'm not here as a cop, Michelle."

She pushed past him. "Save the good cop routine. I don't buy it, and I'm sure as hell not in the mood."

"I'm here to take you back to the hotel. That's all."

"I don't want to go to the hotel. Dammit, I want to go home."

"You're not ready to go back there."

"Oh, I forgot, you're the veritable expert on my innermost feelings—"

He grasped her arm, spun her around to face him. "Look, I'm sorry you got hurt back there. I know that was difficult—"

"Difficult?" She wrenched free of his grip. "That's not the right word, Betancourt. Not by a long shot. It's like a stake through my heart when people talk about my relationship with Armon that way." A hard, humorless laugh broke from her throat. "And I took the bait right out of her hand, didn't I?"

"It doesn't matter."

"That's where you're wrong, Detective. It *does* matter. All of those people back there knew Armon. They want to think the worst. Now they have reason to."

"She knew exactly where to aim to get to you, Michelle. She's out to hurt you, not ruin her father's reputation."

"What's that supposed to mean?" She blinked against the rain. Her face was deathly pale in the light of the streetlamp. Her hands trembled as she shoved the hair from her eyes.

Philip hated seeing her like this. "It doesn't matter," he said gently.

"Oh, I saw how much it mattered the first night I met you. You took one look at me and thought what's that rich old guy doing with this hot little number?"

His heart wrenched as she choked out the words. Not because they weren't true, but because they were. "That's not fair. I'm a cop. It's my job to be suspicious."

"You were judging me. Just like Danielle. Just like all those people back there."

"I wasn't judging you."

"I saw it in your eyes. I knew what you were thinking! Because of the way I look! The way I live! Because of who

I am.'' She rapped her fist against her chest with the last word.

He knew no matter what he said she wasn't going to calm down anytime soon. Sighing, he resigned himself to getting wet. This was going to take some time. She needed to get it off her chest. ''Go ahead, Michelle, get it out in the open. Maybe it'll help you knock that giant chip off your shoulder.''

''Go to hell.'' Her voice rose above the pitch of the rain.

''You've been holding this inside for a long time, haven't you?''

''Leave me alone, Betancourt. This is none of your concern.''

''Let it out, Michelle. You'll feel better if you do.'' Lord knew he was an expert on leaving emotions inside to fester.

''You're just like everyone else.''

''Now who's judging whom?''

She fought the tears, bravely, valiantly, but feature by feature, her face crumpled. The tears came in a rush. Violent, angry tears. ''Do you think those people are going to remember Armon for the good he did in his life, Betancourt? For the wing he donated to Charity Hospital? For the foundation he started for homeless children? Or do you think they're going to remember him as the man who was murdered by his young lover?''

Philip hadn't realized the depth of her pain, or the extent of her bitterness. He sensed there was more buried inside, but he didn't want to press her. Not now. More than anything, he wanted to go to her, hold her, stop the tremors racking her body. But he knew that wasn't what she needed. She needed to stand on her own two feet and face the demons that haunted her.

''I come from the gutter, Betancourt. Do you understand what that means? Do you have any idea how many years it took me to put that behind me? To get where I am? Do you know how hard it is to overcome the stigma attached to being poor and uneducated?''

''You're not uneducated,'' he growled.

''My mother only went to school through the sixth grade, for heaven's sake! I don't even know who my father was.'' A hard laugh squeezed out of Michelle's throat. ''Do you have any idea what it meant to me when Armon picked me up and gave me a chance to make something of myself?''

''You'd already picked yourself up when he met you.''

''I was a waitress.''

''You'd made it to one of the best law schools in the country.''

''I wouldn't have survived.'' She stared at him, vacillating, her arms wrapped around herself.

''Aw, hell.'' Philip reached her in two resolute strides. She stiffened when his arms went around her, but he didn't withdraw. ''Shut up, Michelle. Just shut up. I've heard enough.''

Her flesh was cold to the touch. She shivered violently, her sobs sending powerful tremors through her body. Philip tightened his grip on her. ''Get in the car.''

''Please, just take me home. I want to go home.''

Philip didn't think she was ready to go back there. Not in her emotional state. ''Michelle, your place is probably a mess.''

''I don't care. I'll handle it. Please, just take me home.''

Holding her against him, he couldn't deny her this one thing. He knew he shouldn't be the one to do it. But he was here. He'd witnessed her hurt. Felt her tremors. Looked into the brown depths of her eyes and seen firsthand the pain and bitterness residing there. Who the hell was he to keep her from doing what she wanted?

''All right,'' he said, knowing he'd probably live to regret it. ''I'll take you home. Get in the car.''

Michelle knew the instant she walked through the door coming back was a mistake. It was too soon, and her emotions were strung tight as a piano wire. Even before turning on the light, she knew Armon's death had irrevocably and forever changed the place she'd called home for the last four years. The change was subtle, not anything she could put her finger on. An unpleasant aura that hung low and invisible, like a cloud of noxious gas.

Taking a deep, calming breath, she flipped the light switch and let the sensations wash over her. Pain was the first emotion she could identify, its power diminishing the last remnants of anger from her encounter with Danielle. Betancourt stood silently behind her. He'd insisted on coming inside even though she'd wanted to face this alone. She hadn't known what to expect, or how she would react. She certainly didn't want an audience if it reduced her to a quivering mass of emotions.

She stepped tentatively into the foyer, her gaze sweeping the room. Sofa cushions littered the floor. The flowers in the vase on the coffee table had wilted. Her books, usually displayed on the built-in bookcase, had been haphazardly tossed to the floor. Fingerprint powder marred almost every surface.

She wanted to say something to let Betancourt know she was handling this just fine, that she was every bit as tough and capable as he, but her throat had a vise grip on her voice box. Something on the floor caught her gaze. She looked down, found herself staring at the chalk silhouette of Armon's body.

Her stomach rolled into a slow, sickening somersault. The steady hum in her ears burgeoned into a roar, deafening her, as her blood pumped harder and harder.

The flashback hit with stunning force, locking out the present. A gunshot, so loud it left her ears ringing. Armon, sprawled on the floor. The man in black raising the gun, shifting the muzzle toward her. She felt terror. The presence of death.

The blood left her head at dizzying speed. The room darkened, pitched. Michelle ordered her legs to take her to the sofa, but they refused to obey. She would have fallen if not for the strong arms that wrapped around her waist. Vaguely, she heard Betancourt's voice, felt a rise of embarrassment even as the room dipped.

"Dammit, I knew this was going to happen," he said.

Sweat broke out on her brow. Nausea rolled through her stomach. "Just let me…sit for a moment," she croaked.

Cursing, Philip swooped her into his arms and carried her to the sofa, where he eased her to a sitting position, then pressed her head between her knees. "Put your head down."

Too weak to argue, Michelle obeyed, gulping air, praying she wouldn't be sick.

"Breathe deeply." He sat beside her, rubbing her back with an incredibly gentle hand.

She sucked in a breath, let it out with a shudder. "I saw the man in black. He was here. I know it for sure now."

"Just breathe."

"He was wearing a black leather jacket."

"We'll talk in a minute. I don't want you passing out on me. Okay?"

"Sorry, Betancourt. I thought I could handle this."

"Don't sweat it. I've been where you are right now. Most cops have at one time or another."

"It's different living it, you know?" She thought about the chalk silhouette and shivered. "This place won't ever be the same." The apartment had been her home for four turbulent years. Her refuge from an increasingly complex world that had seen her through life-altering changes, both good and bad. As she fought back nausea, Michelle knew she could never live here again.

"You did all right, Michelle."

She liked the way her name sounded on his lips. She concentrated on that, on the way his hand felt skimming along the curve of her back, and slowly, her stomach settled.

She raised her head. The room stopped swaying. "I want another hypnosis session."

Betancourt scowled at her, but his expression was buffered by concern and, unmistakably, empathy. "I think that's a good idea. I'll set it up."

He was sitting so close she could smell the woodsy scent of his aftershave mingling with the heady scent that was distinctly his. It surrounded her, heightening her senses so that for a moment she was only aware of his closeness. Warmth radiated from his thigh into hers. His hand stilled on her shoulder. She found herself staring into a face as hard and inscrutable as stone. Even his mouth looked hard, but she knew it wasn't. Disturbed by the tug of awareness, she rose. The room shifted, then leveled off.

"Take it slow, Michelle, else you'll end up on the floor."

Bracing a hand against the sofa back, she glanced around the room, hoping she looked more in control than she felt. "You cops could have been a little more careful with my things."

Betancourt rose abruptly, his narrowed eyes sweeping the room. With an oath he strode to the hall, then disappeared into the kitchen.

Michelle heard another curse.

He stalked back into the living room, his face set and angry. "I should have noticed this right off the bat."

"Noticed what?"

"Don't touch anything," he said cryptically, then knelt beside the books on the floor. "The cops didn't do this."

Anxiety quivered through her. "What are you talking about?"

Philip crossed to the foyer, knelt to inspect the front door. "They came in through the back door."

"Who?"

"I don't know." He shot her a hard look. "The kitchen's been trashed. Someone ransacked the place."

"My God." Michelle rose, intending to see the kitchen for herself, but Philip stopped her.

"Not tonight."

"This is my home." She stood her ground, an argument poised on her lips. "I've got a right—"

"You're not up to it."

She knew he was correct; she'd nearly fainted. "Why would someone break in? What could they possibly hope to gain?" A slow, seething anger dribbled into her blood as she considered what had been done. She felt violated, outraged that someone had rifled her belongings, thoughtlessly destroying the sense of security that had taken her so many years to build.

"Do you need to pack some things? You may not be back for a while."

"I don't want to go to the hotel."

Philip plucked a handkerchief out of his pocket and picked up the phone. "I'll get a couple of lab techs out here to see if they can lift some prints."

Michelle watched, a sense of helplessness rolling over her. She wanted her old life back. She wanted this insanity to stop. "It doesn't make sense, Betancourt. I don't have any valuables."

"Maybe they weren't looking for valuables." He punched in the numbers, then leveled a stony gaze at her. "Any idea what they *were* looking for?"

Chapter 7

Philip knew better than to take her to his house. But he was just as uncomfortable walking into the Pontchartrain Hotel with her. A cop going into a hotel room with a suspect might start a few tongues wagging. He knew how it would look if anyone at the department found out he was spending his off-duty time with a murder suspect.

But after the scene at the funeral, after witnessing her near collapse at her apartment, he couldn't bring himself to walk away—even if it was the smart thing to do. They were both soaked to the skin and needed to change clothes. Not to mention that he had a few questions bouncing around inside his head. She wasn't going to like them. But the cop in him figured it would be more effective to hit her when her defenses were down.

In all his years as a cop, he'd never stepped this far over the line. Oh, he'd broken the rules now and again, but he'd always had a solid, tangible reason, like getting some scumbag off the street. This time, however, things were different. Bringing her here, getting closer to her, wouldn't help him solve the case. It would only cloud his judgment, muddy his objectivity. He knew the difference between right and wrong. The hell of it was, he was going to do the wrong thing anyway.

He'd called Cory from the car to report the break-in. His partner had been quick to point out the precarious position Philip had placed himself in. If their commander heard rumblings of indiscretions between Philip and the prime suspect in a high-profile murder case, Philip's job would be on the line.

What the hell was going on between him and Michelle, anyway? Since the moment he'd first laid eyes on her she'd dominated his every thought, invaded his dreams and wreaked havoc on his common sense. Worse, Philip didn't have a clue what he was going to do about it. He wanted her. A hell of a lot more than he wanted to admit. As a man, he didn't care how much evidence piled up against her. As a cop, he now believed she was innocent—at least of murdering Armon Landsteiner. But was he ready to give up a career he loved for the likes of a woman who didn't trust him enough to tell him the truth?

All he could do was work the case. Keep a cool head. Look at the facts with his usual objectivity. Strive for emotional distance. He'd damn well better keep his physical distance.

And the moon was made of cheese.

Annoyed with himself, Philip stalked into the kitchen and pulled a beer out of the refrigerator. He popped the cap, heard the shower turn off, and felt a shudder of heat low in his belly. *Yeah, he was in deep,* a little voice acknowledged. Before he could stop himself, the image of her stepping out of his shower flashed through his mind. Wet flesh and secret curves. The baby-powder scent that had haunted him every night since he'd first seen her. He wondered if her hair would be wet, or if she'd tucked it into a towel. He imagined what it would be like to skim his fingertips over her milky shoulders. Loosen the towel and let it drop to the floor. Drink in the sight of womanly flesh and the kind of beauty that took a man's breath away.

Uttering a curse, Philip strode into the living room and took a long pull of beer. The last thing he should be thinking about was Michelle in his shower. His career was on the line. He had a murder case to solve. What the hell was the matter with him, thinking of her in sexual terms when he should be pressing her for answers?

"I put my clothes in the dryer. I hope you don't mind."

Philip spun, nearly dropped his beer when he saw her standing in the hall just as he'd imagined her a moment ago. A white terry robe fell modestly to her knees. One of his navy-blue towels was wrapped around her head turban style. Philip's clothes were still damp, but the coolness against his flesh didn't keep the heat from rising in his groin.

"That's fine." What the hell had happened to his voice?

She approached him, frowning. "You didn't have to bring me here. I know my being here could cause problems with your job."

She had no idea the kind of problems she was causing him, he thought, shifting his weight from one foot to the other to accommodate his arousal. "Don't read something into it that isn't there, Michelle. You're here because I want some answers."

"You still think I'm lying."

Her smoky voice wafted over him like a drugging cloud. He smelled baby powder and her own womanly scent. Soft. Clean. And so damn sexy that for a moment he couldn't look away. What was it about her that had him acting like a pimply faced teenager with a bad case of hormones? Making him do crazy things that could cost him much more than merely the case? Things like losing himself in that lush mouth in the ladies' room of the police station....

Philip gave her a hard look. "You lied to me."

He made the mistake of letting his gaze drop. Her mouth

opened, revealing the space between her teeth. He'd never seen such a tempting, interesting mouth. He knew how soft it was, remembered every curve, and the sweetness of her breath.

Steeling himself against an attraction that would only cause him trouble, Philip stepped back, determined to keep his mind on the business at hand. "I don't like surprises, Michelle. When it comes to working a murder case, I downright despise them. I have the feeling you've got a few up your sleeve. I'm out of patience. If you want to keep yourself out of jail, I suggest you start talking."

His stare hit her like a physical blow. His gaze was angry, forceful and filled with the kind of hunger that should have sent her scrambling for the front door.

"Thanks for setting me straight on that, Betancourt. For a moment I thought you'd brought me here out of the goodness of your heart."

"Goodness has nothing to do with it. And you've probably realized by now I don't have a heart. I've been patient with you, Michelle. I've put a hell of a lot on the line for you. You owe me the truth."

"I didn't realize you were keeping score."

She turned away, but his hand shot out and clamped on her arm. "No games. I want the truth. All of it. Starting with why you were arrested as a juvenile."

She slapped his hand off her arm. "Maybe you should get out the handcuffs and brass knuckles." Her voice was strong, but his touch had shaken her. Needing a minute to regroup, she brushed by him, hating it that her legs felt like rubber.

A fire blazed in a marble-front hearth. Aside from a futon in the corner, the room was completely devoid of furniture. A leafless plant stood next to the picture window. A set of dumbbells lay scattered in the center of the room. Classic rock and roll hummed from a small radio on the windowsill.

"What happened to your furniture?" she asked.

"My ex took it when she left. I haven't replaced it."

She'd often wondered what kind of a place he lived in, and realized this suited him perfectly. Hard. Cold. Empty. "How long ago—"

"Why were you arrested, Michelle?"

She moved closer to the fireplace, suddenly needing its warmth. "What happened to me as a juvenile has nothing to do with Armon's murder."

"I've had your record subpoenaed. I thought maybe you'd want me to hear it from you."

"You won't get the records. I was a juvenile. They were sealed."

"I'll get them."

She spun to face him. "And what? Use it against me? So you can arrest me for a crime I didn't commit? So some fresh-faced prosecutor can convince a jury I murdered my best friend?"

"No, dammit, to help you!" His voice echoed through the house like a gunshot. "How the hell am I supposed to help you when you don't trust me enough to tell me the truth?"

"By finding the real killer." Her voice was thready and thin.

"I need to know what happened that night, Michelle. I need your memory. Dammit, I need your cooperation."

She met his gaze, felt her breath stop dead in her chest at the power behind his eyes. He could go from dry-ice cold to furnace hot in the span of a heartbeat. He was volatile and unpredictable, with the kind of temper that sent alarm bells clanging in her head. Why couldn't she stay away from him?

"What did Dr. Witt say about the hypnosis session?" she asked.

He scrubbed a hand over his face. "The tests results were inconclusive, but in his opinion you were probably telling the truth.'' One side of his mouth hiked up into a cynical smile. ''Of course, you know hypnosis results aren't always admissible should this go to court.''

''I'm aware of that.'' Taking a deep breath, Michelle took a moment to organize her thoughts. ''There is something else.''

His gaze snapped to hers.

''When we walked into my apartment tonight, I had a flashback of sorts. When I got dizzy.''

Setting his beer on the fireplace mantel, Philip approached her, his jaw set, eyes intense. ''What did you remember?''

''Basically what I saw in the hypnosis session. Only now I know the man in black is real. I know he's the one who shot Armon. I know he aimed the pistol at me. It was almost as if he changed his mind and decided not to kill me at the last second. And he wore a mask. Not a ski mask, but a Mardi Gras mask. Black, I think. The kind that usually has feathers, but this one didn't. I'm certain of that now.''

''That doesn't leave us with much more than what we knew from the hypnosis session.''

''I wasn't sure of the man or the mask then. I am now.''

Philip contemplated her. ''Why did Armon go to see you that night?''

''I don't know.''

''Did you know you're the beneficiary of a life insurance policy?''

The revelation jolted her. Pain flashed across her chest, so sharp and intense that she couldn't draw a breath. ''I didn't know.''

''A small policy to the tune of a hundred thousand dollars.''

Michelle rubbed her brow where a headache threatened to break through. ''My God.''

''Did he ever talk to you about a will?''

''He brought the subject up once or twice, but talk of death and wills made me uncomfortable.'' She laughed dryly. "I never wanted him to think it mattered. The money, I mean, so I never let him talk about it. I just…couldn't handle it."

"Did he say he would provide for you?"

"Yes. But I told him it didn't matter."

"Do you know if he used an attorney?"

Michelle acknowledged the headache, even as her mind skimmed through the names of the dozens of attorneys Armon had used on occasion. "There was a small firm not far from the Warehouse District. He went to Tulane with the senior partner, Dennis Jacoby. Armon had used Dennis to draw up some of the documents when he donated money to Charity Hospital for the wing. Then again for the foundation he set up for homeless children."

Philip arched a brow.

She smiled wryly. "I'm sure that throws a wrench into your perception of the proverbial lawyer, but Armon Landsteiner had a heart of gold. I'm living proof of that."

"What was the name of the firm?"

"Jacoby and Perez. Armon and Dennis Jacoby were friends. They kept in touch. In fact, Armon and I had dinner with Dennis and his paralegal about a month ago, right before Christmas."

"Did they talk about Armon's will?"

"What are you getting at? Do you think Armon's murder has something to do with his will?"

"I'm checking into everything at this point."

"The only people who would have something to gain in regard to a will are Danielle, Derek and Baldwin. They're not murderers, Betancourt."

"If you were listed on the will, it might make you look guilty."

The words lanced her, but she didn't react. "I'm not a murderer."

"So you've said, Michelle. But the bottom line is you keep lying. That's one of my cardinal rules. No lying."

"I haven't lied to you."

"Lying by omission is the same. Worse, probably, because it's so premeditated. Refusing to tell me what that juvenile charge was makes me wonder what the hell else you aren't telling me. One lie usually leads to another, and eventually they get all tangled up. I'll get the truth, Michelle. And if need be, I'll nail you to the wall."

Everything inside her went perfectly still. He wanted to know about Bayou Lafourche; she couldn't tell him. She could still taste the betrayal at the back of her throat, still feel the stinging slap of humiliation and shame. She wondered if Betancourt would betray her, too. "The charges against me were dropped. There is no record. Therefore, your witch-hunt is irrelevant."

"If I found out about your record, someone else can. I'm not the only one looking, Michelle. Armon Landsteiner had friends in high places. Those people want blood. They want an arrest. They don't give a damn who the sacrificial lamb is."

Fear quivered deep in her stomach. "I'm innocent. I've got the truth on my side."

"Then why do you keep lying?" He moved toward her, like a storm cutting a violent path across the gulf, dark, dangerous. "Not everyone cares about justice, Michelle. Not everyone cares about the truth."

She stepped back, felt the heat of the fire against her calves. "You care about the truth. Shove all the cynicism and suspicion aside and you care."

A hard laugh broke from his throat. "Really?"

Her back thudded against cool stone. She felt trapped beneath his gaze, like a sailboat stalled in the path of that approaching storm, awaiting a deadly trip to the bottom of the sea.

"Maybe I care about more than just the truth," he said.

The words sent a bolt of panic up her spine. "Lying now makes you a hypocrite, Betancourt. So please don't." She

wasn't sure what he was trying to say, only that she didn't
want to hear it.

"Don't what? Tell you I'm a hell of a lot more involved
in this case than I should be? That I care what happens to
you?"

The stark admittance sent a ripple of shock through her.
She didn't want to believe him. To fall for that bad-boy
charm now would open her up to the same kind of hurt, the
same kind of betrayal she'd suffered at the hands of another
cop, in another era of her life. "Don't play games with me.
I can't handle it right now."

"You can't handle it?" His eyes glittered menacingly.
Leaning toward her, he braced his arms on either side of
her, pinning her against the wall. "Let me tell you what you
can't handle. Arrest. A trial. Prison time. Do you think you
can handle all that? Have you even considered the possibility?"

Michelle's heart banged hard against her ribs. He was so
close she could feel the warmth of his breath against her
face. His scent surrounded her, pressed into her, filling her
with needs she swore she'd never succumb to.

One side of his mouth curled. "No, you haven't thought
of prison. Just as you haven't considered the possibility that
I might care about what happens to you. You've convinced
yourself that no one could ever care about the poor little girl
from the bayou, haven't you? Isn't that why you carry
around that giant chip on your shoulder?"

"You're wrong about me."

"I hit the nail on the head, only you don't have the courage to admit it."

Her temper ignited. "Don't lecture me about courage."

"You need it, Michelle, because it takes courage to tell
the truth. It really ticks me off when you lie to me."

His mouth was less than an inch from hers, so close she
could almost taste him. Her breath hitched. If he didn't let
up her heart was going to explode.

''That makes you a coward.''

Her hand shot out, connected with his cheek.

His face darkened, but he didn't so much as flinch.

''Don't you dare call me that,'' she said breathlessly. ''You don't know anything about me. What I've been through. What I've overcome—''

''You're tough, aren't you, Michelle? You take care of yourself. You don't need anyone else, do you? You don't need me. You didn't need Armon.''

She couldn't move. Couldn't breathe. Her pulse raced out of control, and the blood rushing through her ears was so loud she could barely hear him. He was using his proximity, his cruel words to confuse her, to overpower her, to disarm her. ''Stop it.''

''Why? Because I'm right?''

''Because you're wrong.''

''Help me help you, Michelle. I need to know the truth. All of it.''

Denial rose up in her, only to free fall when he moved his hands to her face, cupping her cheek. His gaze bored into hers, angry, pleading. The only sound between them was their ragged breathing. But she was helpless to steady hers, just as she was helpless to resist what she knew would happen next.

His body came full length against hers. Michelle's brain stalled. Her heart seemed to explode in her chest. The only information that processed was the pleasure shooting sparks to all the wrong places.

He crushed his mouth to hers with a barely concealed violence that left her breathless. She tasted heat and male frustration. Her knees went weak. To keep herself from sliding to the floor, she put her arms around his neck, felt his muscles cord with tension. Vaguely, she was aware of one of his hands slipping to the back of her head, angling her mouth so that he had better access. He deepened the kiss, a growl rumbling up from his chest. Thoughts staggered through her brain, churning out sensations, emotions, everything but logic. Helpless to resist, she melted against him, opened her mouth. His tongue dipped inside, tasting her, taunting her with the satiny texture of his mouth, his own unique flavor. She welcomed the intrusion. All she could think of was that she'd forgotten how powerful a kiss could be. She fed on him like a starving woman, giving as much as she took, her body all the while humming with arousal.

It barely registered when he took her hands in his. Slowly, with devastating surety, he eased her hands above her head. The act was so unexpected and so incredibly sensual that Michelle let go of her iron-fisted control. A groan bubbled up from somewhere deep inside her. Her swollen breasts ached as her nipples pebbled against the terry cloth of the robe. For the first time she recognized the force of her own arousal, pulsing and wet between her legs.

She'd forgotten how it felt to be touched by a man. This particular man's touch moved her like no other. Feather light, but at the same time as shocking as the snap of a whip. The way his mouth moved over hers was quite simply something she'd never experienced. The result devastated her, shook her to her core. A small corner of her brain denied that she was falling for a cop even as delicious sensations washed over her. But she knew it was true. She felt it in her every fiber. Worse, she knew it in her heart.

Her vision went black-and-white when he trailed wet kisses down her throat. Releasing her hands, he parted the robe. Michelle shivered when cool air brushed over her breasts. Then the heat of his mouth on her nipple stole her breath. Her body clenched, released as he suckled. A groan escaped her. Heat built low in her belly, spreading lower, building, exploding, burning her until she felt feverish. She closed her eyes and let the sensation carry her. White light exploded behind her lids. Control tumbled away, replaced by need that was insane in its intensity. She arched into him, giving him full access to her breasts. Sensation pounded through her as he caressed her nipples with his tongue.

"I can't stay away from you," he panted. "This is crazy, but I want you. I want this. I've wanted you all along."

Michelle barely heard the words. She was beyond hearing, beyond understanding. Insanity descended the instant she felt his hand at the juncture of her thighs. A sound that was part need, part alarm escaped her. But she didn't stop him. Her thighs opened of their own accord, cool air rushing over wet heat.

She cried out when his finger found her, slipped into her very center and went deep. He stroked her there, and she met him stroke for stroke. All the while his mouth worked dark magic on hers. The pleasure overwhelmed her; it was too much, too soon. Then she was falling...tumbling end over end....

The climax swept over her with stunning force, shocking her. Even as she tumbled into oblivion, Michelle knew she'd crossed a line that could never be recrossed. Another mistake. Another lie. Another cop.

Philip hadn't meant for things to go this far. But they'd spiraled out of control so quickly, he'd been helpless to prevent what had been inevitable from the moment he'd first met her. He wanted to blame lust. The fact that he'd been alone for a long time. It was easier to think he'd put everything he'd ever worked for on the line because of long-neglected male needs and good old-fashioned lust.

But he knew better.

He also knew he couldn't let it go any further. Both of them would be irrevocably damaged if he did. Her emotionally. Him professionally. He refused to consider anything deeper than that.

Even as his rock-hard erection strained painfully against his slacks, he eased himself away from her. "This is insane."

Perspiration slicked her forehead. She blinked at him, her brown eyes wide, her expression stricken.

He'd never seen a woman look quite so beautiful—or wanted anyone quite so badly. The need ate at him like a voracious creature hollowing him out. "I'm sorry. I…that was a mistake."

Clutching the lapels of the robe together with white-knuckled hands, she stumbled back. "You're right. Oh, I…you're right. I've got to go."

Philip saw panic and humiliation in her eyes, moved to stop both before she did something rash. "I want you, Michelle. But I'm a cop. I can't be putting my hands all over you during an investigation—"

"Is that what you were doing? Putting your hands all over me?"

Oh, hell. Had he said the wrong thing?

"Maybe you wanted to see if you could get a confession out of me. Maybe you wanted to knock that chip off my shoulder. Or maybe you thought I was a sure thing. I hear those bayou girls put out if you push the right buttons."

Anger stabbed through him with surprising force. "Don't ever let me hear you put yourself down like that again."

"You're right. I don't have to put myself down. I have you to make me feel like dirt." Spinning away, she ran toward the guest bedroom, where he'd left her overnight bag.

Philip followed, cursing, starkly aware that her scent was still on him—and that his arousal showed no signs of abating anytime soon. "I shouldn't have let that happen, Michelle. I'm sorry. You know I did the right thing by stopping it."

She slammed the door in his face.

He silently counted to ten, willing his temper to cool. "I've got a murder investigation to conduct."

Silence.

He waited a beat, then tried the knob, found it locked. "I

can't do this case justice if I don't have an objective bone in my body.''

The door swung open. Surprised, Philip backed up a step. She'd thrown on a pair of jeans and an oversize shirt. Her damp hair was piled in an unruly mass atop her head. Her gaze was cold enough to freeze Lake Pontchartrain. ''Your number one suspect will no longer be a problem, Detective. If you have any more questions, you can deal with me through my attorney.''

She looked angry and vulnerable at once. He knew he'd hurt her, humiliated her, in fact. But in the long run, he'd saved them both a lot of heartache. Even so, in a little corner of his mind, he knew no other woman had ever appealed to him as much as Michelle did.

''You don't have an attorney,'' he pointed out.

''I'll get one.'' Tossing her bag over her shoulder, she shoved past him and headed for the door.

Feeling like an ogre—and a fool—Philip trailed her to the foyer. ''Let me take you home.''

A droll laugh escaped her lips. ''I'll take my chances with the muggers. They're more straightforward. At least I'll know where I stand.''

''I'm calling you a cab.'' He wanted to stop her, but he knew better. If he touched her, he might not be able to let her go.

She opened the door, stepped into the night. ''Go to hell.''

Michelle had never been so humiliated in her life. Even as a child, growing up in that tiny shanty without proper plumbing, she'd never been as humiliated as she was walking away from Betancourt's house. She wanted to blame it on him, but she knew her own weakness had driven her into his arms. When it came to Betancourt, she no longer trusted her self-control. She certainly didn't trust her judgment.

How could she have been so stupid? She knew better than to surrender to physical needs. Ten years ago the power of those needs had nearly destroyed her. She refused to let another cop ruin her life.

A fresh wave of shame sliced through her. A single, earth-shattering kiss and she'd melted, her resolve forgotten, her dignity trampled beneath desire. A single caress from those magical hands, and he'd brought her to the most explosive climax she'd ever experienced.

Then he'd pulled away.

Michelle's face heated as the memory burned through her. Why had she put herself in that position? She should have known what kind of a man he was. He was a cop, for heaven's sake. He would do anything to solve his case, including seduce her. Had she really thought he would want anything to do with Michelle Pelletier from Bayou Lafourche, Louisiana?

No, she thought dully, Detective Lieutenant Philip Betancourt wouldn't want anything to do with a woman like her. What had she been thinking, opening up to him like that? How would he feel after finding out what had happened in Bayou Lafourche?

If he hadn't pulled away, she would have made a fool of herself for sure. She should be thanking him for keeping her from making a mistake she would have regretted the rest of her life.

But the hell of it was she'd wanted him. Apparently more than he wanted her. The realization that she wasn't attractive enough or sexy enough to keep his attention hurt. Worse, she hadn't wanted to quit. She'd wanted another taste of that hard mouth, wanted to feel his callused palms against her breasts, his long fingers moving within the deepest reaches of her....

Blinking back tears, Michelle quickened her pace. She was tired and emotionally wrought. Her feet hurt. The way the lightning was splitting the sky, she was going to get soaked again.

"Oh, this is just peachy," she grumbled, cutting south on Carrollton and heading toward St. Charles.

She didn't want to go back to her apartment. The reality that she didn't have anywhere else to go struck her hard, sent shards of panic cutting through her. For the first time in a long time she felt completely and utterly alone.

She didn't even realize where she was heading until she found herself standing outside the wrought-iron gates of St. Louis Cemetery. Not caring about the rain or the derelicts known to prowl the cemetery after dark, Michelle tossed her overnight bag over the top of the gate. Bracing her foot against scrolled iron, she hoisted herself up, dropping soundlessly to the other side. She wanted to say goodbye to Armon in private, without the threat of Danielle or Baldwin or Derek, or the prying eyes of his colleagues.

Light rain fell as Michelle made her way past a row of live oaks and some small crypts bleached white by the subtropical sun. Her footfalls were nearly silent against the wet grass as she cut between rows, careful to stay clear of the shadows where muggers were known to hide. She neared the Landsteiner family crypt, then stopped cold when she caught sight of a shadow darting from behind the tomb.

Chapter 8

Ducking into the shadows of a crypt, Michelle fought down an uncharacteristic jab of fear. She wasn't afraid to walk the streets at night, had done it many times since she'd moved to New Orleans. She was cautious—as well as street savvy—but tonight her hair stood on end as she pressed her back against the cold, wet tomb.

Footfalls sounded a few yards away. Heart pounding, she watched as a shadowy figure moved slowly past her. A man. If he turned, she would be in plain sight. She held her breath. He continued on, disappearing into the night like a phantom.

For several minutes she stood motionless, listening. She heard nothing but the sound of the rain and the hiss of tires against wet pavement coming off Esplanade. Relief swamped her. Telling herself she was being silly for hiding when no one had threatened or approached her, Michelle slung the overnight bag over her shoulder and stepped out of the shadows.

Maybe she would forgo the visit to Armon's crypt. Maybe

she would just go back to her apartment, come back tomorrow when it was light and—

Strong fingers dug into her shoulder. A scream tore from her throat. She spun, punched blindly. A grunt sounded as her fist connected with a solid body. Wrenching free, she broke into a dead run. Clutching her bag, she ran as she had never run before. Angels and crosses blurred by, their shadows forming ominous shapes. Footsteps sounded behind her. Adrenaline kicked through her muscles. She changed direction, slid on gravel and nearly went down. Recovering, she darted between two crypts, only to realize she'd lost her sense of direction in the darkness.

Oh, God. Oh, God. What now?

Panting, she looked around wildly. She was standing in the middle of a wide path. Mist hovered around the crypts like spindly fingers. Light slanted through the branches of a gnarled live oak. Which way was the entrance?

The sound of shoes against gravel sent a scream to her throat. Michelle spun, watched the figure emerge from between two vaults. The scream wouldn't come. A choking sound bubbled up from her chest. Then she was running, animal sounds coming from low in her throat. Rain slashed down, blinding her. The gate loomed into view. Ten yards. Oh God, how was she going to get over the gate? He would be on her before she could get over the top.

Headlights washed over her, blinding her. Michelle flung herself at the gate, her arms absorbing the impact. Her fingers closed over iron. "Help me!" Terror clawed at her. Wedging her foot in the grillwork, she pulled herself up and over the top.

Strong arms caught her as she plummeted down. "Michelle! Whoa. Easy."

She fought the hands gripping her. "Let go of me!"

"It's me, Philip. Hold still, dammit. Stop fighting me!"

Recognition spiraled through her, followed by relief so powerful she nearly collapsed. "He was there. A man. At

Armon's crypt. He—he tried to…'' She remembered the way the man's fingers had closed over her shoulder, realized she didn't want to finish the sentence. "I got away, but he came after me."

With one arm clamped protectively around her shoulder, Betancourt shone his flashlight through the gate at the end-less rows of weathered crypts. "There's no one there now. You're safe."

Michelle looked over her shoulder, saw shadows dancing in the beam of the flashlight. "He was so close I could hear him breathing."

Betancourt extinguished the flashlight, turned her to face him, his dark eyes assessing her in a single sweep. "Are you all right? Did he hurt you?"

"I'm fine. He didn't hurt me. I ran."

"Did you recognize him?"

"No. It was too dark."

Philip's eyes hardened. "You know better than to come out here at night. You're not some tourist just off the bus."

Censure sharpened his voice, but she let it roll off her. She was too shaken to care if he was angry or not. "This guy wasn't a mugger or some crazed vagrant just hoping for a victim to stroll by."

"What does a mugger look like, Michelle? They don't wear signs, you know."

She saw the man clearly in her mind's eye and shivered. "He was wearing a suit."

"A suit?"

"And shoes with leather soles. I could tell by the way they sounded on the gravel."

"I'm surprised you don't know the name of the maker." Jaws working, Philip turned his head again to sweep the cemetery with his gaze.

She resisted the urge to look over her shoulder once more. She figured she'd be looking over her shoulder for a long time.

"Whoever it was, they're gone. It's over."

Something in the way he said the words made her think of the scene back at his house, and a wave of embarrassment cut through her fear. "How did you know I was here?"

His gaze latched on to hers. "Logic. I drove by your apartment, and you weren't there. I thought you might be here."

It perturbed her that he'd figured her out so easily. Still, she was glad he'd shown up when he did.

"You've got to stop running the streets at night, Michelle."

Annoyance rippled through her. "I don't own a car, Betancourt. I walk. Unless I win the lottery, that's not going to change anytime soon. I'm careful. I keep my eyes open. I know these neighborhoods like the back of my hand. I know what I'm doing—"

"Yeah, it looked like you knew what you were doing when you ran up to that gate screaming your head off."

He had a point. "Nothing like this has ever happened before."

"All it takes is once. This was stupid, Michelle. You know better than to put yourself in this kind of position. You could have been hurt, or worse."

"That would be a big loss to the world, wouldn't it?"

A sigh of what could have been frustration whistled between his lips. "Look, I came looking for you because I wanted to apologize for some of the things I said to you. Uh...for what happened back at my house."

The image of her writhing in his arms as he brought her to climax flashed through her mind, and a hot blush crept up her cheeks. Michelle turned, started to walk away. "That was a mistake. Don't say anything else. I don't want to deal with it right now."

He stopped her with a gentle touch on her shoulder. "You're an attractive woman, Michelle, and I...we got carried away. I want you, but you're vulnerable right now. I don't want to take advantage of that. It would be not only unprofessional, but unethical. I'm in the middle of an investigation, and I can't afford to...get involved.''

The words stung. Turning to him, she forced a smile, but her face felt like plastic. "Let's just leave it at that, shall we, Betancourt? No big deal."

He contemplated her, his face inscrutable. "Come on. I'll take you back to the hotel." Picking up her overnight bag, he set it in the back seat of his unmarked car.

Michelle didn't want to go back there. She felt out of place among the old-world elegance and richly dressed patrons. But she wasn't ready to go back to her apartment. One more night at the hotel, she promised herself. Tomorrow she would start looking for a new apartment. Tomorrow she would launch her own investigation into the murder of Armon Landsteiner.

"How close are you to an arrest in the Landsteiner case, Lieutenant Betancourt?"

Cold Case Squad Commander Hardin Montgomery was the last person Philip wanted to deal with at seven o'clock in the morning. He hadn't slept, hadn't shaved, hadn't even had his first cup of coffee yet, and Montgomery was already breathing fire.

"Sergeant Sanderson and I are following up on leads. We're looking into the possibility of a will. We're checking alibis and backgrounds. You've already seen the reports from the lab and medical examiner." He'd copied Montgomery on everything. So why in the hell had the old fox called him into his office for an early morning grilling session?

"What about the young woman Landsteiner was involved with? Last report I read, she was your number one suspect. You haven't mentioned her."

Philip went on full alert. Montgomery might be fat and lazy, but he wasn't stupid. "She's still a suspect."

"Why haven't you arrested her?"

"The lab reports were inconclusive. She didn't fire the gun that killed Landsteiner. There were no powder burns on her clothes or her hands."

"Couldn't she have changed clothes, worn gloves?"

For the most part Philip liked Hardin Montgomery. But the commander didn't like to make waves, even if it meant standing up for what was right. He let individuals with a higher authority jerk his chain at their leisure. Philip wondered who was jerking his chain this time.

"It's possible," Philip said.

"We've got motive, means and opportunity, Lieutenant. What's the delay?"

"I'd like some more physical evidence before I make an arrest, sir."

Montgomery didn't look happy. "She's got a record, for God's sake."

"We're working on getting the records released. She was a juvenile at the time. Judge Thomas issued a subpoena."

"I'll see what I can do to expedite that. Maurice Thomas and I go way back." Montgomery rubbed a hand over his beefy neck and grimaced at the reports in front of him. "Dr. Witt's report said his session with Miss Pelletier was inconclusive. She could be lying about the memory thing."

"Or she could be telling the truth. There's another witness claiming to have seen the man in black running from the house. Plus, her apartment was broken into and ransacked last night."

Montgomery's brows knitted. "You think it's connected to the case?"

"I think it's likely. Lab team couldn't lift any prints." Philip considered telling him that Michelle had been accosted in the cemetery as well, but he knew that bit of information would raise questions about his own presence, so he remained silent.

"Look, Lieutenant, to make a long story short, I've got

politicians breathing down my neck. We don't need any more PR problems.'' He looked at Philip over the tops of his bifocals. ''Frankly, Lieutenant, you don't, either. Not after the Rosetti fiasco last year.''

Anger lashed through Philip, but he didn't let himself react. ''I was cleared of any wrongdoing, Hardin.''

''We're talking PR, Lieutenant. I want this thing wrapped up yesterday. Understand?''

Philip nodded. As he left Montgomery's office, he realized someone wanted Michelle to fry regardless of guilt or innocence.

Philip's temper simmered all the way to the division's community coffeepot. Who the hell had Montgomery been talking to? he wondered as he poured engine sludge into his cup. Baldwin Landsteiner? Or was the pressure coming from higher up? Armon Landsteiner had had a lot of friends in high places. The police commissioner. City Hall. The mayor. Rumor had it he'd even wined and dined a congressman or two in his Garden District mansion on occasion. But who would want the case closed with the wrong person behind bars?

Philip had lost his objectivity, and that scared the hell out of him. As hard as he tried, he couldn't stop thinking of the way Michelle had melted in his arms the night before. He remembered every shudder, every sound. He remembered the warmth of her breath on his ear, the feel of her body when he'd stroked her and she'd let go of her control.

He cared about her a hell of a lot more than he should.

Michelle was the most desirable woman he'd ever known. Not just physically, but in spirit. Beneath the thin veneer of street toughness—and that chip she wore so steadfastly on her shoulder—resided a deeply emotional woman whose heart had taken a beating. Her life hadn't been easy. She had demons. She'd been hurt, but he didn't know why, or by whom.

Still, she'd lied to him. Not outright, but by omission. Philip couldn't live with that. Just as he hadn't been able to live with Whitney and her lies. Her betrayal had bled him dry of tolerance for deception. He wouldn't set himself up for another slash of the feminine sword.

Philip ground his teeth and acknowledged the fact that he'd lost more than just his objectivity. The moment he'd touched Michelle, he'd lost his logic, his professionalism, his ability to think clearly. How the hell was he going to solve this case when he couldn't keep a handle on his own lust? What if he was wrong about her?

Aside from his personal contact with her, he'd handled the investigation by the book. But his professionalism stopped there. If push came to shove, he wasn't sure he could bring himself to arrest this woman who'd slipped under his skin. How long could he put off Montgomery? A day? A week, maybe?

Michelle wasn't a flight risk, Philip assured himself. The guidelines didn't dictate an immediate arrest. The absence of powder burns and the corroboration of another witness who'd seen the man in black were the only things saving her from arrest. Still, Philip had to ask himself if he was willing to put his career on the line for a woman who couldn't tell the truth.

Coffee in hand, he took the elevator down to central evidence and signed a procurement slip for the files he'd taken as evidence from Armon Landsteiner's home. Back at his desk, he flipped through the phone book, then dialed the number for the Jacoby and Perez law firm.

He identified himself, and the receptionist put him on hold. Impatient, Philip muttered a curse, then absently paged through the stack of canceled checks from one of Landsteiner's old bank statements. His finger stopped on one made out to Tulane University. The hairs on the back of his neck prickled.

"May I help you?" a professional-sounding female voice asked.

Pulling out the check, Philip turned his attention back to his phone conversation. "I'd like to speak with Dennis Jacoby."

"Uh...who's calling?"

He identified himself, using his full title in case she got any ideas about screening her boss's phone calls. Damn lawyers.

"I'm sorry...Detective, this is Emma Thorpe, Mr. Jacoby's paralegal. There was a fire last night at the office." Her voice cracked. "Mr. Jacoby was....killed. He died about an hour ago at Charity Hospital."

Philip's interest flared. Hell of a coincidence that the man Michelle believed had drawn up Armon's most recent will had been killed. Only Philip didn't believe in coincidence.

After getting as many details as he could, he dialed the fire marshal, got voice mail, left a message.

He looked down at the check he'd pulled from the bank statement. It was dated several months before Michelle had come to New Orleans from Bayou Lafourche. Another coincidence that didn't sit well in his gut. Philip wondered why Armon Landsteiner had written a $25,000 check to Tulane University. He flipped through the remaining checks with renewed interest, and found one made out to Honeycutt Investigations. Scrawled on the For line was "Bayou Lafourche."

"I'll be damned." Philip was familiar with the private investigation firm. They'd had a good reputation, but went out of business over a year ago. Honeycutt had hired on with another firm. Why had Armon Landsteiner engaged a private detective to go sniffing around Bayou Lafourche, Louisiana, *before* he'd ever met Michelle?

Pulling the yellow pages from his desk drawer, Philip paged to the private investigator section, located the firm where Honeycutt worked and dialed the number.

Cory arrived just as Philip finished setting up an appointment.

"Since when are you keeping banker's hours, Sanderson?" When Cory didn't answer, Philip looked up, realized immediately something was wrong. "Rough night?" Pulling a bottle of aspirin from the top drawer, he handed it to his partner.

"I'd say two hours with Public Integrity is pretty freaking rough, Betancourt, wouldn't you?"

An alarm bell went off in Philip's head. The Public Integrity Division was the city's equivalent of internal affairs. "What the hell are you talking about?"

"Ken Burns got me walking into the building, and I've been up in their little interview room playing twenty questions ever since." Cory shot Philip an accusatory look. "They've got a hell of a lot of questions about you, Betancourt."

"About Michelle?"

"The whole Landsteiner case. Burns said it was just an informal interview, but, man, I knew better. Nothing's informal when it comes to PID. I danced around as much crap as I could, but they're after you big-time. You better watch your back."

Philip should have expected this, especially after the way Montgomery had grilled him this morning. Still, the fact that PID had gotten involved irked the hell out of him. "Something isn't right with this case, Cory."

"Yeah, and she's got big brown eyes and a body to die for—"

"That's not it." Philip relayed the information about the checks, and the fire at Dennis Jacoby's office. "I put a call in to Honeycutt." He glanced at his watch. "I'm meeting with him in twenty minutes."

"You want me to check in with the Tulane administrator? See what the check was for?"

"I'd appreciate that."

Philip swallowed a small rise of panic when his phone rang. He answered with a curt utterance of his name, fully expecting one of the PID investigators.

"Hi, Philip. This is Tina over at the courthouse. Judge Thomas asked me to give you a call to let you know we're sending over some records on the Landsteiner case via courier."

Philip looked down at the check on his desk. "The juvenile records on Michelle Pelletier?" he asked.

"Yes."

"What was the charge?"

Papers rustled on the other end of the line. "Ten years ago in Lafourche Parish Michelle Pelletier was arrested for murder."

Shock rippled through him, followed by crushing disappointment. "Was she convicted?"

"No. Didn't even go to trial."

That was something. Philip thanked the woman and hung up the phone. Murder. He almost didn't believe it. Almost.

He looked up, found Cory looking at him quizzically. "Your house didn't burn down or something, did it, Betancourt?"

"Cory, the juvenile charge against Michelle was for murder."

"No wonder she didn't want to talk about it. That's going to bury her."

"Yeah." Philip looked at his watch again. He wanted to talk to Montgomery to tell PID to back off, but he needed to meet with Honeycutt, then swing by to see the fire marshal about the blaze at Jacoby's office. After that he was going to confront Michelle and get the truth from her once and for all.

Michelle couldn't believe her eyes as she stood on the sidewalk and stared at the charred remains of Dennis Jacoby's office. The building was unrecognizable. The roof had collapsed, the windows shattered. Soot and ash blackened the bricks. A band of yellow crime scene tape stretched across the front of the building. She wondered if anyone had been hurt in the fire, if any records had been destroyed.

Betancourt would know.

Sighing, she turned and faced the midday traffic humming along Poydras. Despite everything, thoughts of Betancourt invariably invaded her mind. She hadn't had a moment's peace since she'd first laid eyes on him the night Armon was murdered. Betancourt, with his suspicious eyes and cynical view of the world, was trouble no matter how you cut it. He was a cop. She was a suspect. It should have been infinitely simple.

Only nothing was simple when it came to Philip.

Every time he looked at her with those stormy gray eyes, her heart stuttered in her chest. His touch sent her body to the clouds, her mind into an emotional tailspin. His kisses sent shivers of pure delight through her. When his hands molded her body, when his fingers stroked her, control and the last vestiges of her dignity fled.

Michelle knew better than to succumb to those male charms. She knew better than to surrender to her own weakness. She'd been around the block enough times to know last night was a mistake. She'd been emotionally distraught, having just attended Armon's funeral. Betancourt had taken advantage of that, hoping she'd open up and spill her guts.

The hell of it was she wanted him anyway. Her body didn't give a damn about logic or self-preservation. She didn't even want to think what might happen if her heart got involved.

The thought made her shiver.

Michelle knew how to protect herself. She couldn't let her guard down now. Not when she had another cop with an agenda hounding her. She'd survived Bayou Lafourche. She'd survived those first years in New Orleans. She'd survive this, too.

Spotting the *Times Picayune* box on the corner, Michelle started down the sidewalk at a brisk clip, digging a quarter out of the pocket of her jeans as she went. She needed to start looking for an apartment.

"Why am I not surprised to find you here?"

Her stomach plummeted at the sound of Betancourt's voice. She spun, found him standing right behind her, the sun casting his face in shadows. She couldn't read his expression, but she could tell by his voice he was angry.

"I—I just…" Raising her chin, she looked him directly in the eye. "I wanted to speak with Dennis Jacoby about Armon's will. There's no law against that, is there, Detective?"

"No, but there is a law against lying to the police." His fingers clamped around her arm. "You know, Michelle, I'm getting pretty damn tired of being lied to."

The sudden contact sent a shock wave through her. By the time she got her wits about her, it was too late. He had his car door open and was forcing her into the passenger seat. She tried to wrench free, but his grip was like a vise.

"Stay put, or I'll cuff you." He slammed the door on her protests, crossed in front of the car and got in.

Michelle considered getting out and walking away, but she knew that would be fruitless. Betancourt was a cop; he had every right to force her to talk to him.

"You know, you're not even that good of a liar." A dry as dust laugh broke through his tight lips. "I should have seen right through it."

"I haven't lied—"

"You were arrested for murder." He turned on her, leaning so close she could feel the fury coming off him. "Did that little detail slip your mind?"

The words hit her like a sledgehammer. Her breath left her lungs, left her gasping and speechless.

"Don't you just hate it when the truth comes out?" he snarled.

"I—I was only seventeen. The charge was—"

"Save the excuses. I asked you for the truth. All I ever wanted from you was the damn truth." Turning away, he started the car. The tires screeched as he pulled onto the street.

She'd known he would find out sooner or later. She knew she should have told him. But the shame and the fear ran so deep she hadn't been able to. Maybe he'd been correct in calling her a coward. Maybe she wasn't as brave as she'd once thought.

"Where are you taking me?"

"I ought to take you to jail. Maybe a few hours in a cell will teach you the value of honesty."

A quiver ran the length of her. She pressed her hand to her stomach. "That's not funny."

"Who's kidding?" His jaws worked angrily as he maneuvered the car through traffic. "I'm taking you someplace quiet where we can talk."

"Like the police station?" she asked tightly. "I'm sure you're quite fond of that little interview room."

"That can be arranged."

Grinding her teeth in anger, Michelle folded her arms and leaned back against the seat. "That won't be necessary."

"I didn't think so."

Ten minutes later, Philip pulled into his driveway, got out of the car and jerked open her door. "I'm a damn fool for bringing you here. I learned a long time ago you can't help someone who doesn't want to be helped."

"You don't want to help me, Betancourt, you want to ruin my life."

"Like you can read my mind."

"No, I just know your type."

"You don't know the half of it." He opened the front door. "Get inside."

Knowing she didn't have a choice, Michelle obeyed. "I won't let you bully me."

Betancourt locked the door behind them, then motioned toward the futon. "Sit down."

Michelle lowered herself onto it, then folded her hands to keep them from shaking.

He sat on the other end, leaned forward and put his elbows on his knees. "I went to bat for you, Michelle. I gave you the benefit of the doubt, and you made a fool of me. My commander thinks I ought to arrest you for the murder of Armon Landsteiner. I brought you here so you could give me one good reason why I shouldn't."

She'd never seen him like this. Yes, she'd known Betancourt was volatile, even unpredictable. But she'd never seen this cold, angry side of him. "I didn't kill him."

"You've already said that, only I'm not sure I believe you anymore. Nothing you're telling me is adding up. My patience is too thin for half-truths. Lie to me again, and I'll arrest you."

Michelle winced, felt her breaths coming quick and shallow. She tried to calm herself, but Betancourt was frightening her. "I don't want to go to jail."

"I don't want to put you there, but I will. So help me, if you don't start talking, I won't have a choice."

Too restless to sit, she sprang to her feet and paced the length of the living room. Dread sat like a lead weight in the pit of her stomach. "I guess this is the moment of truth, Betancourt." Struggling for composure, she squared her shoulders and turned to him. "Are you sure you can handle it?"

He stared at her through eyes as dark and cold as the nighttime depths of the gulf. "Bring it on, and we'll find out."

Chapter 9

Because her knees were shaking, Michelle went back to the futon and sat. She didn't want to talk about what had happened in Bayou Lafourche. She didn't want to talk about Nicolas or Deputy Frank Blanchard. Most of all, she didn't want to rehash her own mistakes—and the fact that she seemed determined to repeat them.

She hadn't consciously thought of that day or the darkness that followed in years. She'd blocked it from her mind, almost convincing herself none of the ugliness had taken place. That no one had died. That a man to whom she'd given her naive heart hadn't used her, then destroyed a part of her that could never be revived.

"Talk to me, Michelle." Impatience edged Betancourt's voice. "The truth. No holding back."

She sucked in a deep, shuddering breath. "My mama got sick when I was fifteen. A little over a year later she was diagnosed with lymph node cancer. She died when I was seventeen. She was only forty years old." Michelle studied her hands, hating it that they were shaking. In a corner of her mind, she wondered if she'd ever be able to think of the past and not feel it like a stake through her heart.

"My older brother, Nicolas, blamed the cancer on the conditions at the chemical plant where she worked. Mama tried so hard to support us, taking all the dirty jobs, working all the overtime. There were so many chemicals, and the management was lax about safety. When she died…Nicolas needed someone to blame. We both did, I suppose."

The pain wasn't as sharp as it had once been, but Michelle still felt it, like the tip of a sword sinking slowly into her chest, through flesh and muscle and bone, penetrating the armor around her heart and cutting it to shreds.

"The plant wouldn't even help pay for her funeral. That was the final straw. Nicolas…went a little crazy after that." She looked at Betancourt, wondered if any of what she was saying had penetrated that hardened heart of his, if it would make a difference, if he was even capable of understanding why she hadn't wanted to tell him about her past. "In the days after her funeral, Nicolas…spent a lot of time alone. Out in the swamp. In his cabin along the bayou. He quit his job at the plant, then dropped out of sight."

As she resurrected the ghosts and the ugliness, the pain rushed back like rancid water gushing out of a black hole in her soul. "A week later, he came home. He had a box with him, and told me he was going to the plant to clean out his locker. Nicolas has a bad temper. I didn't want him to start a fight, or do anything crazy. So I told him if he was going to the plant, I was going with him. We fought, but he finally agreed.

"We went to the plant. He cleaned out his locker. An hour after we left, an explosion devastated half the plant—" Her voice broke as the memories pummeled her, bringing with them the shame of what had happened next. "It was Sunday, and that portion of the plant was usually closed. But on this particular Sunday a maintenance worker…a man with a family…"

She couldn't finish the sentence, couldn't look at Philip, couldn't bear to see the disgust or revulsion in his eyes. "The man died. The next day, the police arrested us. Nicolas and I were charged with murder. I spent two days in jail before I was cleared. Two months later, Nicolas was convicted of manslaughter and spent ten years in prison. I tried to visit him in prison, but he refused to see me. I haven't seen him since the trial."

She couldn't bring herself to tell him about Deputy Frank Blanchard, or the betrayal that had nearly destroyed her. Philip didn't need to know that part of the story.

She stood, vacillating, her heart pounding furiously in her chest. Tears burned behind her eyes. God, she'd thought she'd come to terms with this.

"Oh, man." Philip pinched the bridge of his nose between his thumb and forefinger.

Knowing she was going to lose the battle with her emotions, Michelle turned away and started for the door. "I have to go."

"Wait a minute."

She didn't stop. She didn't want him to see her like this, scraped raw and out of control. "Leave me alone." She was halfway to the door when his hand closed gently around her shoulder.

Wordlessly, he turned her to him. "Come here."

The words surprised her; she'd expected disgust from this man who saw the world in stark black-and-white. As a homicide detective, he knew firsthand the ugliness people were capable of. He understood the darkness, and he lived with it. But here he was, offering her a solid embrace, even after he knew the truth.

"So now you know, Detective. My big dark secret. I have an arrest record. For murder." Blinking back tears, she raised her chin and looked him in the eye. "I'm sure that fits nicely with your profile of a cold-blooded murderer."

"Nothing fits when it comes to you." He studied her through shuttered eyes. "Did you know about the bomb?"

"I knew Nicolas was capable. I knew he was hurting. But I never—"

"You've been blaming yourself for this all these years?"

The words took her aback. Had she been blaming herself? Possibly, she thought. But it wasn't for the reason Betancourt suspected. He didn't know about Deputy Blanchard, or the role she'd played in getting her brother convicted of manslaughter.

"Nicolas didn't do it," she said.

"He had motive, means and opportunity."

"He told me he didn't do it. I believe him."

"A jury thought differently."

Because of her, but she didn't want to get into that now. She'd told Philip what was relevant. He didn't need to know the rest. The shame was too great.

"Did you testify against him?"

Guilt welled up inside her, like blood from a wound. Guilt for the maintenance worker's death, but mostly for the brother she'd turned her back on when he'd needed her. All for the likes of a cop who'd used her, then betrayed her.

"Yes," she said.

"You've been holding this inside you ever since, haven't you?" Slowly, he eased her close to him, then wrapped his arms around her.

She hadn't realized how badly she needed to be held. The simple gesture threatened her thin hold on control. "If you do one more nice thing, I'm going to lose it, Betancourt."

"Hey, I'm the cop without a heart, remember?" A smile played at the corner of his mouth. "I don't do nice."

A tension-easing laugh broke from her chest. "I'm in a lot of trouble, aren't I?"

"Probably."

"Don't cushion the blow on my account."

"The D.A. probably knows about your arrest record."

Raising his hand, Philip stroked the back of her head. "Did Armon know?"

Michelle winced. "I never told him."

"That's a hell of a burden to be carrying around. I'm sorry you had to go through that."

"I wanted to tell you—"

"You should have."

"I was afraid you wouldn't believe me."

"Shh. I'll flog you later. Let me just hold you a moment, okay?"

His arms were solid and warm around her. Michelle leaned against him and pressed her cheek against the collar of his suit jacket. The woodsy scent of his cologne surrounded her, mingling with the subtle scents of soap and shampoo and his own distinctly male essence. For the first time in a long time, Michelle felt…safe. It was a glorious feeling, and she wished she could freeze this frame of time, knowing another might not ever come.

"I might have been able to stop it, Betancourt. If I'd reached out to Nicolas. If we hadn't gone to the plant—"

"You didn't know what your brother had planned." He stroked her hair. "That's why the charge against you was dropped. That's why it never went to trial."

"Nicolas was…inconsolable after Mama died. If I'd approached him—"

"You were a seventeen-year-old kid. You'd just lost a parent. You sure as hell couldn't control an older sibling bent on self-destruction."

Michelle closed her eyes. The logical side of her brain knew he was right. But her heart broke because she knew that Nicolas was innocent. It tore her up inside knowing she'd played a role in sending him to prison.

"It hurts, Betancourt. All of it. Nicolas. That maintenance worker. It hurts that Armon died and that people think I'm responsible. I can't live with that."

"I know you didn't kill Landsteiner." Easing her to arm's

length, Philip leveled a heady gaze at her. "I know that now."

The words stunned her, overwhelmed her. Chest constricting, Michelle searched the gray depths of his eyes for the lie, but found only honesty.

"Is that everything, Michelle? Have you told me everything? Because before I can help you, I have to know the whole truth."

She considered telling him about Blanchard, but a little voice of reason stopped her. She'd told him everything that was relevant. He believed her. That had to be enough.

"That's it," she said.

He studied her, his gaze hard and inscrutable. "I believe you."

No one except Armon had ever believed in her. Blinking back fresh tears, she nodded. "That means a lot to me."

"I'm going to solve this case, Michelle. If it's the last thing I do, I'm going to find out who murdered Armon Landsteiner. But I'm going to need your help."

"Aside from getting my memory back, I'm not sure what I can do."

"I think the murder has something to do with Landsteiner's will."

Her gaze snapped to his. "His will…you mean Armon's family?"

"Armon told you in passing he was having a new will drawn up. A will that would supersede his old one. The lawyer most likely to have drawn up that new will, Dennis Jacoby, was killed this morning. His office burned to the ground."

Michelle recoiled. She hadn't known anyone had died in the fire. She'd seen the burned out shell of the building, yet she'd never suspected foul play…or that he had been murdered. The implications staggered her. "You think someone murdered Dennis Jacoby and destroyed his office to prevent the will from ever coming to light?"

"It's possible."

She and Armon had had dinner with Jacoby last month. He was a nice man with a wife and children. Her heart wrenched. "Two people murdered in the span of a week over a will? I don't understand."

Betancourt's jaws worked as he considered the question. "Maybe old man Landsteiner decided to leave some of his riches to someone more deserving than his own conniving offspring."

The words struck her like a whip. "Me."

He nodded.

"Oh, my God." Pain congealed in her chest, so sharp and deep she nearly doubled over with it. "Oh, Armon."

"There's more," Philip said. "Sit down."

Michelle knew instinctively she wasn't going to like what he had to say. Mentally, she braced. "What?"

He guided her to the futon, then sat down beside her. Taking her hands in his, he looked deeply into her eyes. "I was going through some of Landsteiner's personal papers this morning. Just routine stuff. Bank statements. Insurance policies. Correspondence. I didn't really expect to find anything. Until I came to a check made out to a private investigator he hired over five years ago to find you."

Everything inside her went perfectly still. "That's impossible."

"A year before you left Bayou Lafourche for New Orleans, Landsteiner hired a private detective to find you."

"Five years ago?" Disbelief whipped through her. "That's not true. It can't be. There's got to be some kind of mistake. I didn't know Armon five years ago. I didn't meet him until—"

"I talked to the detective this morning, Michelle. It happened. He also made reference to Nicolas." His gaze burned into hers. "That's your brother's name, isn't it?"

The words hit her like a set of brass knuckles, so brutal

they took her breath, so unexpected she could only stare at him, speechless. "I don't believe you."

"You know I don't have a reason to lie to you." Never taking his gaze from hers, Betancourt tightened his grip on her hands. "Landsteiner funded your scholarship to Tulane."

Denial reared up inside her. She tried to pull away, but he held her hands firmly in his. "You're lying. I earned that scholarship with my GPA. I've got the paperwork to prove it. Armon couldn't have…he wouldn't have…"

"I saw the check with my own eyes."

"He didn't lie to me, damn you. I met him at the restaurant a few months after I moved to New Orleans. He couldn't possibly have arranged that." But even as she said the words, she wondered if she'd known Armon as well as she once thought. Who had he really been? That kindhearted, compassionate man who had plucked her from obscurity and given her hope? Why had he chosen her when there were dozens of other disenfranchised young people who'd needed someone to care?

"After he found you in Bayou Lafourche, and realized you attended the community college, he arranged for your scholarship. All of it was done under the table, so to speak. Then he waited six months, sought you out and hired you at his firm."

Her world crumpled like wet paper, the words shattering everything she'd ever believed about Armon, about herself. "I don't believe any of it. You're wrong about Armon."

"I'm investigating his murder, for God's sake. Lying doesn't enter the picture. Maybe all this has something to do with why he was murdered."

The words didn't register at first. Then, slowly, a second scenario dawned on her, and she clung to it. Anything was better than believing her entire life was based on a lie.

Blood thundering, she turned her gaze on him. "Oh, you're good."

"What are you talking about?"

Anger speared through her when she realized she'd nearly fallen for it. She wrenched free of his grasp and lurched to her feet. Her hand grazed a lamp, sent it tumbling, but she didn't even look at it. "You'll do anything to solve this case, won't you, Betancourt?"

He moved toward her, jaw set, intensity burning in his gaze. "I'm sure this will throw a wrench into your tainted view of the world, Michelle, but I happen to care about you."

He wasn't the first cop to say those words to her. The fact that she'd almost fallen for it a second time infuriated her. "You care about me as long as I fit neatly into your agenda."

"If I didn't care about you I wouldn't have risked my job or my reputation bringing you here. I sure as hell wouldn't have gone to bat for you in the commander's office this morning. If it was up to him, Michelle, you'd be in a cell right now."

The thought of being thrown in jail for a crime she hadn't committed sent a shudder racing through her. The same thing they'd done to her brother. Maybe it was a just punishment considering she'd helped the cops put him there.

"You don't follow the rules, do you, Betancourt?"

His eyes narrowed, flashed darkly. "I don't know what you mean."

"That's what I've heard about you. You walk that thin line, straying to whatever side suits your objective." A harsh laugh tore from deep in her chest. "Yeah, I read about the Rosetti case. Maybe we both have something to atone for."

He flinched, and Michelle knew she'd hit a nerve.

"Don't push it." His voice was low and dangerous.

"No wonder they call you the terminator. You always get your man, don't you? You don't give a damn about who you trample in the process, as long as you get the end result."

He was on her in two strides. "I may not follow the rules, but I sure as hell know the difference between right and wrong."

His fingers dug into her biceps. His strength overwhelmed her, his gaze boring into her like a laser. She backed up, but he went with her. She struck back the only way she knew how. "Some men get turned on by the thought of a roll in the hay with a woman from the wrong side of the tracks. It's a power thing, I think. Is it a power thing with you, Betancourt? Or am I just a convenient suspect? Maybe you're hoping I talk in bed."

"You're pushing the wrong buttons, Michelle."

"You're playing with my feelings, and I don't like it."

Incredulity entered his eyes. "Now where the hell did *that* come from?"

"You're the rocket scientist. You figure it out."

He blinked, then scrubbed a hand over his five o'clock shadow. "I care about you," he growled.

"You care about the case. Whether or not my life gets ruined in the process is inconsequential."

"Your life is what I'm trying to save!"

That stopped her. Michelle stood frozen, staring at the tall, steely eyed man in front of her. A lock of black hair had fallen onto his forehead. He was breathing hard, just as she was. His fingers were still clamped over her biceps. Her flesh tingled beneath them, as if an electrical current flowed from him into her.

His dark eyes searched hers. "You really haven't ever had anybody care for you, have you?"

Michelle dropped her gaze, embarrassed and oddly ashamed that he'd guessed correctly. She wanted to deny the truth of the statement, deny that it disturbed her, but she just didn't have the strength. "Armon cared for me." She hadn't even realized she was going to say the words, but they were there, in her heart, a constant in the backwaters of her mind.

"Did you fight him, too?"

"Armon wasn't a threat."

"And I am? Is that why you're fighting me, when you know I'm trying to help you?" Philip raised his hand, brushed his thumb over her cheek.

The caress touched her more deeply than it should have. Michelle averted her face. "Don't toy with my feelings."

He maintained contact. "I wouldn't do that to you. Not knowing what I do."

"But you're not above using me."

"I'm not above breaking the rules. Maybe that's what I do best." His lips curled in derision. "But that's not why I'm here. That's not why you're standing so close I can smell you, feel the heat coming off you. I'm here because I care about what happens to you."

"Stop it." She didn't want to hear those dangerous words, couldn't bear it. Not now.

"I wish I could take away the pain you've suffered over the years. I wish I could right the wrongs. But I can't. All I can do, all I'm equipped to do is find the person who killed Armon."

The touch of his thumb against her cheek moved her as no other touch could have. She wanted to believe he cared. Oh, how she needed someone to care for her right now. She'd been alone so long it seemed an eternity. Until Armon, there hadn't been another human being who cared whether she lived or died.

"I don't want anything more," she said.

"Maybe I don't, either. Maybe that would be too dangerous for both of us."

The image of her writhing in his arms as he'd brought her to climax sent a wave of heat slicing through her. There was no doubt they shared a volatile physical attraction. She'd experienced it twice, and the power of the feelings he unleashed frightened her. She wasn't reckless or impulsive. Nor was she a risk taker, though fate had seen to it she'd been forced to take a few in her time. What worried her most was that she no longer trusted her vise grip on self-control. What was it about Betancourt that had her wanting to jump headlong off the precipice she'd clung to for so long?

She wasn't a sexual creature by nature, yet she'd reacted in a wholly sexual way, despite her efforts to resist. In doing so, she'd made herself vulnerable, and that was a mistake. Betancourt was the kind of man she could lose her heart to, perhaps already had. She didn't want to think about that now; she was too raw, too vulnerable. She'd learned how to be alone over the years, and she was good at it, had it down to a fine art. But when he looked at her like the sun rose and set in her eyes, when he touched with such gentleness that it brought tears flooding, she wanted to cast her self-imposed emotional isolation aside. For the first time since the day she'd walked away from Bayou Lafourche, she wanted to let go. She wanted to feel loved. Free. Alive. Because she knew as surely as she felt his palm at her cheek that her days as a free woman were numbered.

His hand combed through her hair. "I've always been drawn to danger."

Alarm bells trilled in her head, but Michelle ruthlessly shoved them aside. "Not me. I know better, Betancourt."

"Do you?"

Angling her head, she pressed her cheek into his palm and closed her eyes. "But I don't always follow my own good judgment."

Philip was out of control, and he knew it. She was inside his head, dangerously close to his heart. The hell of it was that, for the first time in his life, he didn't care. He was powerless to stop the raw need hammering away at the last of his own good judgment.

Sunlight streaming through the window highlighted her sun-streaked hair. Her eyes were closed, her lashes thick and dark against the pale skin of her face. Her imperfectly shaped mouth, which haunted his dreams night after night, looked soft and inviting. He wanted to kiss her, wanted to devour that mouth, feel her open beneath his lips, taste her, savor the sweetness he knew resided there.

Her beauty was subtle, but powerful. As he gazed down at her, the full force of her struck him squarely between the eyes. She affected him as no other woman ever had. Need and lust and a tangled array of emotions he didn't want to think about collided, exploded, sent his logic scattering. He wanted to run his fingers through that wild mane of hair. Wanted to touch her lush mouth. With his fingers. His lips. His tongue. He wanted to make her eyes glaze over with pleasure.

Turbulent need boiled up inside him, engulfing him, arrowing straight through his chest to a place he didn't want to acknowledge. He stroked her cheek, finding her flesh like velvet beneath his fingers. Supple. Flushed. His fingertips traced along her jaw, touched her mouth. Her lips parted. Soft. Wet.

He couldn't believe no one had ever loved this woman. She was such a gift. Full of hope in the face of insurmountable odds. Full of secret dreams as big as the sky was endless. She soothed his cynical heart as no one else ever had, almost made him believe that good prevailed over evil, and that people were basically decent.

"I think the last of my good judgment just went out the window," he growled.

"There's no room in this relationship for good judgment, Betancourt."

"Ah, a little cynicism for the soul. That makes me feel a lot better."

Her tentative smile devastated him. "I thought it would."

"I've never wanted anyone the way I want you."

"No one's ever said that to me before, Betancourt."

Emotion coupled with physical sensation, making his voice thick and slow. "I'm not going to let you go to jail.

You've got my word on that. I'm going to solve this murder. Then I'm going to show you what it feels like for someone to care."

"I'd like that." She looked at him from beneath her lashes. "About last night...I've never done anything that...reckless before. I'm not impulsive."

He smiled, charmed and oddly humbled. "What we did wasn't *that* reckless."

"For me it was."

"Sometimes reckless is good."

"Most times it just gets you into trouble."

He wanted her so badly he was shaking. He wanted her with heart and soul and everything that made him a man. The physical need pulsed through him, settling low in his groin, where his erection strained painfully against his trousers.

Cupping her face with his hands, he lowered his lips to hers. Her mouth opened, welcoming him. Surprise rippled through him, followed by a small explosion of pure lust. He felt her hands on his back, then his buttocks, and his control tumbled away. He kissed her deeply, thoroughly, tasting heat spiced with his own frustration. Need clawed at him, sending fire to every nerve in his body. His fingers splayed through her hair, skimmed down her back, then lower. Her waist was narrow. Her backside was firm, high and curvy.

An involuntary shudder went through him. He hadn't been with a woman since his divorce last year, and the power of his reaction to Michelle stunned him. It had never been like this with Whitney, not even in his wildest dreams.

Holding Michelle's hips firmly in his hands, he pressed himself against her, and an involuntary groan rumbled up from his chest. "I want you. Here. Now."

Looking at him through heavy-lidded eyes, she worked the buttons of his shirt with trembling fingers. Her hands slipped past the buttons, brushed across his nipples.

His vision blurred, dimmed. He wanted her beneath him,

writhing and wet and open. If he didn't get inside her right now, he was going to explode.

He tumbled her onto the futon, feasted on her mouth like a starving man on a banquet of sweet, succulent fruit. He couldn't get enough, would never get enough of Michelle. Slipping his hands beneath her T-shirt, he molded his palms to her breasts. They were wide and incredibly full for such a slight woman. A soft cry broke from her mouth, and he kissed her harder, deeper. He struggled for a moment, trying to find the fastening of her bra, felt a tug of embarrassment when he couldn't.

"It's a rear closure," she whispered in a breathy voice.

"I'm a little out of practice." Philip grinned, unfastening the hook when she leaned forward. "In a lot of areas."

"Yeah, Betancourt, me, too. Think we can manage this?"

"No doubt about it."

Her bra snapped open. Leaning over her, Philip tugged her T-shirt over her head. His heart beat wildly in his chest. Blood roared like a waterfall in his ears. He'd never seen such beauty. He cupped her breasts, trapping her small nipples between his thumb and forefinger.

Michelle arched up, a cry breaking from her lips. Philip felt her stiffen, then relax back onto the futon. Pulling back, he trailed kisses down her throat. The tempo of her breaths increased. He took a nipple into his mouth, suckled hard, teasing the hardened tip with his tongue. Her hips moved against him, and he thought for sure it was all over for him, but he maintained his control if only by a thread. That would have been a hell of a way to end the most erotic experience of his life.

Raising up on his knees, Philip fought the jacket from his shoulders, tossed it on the floor. His shirt went next. He looked down at Michelle, saw her as he'd seen her in his fantasies. Dark eyes glazed with pleasure. Anticipation etched in every feature. Her mouth bruised from his whiskers. Her generous breasts bared, the nipples hard, dark peaks.

He reached for the snap of her jeans, wondering if she was already wet, pulsing for him....

The knock on the door had Philip reaching for his shoulder holster. Damn, it wasn't there. Michelle jerked beneath him, her eyes flashing to the front door.

"Expecting company?" She looked wildly around for something with which to cover herself.

"Hell no." Philip sprang off the futon, snagged his shirt from the floor. He was dizzy with passion, and stood there for a moment, taking a lingering look at her, letting his head clear.

Who would be knocking at his door in the middle of a weekday?

He slipped into his shirt, then walked to the door and checked the peephole. Cory stood on the other side, looking like he wanted to throttle someone. Philip cursed, knowing that someone was him.

He looked over his shoulder at Michelle. "It's Cory," he said quietly. "I'm, uh, sorry. You can get dressed in my bedroom if you want."

She already had her shirt on. Philip stared at her, thinking he'd never seen a woman look quite so beautiful.

The doorbell blasted.

With an oath, Philip swung open the door. "This better be good, Sanderson."

Cory pushed his way inside without greeting him, without speaking. He took a look around the room, then turned accusing eyes on Philip. "I came to save your butt, my friend." Anger resonated in his voice. He poked a finger into Philip's chest. "From the looks of you, I'm too late."

Philip shifted his weight from one foot to the other. Damn, he was still aroused. How much more obvious could you get? But he wasn't sorry for what had happened between him and Michelle. He wasn't sure what he was going to do about it—or how it would affect the case—but he wasn't sorry. The only thing he was sorry for at the moment was that they hadn't finished what they'd begun.

"I'm not in the mood for a lecture, Cory. What do you want?"

"Montgomery's looking for you and he's on the warpath. Said he's been paging you for the last two hours." Cory's eyes swept to the pager lying on the floor next to a lacy white bra.

Philip's eyes followed his gaze. Chagrined, he let out a pent-up sigh and cursed. "Do you know what he wants?"

"I don't know exactly, but I'd guess it has something to do with a certain suspect you're getting involved with. For a police detective you've been pretty damn stupid."

Philip knew he was right. He'd laid his career on the line for Michelle. But, dammit, he no longer saw her as a suspect. The problem was, Commander Montgomery did.

"Thanks for the heads up."

"Do yourself a favor, Betancourt. Get it out of your system. Get *her* out of your system. Go down to the Quarter and find yourself a whore, if you have to. Then pull yourself together and get back to work, else you're going to screw your career up big-time."

"I don't owe you an explanation."

"I'm not sure I want to hear one."

Shoving his hands into his pockets, Philip looked at Cory long and hard. "She didn't do it, Cory."

"Next you're going to be reciting poetry."

"I'm serious. Something about this case stinks. I'm going to get to the bottom of it."

Cory raised his finger, punched Betancourt's chest again. "Do it on your own time, my friend. I ain't going down with you on this one. Understand?"

Without another word, Cory turned on his heel. Philip watched him leave, wondering what in the hell he'd gotten himself into.

Chapter 10

Michelle knew better than to tempt fate, even if Betancourt didn't. If it hadn't been for that fateful knock on the door, they would have made love. Her emotional side knew how glorious that lovemaking would have been—she'd wanted him with a fierceness she hadn't known existed—but her intellectual side knew giving her heart to a man like him would be a fatal mistake.

She'd sworn the day she left Bayou Lafourche she'd never make herself that vulnerable again.

Unlocking the front door of her apartment, Michelle walked inside, trying not to notice the mess left behind by the police, then turned to watch Betancourt drive away. She didn't want to be here, didn't want to face the horror of knowing what had happened in this very room. But she didn't have anywhere else to go. She didn't have a job, couldn't afford the hotel another night.

So Betancourt had brought her here.

The ride from his house had been tense and silent. She'd heard every word his partner had said, knew how bad the situation was. She couldn't help but wonder what Philip faced at the precinct.

As much as Michelle didn't want to admit it, she cared for him. A devastating reality, considering a relationship was the one thing they could never share. She refused to get involved with a cop, especially a cop with an agenda, no matter how attracted she was to him. Deputy Frank Blanchard had taught her that lesson long ago.

Her body wasn't happy about the situation. The responses Betancourt provoked left her shaking and weak. He'd nearly brought her to fulfillment again, and they hadn't even undressed. A blush heated her cheeks at the memory of her wanton reaction. How on earth was she going to handle this?

She and Betancourt came from different worlds. He was a career cop; she was a woman from the wrong side of the tracks, with a damaged heart and a criminal record to boot. A volatile mix to begin with, but sex would only make things infinitely worse. He would turn her world upside down. Michelle knew she would be the one who ended up hurt.

Shoving the thoughts aside, she walked to the bathroom and turned on the shower, going heavy on the cold water. She couldn't think of him in physical terms. She definitely didn't want to think of him in terms of a relationship. Both were impossible; either would destroy her. For now she had to concentrate on clearing her name and on unraveling the mystery surrounding Armon.

How was it that Armon had hired a private detective to find her before she'd ever met him? Michelle couldn't quite bring herself to believe it was true. What possible motivation could he have had, when she'd been a complete stranger? In the years she'd known him, Armon had never lied to her, never given her a reason to doubt him. Still, the questions remained. Why had he written a check to Tulane? Had the money been a simple donation? Or had he, as Betancourt suspected, financed her scholarship?

As the water pounded down on her, Michelle considered contacting the Landsteiners. But she knew they probably wouldn't help. The next logical step would be to find the private detective Armon had supposedly hired, but she didn't even know the name of the firm. Another dead end.

Sighing in frustration, she turned off the water and tugged on her robe. Restless, she paced to the living room, hating it that the only other person who might be able to help her was the one person she didn't want to see. Nicolas. The brother she'd loved with all her heart—and betrayed for the likes of a cop. She'd thought of him a thousand times over the years. Often enough for her to know the past hadn't tarnished her love for him. Often enough for her to know it was guilt that kept her away. Would he help her?

Betancourt had told her the private detective made mention of Nicolas. Was it possible her older brother had been somehow involved? If he was, would he put aside his hatred for her long enough to help unravel the mystery surrounding Armon?

Michelle knew he'd been released from Angola just six months earlier. She'd checked on him periodically over the years and knew he'd resettled in Bayou Lafourche. Though she'd never had the courage for a face-to-face meeting, a small part of her had hoped Nicolas would seek her out after his release. He hadn't.

She looked down at her hands, realized they were shaking.

The clock above the stove in the kitchen chimed. She still had time to rent a car. Foreboding churned in her stomach as she crossed to the coffee table. Snatching the phone book from the drawer, she flipped to the car rental agencies and picked up the phone. If she hurried, she could be in Bayou Lafourche before dark.

"Sit down, Lieutenant."

Philip's palms were wet with sweat as he took the chair opposite Commander Hardin Montgomery's desk. He'd known the instant he walked in that something was dreadfully wrong. That feeling of doom had augmented a hundred times when he'd spotted Lieutenant Ken Burns of the Public Integrity Division lounging in the remaining chair.

"What's this about?" Philip asked.

"I think you know what this is about, Lieutenant."

Philip noticed Burns's smug look and squashed his temper. "Humor me."

Frowning, Montgomery took off his bifocals and tossed them onto his desk. "PID is bringing formal charges of sexual misconduct against you in relation to the Landsteiner case."

The words hit him like a sledgehammer. He'd expected repercussions from his improper contact with Michelle, but he hadn't expected this. Sexual misconduct meant a mandatory administrative leave. His caseload would be passed to another homicide team.

Philip's chest constricted as the full meaning of the action struck him. "Wait a damn minute—"

"Effective immediately, you are on administrative leave with pay, pending further investigation. Your current caseload has been turned over to a cold case team." Montgomery looked at his watch. "A felony warrant has been issued for Michelle Pelletier."

Philip flinched as the words tumbled over him. "She didn't do it."

The commander's eyes narrowed. "You've lost your objectivity, Lieutenant, and I won't have you jeopardizing this department the way you did with the Rosetti case. You can leave your sidearm and badge with me."

Rising, Philip put his hands on the other man's desk and leaned forward. "What's really going on here, Hardin?"

"You heard me, Betancourt. Your gun and your badge. Now."

Philip's temper spiked. A nasty curse slid from his lips.

"I'm in the middle of a case, for God's sake. I can't turn it over to someone who isn't familiar—"

"You'll pass on all your notes and pertinent reports—"

Philip spun, faced Ken Burns. "Who pointed you in my direction, you sniveling lapdog? How much are they paying you?"

Burns started to laugh.

Montgomery rose. "Lieutenant!"

Fury had him turning on his superior. "Someone doesn't want the Landsteiner case solved, Hardin. I've done some digging. Michelle Pelletier is no longer a suspect in my mind. There was a new will drawn up, but no one can find it. The lawyer who—"

"Sit the hell down, Betancourt!"

Neither man sat. Breathing heavily, face suffused with temper, Montgomery opened a brown clasp envelope, opened it and passed the contents to Philip.

A wrecking ball of dread dropped into Philip's stomach as he accepted the photographs. He didn't have to look at them to know what they contained. They'd been taken through the French doors of his house the night of the funeral, when Michelle had ended up at his place. The images were clear and damning. Shame and fury cut him. Michelle in his arms, head thrown back. He closed his eyes, let the remaining photos drop to the desk.

Hardin cleared his throat.

Burns chuckled. "That's some interrogation technique you've got there, Betancourt. Maybe you could give a seminar."

In an instant, he had Burns by the collar. "You son of a—"

"Get your hands off me!" Burns bared his teeth.

"You can't use those photos!"

"I don't need to!"

Philip shoved him toward the door. "Get out before I throw you out."

Burns opened his mouth to say more, but Philip grabbed him by the collar once more and hauled him to the door.

"I'll have your badge for this," Burns squealed.

"You already do." Philip kicked the door open and shoved him into the hall, where a dozen eyes looked on. Wordlessly, he slammed the door and turned back to Montgomery.

The commander swallowed. "You're in trouble, Betancourt. What you just did to Burns isn't going to help matters."

"Screw Burns. I want to know what the hell is going on with the Landsteiner case."

"PID isn't going to publish those photos, Philip. That would be a PR nightmare for the whole department. You are on administrative leave. I can't help you. My hands are tied."

"Who's pressuring you, Hardin? Baldwin Landsteiner?"

Montgomery rose, leaning forward until his face was mere inches from Philip's. "You're out of your league, my friend."

Despite the fury pumping through him, Philip smiled. It felt like a snarl on his face, but the effect was the same. "So are you, Hardin. Watch your back."

The door behind him opened. Philip turned, spotted Burns and the two uniformed police officers. He looked at Burns, tamped down a burst of rage. "I see you brought backup."

"He was just leaving," Montgomery stated.

Philip pushed past the three men without saying a word.

Michelle wasn't home, and Philip was in no mood to wait. He'd been trying to call her for an hour, had spent the last twenty minutes parked on the street in front of her apartment, waiting. Where the hell was she?

He told himself his need to see her stemmed from what had happened at the precinct. That he wanted her to know there was a warrant out for her arrest. Only he knew better.

A curse escaped him, his voice sounding hollow and strange in the silence of his car. The truth of the matter was he couldn't stay away from her. She'd gotten under his skin, something he'd promised himself he'd never allow. He'd never been one to put much weight in relationships with women. With two ex-wives under his belt, he hadn't the inclination to try again. His first love was his job, always had been, always would be. He could count on his job. He was good at it.

The hell of it was he'd thrown it out the proverbial window for the likes of a woman who couldn't seem to tell the truth. The irony stuck in his craw like a tack.

He told himself the tightness in his chest would go away if he could do like Cory said and get her out of his system. A night of mindless sex, and come morning he'd walk away and never look back. Lust was simple, easy to understand. His feelings for Michelle were anything but simple.

Another harsh sound escaped him, and he realized with some surprise that he'd laughed. Who was he fooling? Not himself. He was in chest deep with her and getting sucked in deeper every time he laid eyes on her. For the first time in his life, he needed someone. A woman. He damn sure wasn't happy about it.

"Where the hell are you?" he growled in the silence.

The thought of her going to jail tore him up. He'd been inside women's prisons before. He knew firsthand how the female inmates were treated. He didn't want to think about that. There was still time to solve the case. Still time to clear her name. To save her life.

Restless and angry, Philip left the car and took the steps two at a time to the door. He knocked, but he knew she wasn't home. It took him less than two minutes to pick the lock. He knew better, but a flimsy little lock wasn't the kind of thing that could keep him from a woman who left him half-insane with the need to touch her just to make sure she was real.

The apartment held her essence. Philip felt it as powerfully as her presence. He walked through the foyer to the living room, listening, soaking up the sensation of being close to her. A scratch pad lay facedown on the coffee table. Planning to leave her a note, he picked up the pad and froze.

The names and phone numbers of three car rental agencies were scribbled on the left side of the sheet in Michelle's handwriting. At the bottom, the name Bayou Lafourche was written in bold lettering, then crossed out.

"I'll be damned." Reaching for the phone, Philip hit the redial button. A woman answered with the name of a car rental agency. He hung up without speaking.

Bayou Lafourche was the last place he'd expected her to go. He wondered what she hoped to find there, besides demons.

He stared at the pad, knowing he didn't have a choice but to go after her. He wasn't going to let her become a fugitive. He doubted she knew about the warrant, but it wouldn't look good if the NOPD found out she'd left town. Some hotheaded cop with more bravado than brains might think she'd decided to run.

Michelle felt the stares like pinpricks the moment she walked through the door. Located on the south side of town, at the edge of the slowly moving bayou, the Black Tattoo Tavern wasn't the kind of place she would normally venture. But it was exactly the kind of place she'd find her brother. She tried to shrug off the stares as she made her way to the bar, where a man with shoulders the size of truck tires wiped glasses with an off-white towel.

Squaring her shoulders, she expelled a breath and approached him. "Excuse me, I'm wondering if you know where I might find Nicolas Pelletier." Her voice withered to a squeak as narrowed aquamarine eyes swept the length of her.

"This his lucky day or somethin'?" The bartender grinned, exposing hit-or-miss teeth and a flash of gold.

She didn't want to pass on more information than necessary, but she thought the man might be more apt to help her if he knew she was family. Bayou Lafourche was tightly knit, the people family oriented, though she wondered if the concept had reached all the way to the Black Tattoo. "I'm his sister."

"Non, il est pas là." No, he's not here.

"Ça c'est malheureux." That's too bad. She watched his eyes widen, and almost smiled, knowing he'd expected his Cajun French to deter her. "Do you expect him?" she fired back in rapid French.

"He'll be in 'fore closing."

"I'll wait."

"He's trouble, that one."

Lord, how she knew that. "Thank—"

"Must run in the family." Betancourt's voice cut through the air like a gunshot.

Michelle spun, an odd mix of shock, pleasure and dread rippling through her. The late afternoon sun streaming in through the window silhouetted his imposing form. Faded jeans hugged his long legs, accentuating a part of his body she didn't want to think about. A black leather jacket lent him the look of a renegade instead of a cop. The frown etched into his features told her he wasn't happy to be there. The word *dangerous* came to mind, but she quickly shoved it aside. She could handle Betancourt.

"You look like you just saw a ghost, Michelle. What's the matter? Not expecting me?" he asked in a low, even voice.

"How did you find me?" She wondered if he'd followed her as a man who cared, or a cop who needed to bring in a suspect.

"I broke into your apartment." He smiled, but it wasn't

a friendly one. "You'd think a woman on the run would be more careful with her notes."

Anger glided through her, and she clung to it. Anything was better than the quick jab of attraction that had her head spinning. She knew she shouldn't have run out on him. But the way she figured, she hadn't had a choice. "You had no right—"

"Oh, hell, yes I did." Without warning, he grasped her hand and guided her toward a corner booth. "You're a suspect in a murder investigation. You can't leave town on a whim."

"I'm not going to sit around New Orleans and wait for you to arrest me."

His flinch was barely discernible, but Michelle saw it and felt a chill creep over her. Had he come here to arrest her? "I have to know why Armon did the things you say he did," she said. "I deserve to know."

He eased her into the booth, then slid in opposite her. Dark gray eyes settled on hers, bored into her. "I'm off the case, Michelle."

"Off the case?" Trepidation vibrated through her. "Why?"

"Misconduct." His jaw tightened. "Sexual misconduct. Montgomery put me on administrative leave."

She gasped. "Sexual…" After what they'd done back at his house, she couldn't finish the sentence. Her cheeks heated. "But how could they—"

"Someone supplied the commander with photos."

The air left her lungs in a rush. "Photos?"

"Of us. Together. The night after the funeral."

The night she'd writhed wantonly in his arms while he stroked her to climax. "Oh, no." She pressed her hand to her stomach. "Oh, no. I didn't mean for this to happen—"

"No, dammit, it's not your fault. I was reckless. I knew better…."

"We both did." Left unsaid was the fact that they'd been

helpless to resist the power of the attraction between them. Every time she saw him, all she could think of was how right it felt to be in his arms. Now he was going to pay the price.

"What's going to happen with your career?" she asked.

"I'll survive, but they won't make it easy on me. Montgomery doesn't want any negative PR. But the damage is done."

Lowering her head, she rubbed at her temples. "Betancourt, you give me a headache every time I talk to you."

"Obviously, I've been giving someone else a headache, too."

The tone of his voice snapped her gaze to his.

"Something about this case stinks, Michelle. Someone wanted me to go away. That same someone wants you to fry."

It took several seconds for the words to register. "You think someone's framing me?"

"I should have seen it a long time ago."

The ramifications of such a theory were enormous. But foremost in her mind was the realization that Philip no longer doubted her. Hope swirled through her. "Who?"

"I don't know. I've been looking in all the wrong places. That's why nothing's adding up." He scrubbed a hand over his jaw, looked at her over the tops of his fingers. "We've got a more pressing problem."

She'd never seen such a penetrating gaze. His intensity was palpable. "I don't see what could be more pressing—"

"A judge issued a felony warrant for you."

The words echoed in her head like a scream. The reality of jail time stabbed through her with such ferocity that for a moment she couldn't speak, couldn't breathe. Panic rose in her chest, but she choked it back, swearing she wouldn't succumb.

"I don't want to go to jail."

Reaching across the table, Philip took her hand. "We've got a little time. We'll work through this."

She wanted to explain to him that there was no working through the old scars, but she didn't. She hadn't told him about Deputy Frank Blanchard or the pain he'd caused her. She couldn't expect Philip to understand.

"Someone wanted me off the case. Someone who knew you and I had gotten…close. So they hired a grunt to dig up dirt."

"What about your partner?"

"No way. I trust Cory with my life."

"Someone in the department?"

"Or someone in a position to pull strings." He turned her hand over, rubbed his fingers over her palm. "I think someone in a position of power murdered Armon Landsteiner. I think they knew about your relationship with him, and capitalized on it, knowing you would be an easy frame."

"Because of my background," she concluded.

He nodded. "I won't let them get away with it."

"You're off the case," she pointed out.

"A technicality. I can work around it." A grimace tightened his jaw. "The logical suspects are his children. Do you think any of them are capable of murder?"

The way they'd treated her the day after Armon's murder scrolled through her mind. The extent of their hostility had shocked her, but she still couldn't reconcile herself to them committing murder. "No. Not their own father. Not in cold blood. Besides, all of them are successful in their own right. They're financially set. What would they have to gain?"

"The one thing nobody ever seems to have enough of."

The thought disgusted her. "Money."

"You'd be surprised what people will do for it."

"What about the firm?"

His eyes narrowed. "In this case that's probably more feasible than the money angle."

Outrage that Armon's life might have been snuffed out in the name of greed rolled slowly through her. "I hate this."

"That doesn't explain why you're being framed." He brooded for a moment. "Did any of them have a grudge against you?"

"Danielle never liked me. If Baldwin or Derek held a grudge, I certainly wasn't aware of it." She paused, mentally recounting the scene in the conference room. "Danielle seemed to take Armon's death particularly hard."

"She was also the first to sink the knife in your back."

"Baldwin argued with Armon occasionally. More than the other two."

"What about Derek?"

Michelle shook her head. "He's the last person I'd ever suspect of murder. He's low-key and has a very kind heart. He's probably more like his father than the other two. And he really cares about the firm."

"I'll bet," Philip said darkly.

Thunder rumbled in the distance, culminating with the patter of rain against the tin roof. Michelle looked out the window at the rain coming through branches of a cypress and tried to remember how long it had been since she'd heard the sound of a bayou storm.

"Do you miss it?"

The question caught her off guard. For a moment, she just stared at him, amazed by his ability to read her thoughts. "I love New Orleans."

"That's not what I asked."

She wasn't sure why she'd danced around the question. Too many mixed feelings about where she was from, she supposed. "On days like this, yes, I miss it a lot. The beauty. The peace. I miss the people most."

"You've been running for a long time, Michelle."

She considered the statement, realized with some surprise it was true. "Maybe."

"Why did you leave?"

She glanced at him sharply. "Come on, Betancourt. It may be beautiful here, and the people may be friendly, but poverty has a way of wreaking havoc on people's lives."

"Is that why you left?"

He wasn't going to let it go, she realized, and wondered how long she'd be able to keep the truth from him. "Let's just say my dreams were too big."

"There's nothing wrong with big dreams."

"As long as they don't get crushed."

"Did yours get crushed?"

She didn't want to talk about her past. Fearing his perceptivity, and what might show in her eyes, she looked out the window. "You know, my mama had dreams. I remember her talking about getting out of Bayou Lafourche, and moving to Shreveport or New Orleans. But it never happened. As the years passed, she stopped talking about it. Her dreams just dwindled until they were nothing. Life just…crushed her." She paused, remembering, trying not to feel the desperation that had been part of her for as long as she could recall. "I saw my own fate when I looked into her eyes. And I knew if it was the last thing I ever did, I'd get out."

"You've come a long way. That's admirable."

"I got out. That's what matters."

"But it took some time. You went to work at the Fortrex Plant after you graduated from high school."

Michelle's nerves jumped. He'd done more than just a cursory background check on her, she realized. "You did your homework, Betancourt."

"I always do."

"What else do you know about me?"

"Not enough." His smile eased some of the tension that had crept over her. "Tell me about the plant where you worked."

She looked down at her hands, stilled them. "After Mama died, I went to work at Fortrex. I hated it. I hated everything about the place, but I especially hated the smell." She hadn't smelled that thick, sweet stink since she'd been back, but the breeze was westerly. When it shifted around from the south…

"I worked the solvent vats for almost five years, did some assembly work, mostly third shift. I made a living, but most of it went for Mama's hospital bills. It was sort of like trying to dig your way out of a hole, only to have the walls keep caving in." The old pain tightened like a clamp around her chest. It surprised her that she was still vulnerable to it. Here she was, a year away from taking the bar exam, yet she still felt threatened by her past, as if it were a living thing, rising up to swallow her whole.

"You went to the community college while you worked."

She nodded, caught up in memories.

"You never stopped trying. Even with the odds stacked against you, you never gave up." He squeezed her hand. "Why are you so hard on yourself? That's admirable. You realize that, don't you?"

His hand covered hers completely. Warm. Strong. Steady. For the first time ever, Michelle fully realized just how far she'd come. She'd managed to gain some semblance of control over her life; she was on the verge of truly making it. But now, everything she'd worked for—her dreams, even her freedom—lay in the balance.

"If it hadn't been for Armon…" Her voice trailed off when the front door of the tavern swung open. Sheets of rain lashed at the plank floor. Michelle stiffened, felt her blood run cold when a vaguely familiar figure stepped inside.

Nicolas.

Reckoning day at last.

Chapter 11

Michelle had imagined a reunion with her brother happening a number of ways. Sitting here in this dank little bar with a cop sitting across from her and an unsolved murder on her mind wasn't one of them.

Everything inside her went still and cold as Nicolas slammed the door behind him and headed for the bar. There was an inherent wildness about him, from the graceful way he moved to the cunning in his eyes. He was taller than she remembered, and a hell of a lot bigger. Not just in size, but in the way he filled the room.

Michelle watched him, taking in the catlike grace of his stride, the inscrutable eyes. Rain dripped from the brim of a crumpled cap onto shoulders as wide as a cypress trunk. It was cold outside, but he wasn't wearing a coat, and he didn't seem bothered by the inclement weather. A tattoo of a woman's breast stood out starkly on his left biceps.

At the bar, he ordered a drink, leaning forward when the bartender spoke to him. His body stiffened slightly, then he turned and looked right at her.

Michelle's heart stuttered, rolled, then beat out an ever-increasing staccato rhythm. But she maintained eye contact, not missing the insolence or the quiet hostility shimmering in his gaze. A silent communication passed between them. The message was unmistakable: you don't belong here.

Across the table, Betancourt shifted in his chair. "From the way you just started shaking, I'd say that's Nicolas."

She swallowed. "Yes, that's my brother."

"Easy. Stay cool."

Nicolas started toward them.

Giving her hand a final squeeze, Betancourt released her. "Are you sure you're ready for this?"

She nodded jerkily. "I don't have a choice."

Nicolas reached the table, flicked a dismissive glance at Betancourt, then sneered at Michelle. *"T'as du gout."* You've got a lot of nerve.

She met his hostile gaze with one of her own. "I need to talk to you. It's important."

"Funny, you didn't have anything important to discuss with me for ten years, now you come all the way to Bayou Lafourche, *chèrie?* You must want somethin' pretty bad."

Michelle felt her face flush, but she didn't look away. "I tried to visit you in Angola, but you refused."

"I must have been busy that day." A dark smile curved the corner of his mouth. "You never came back, though, did you, *chèrie?*"

She wouldn't let him make her feel guilty for not visiting him in prison. They both knew it would have been hypocritical of her. After all, she'd been the one to put him there. "I don't have any regrets, Nicolas. Do you?" It was a lie; she had plenty of regrets, and they'd almost hollowed her out over the years. But he didn't need to know that.

"Oh, yeah, I got regrets. The only difference 'tween you and me is I ain't afraid to admit them." He smiled, but the humor didn't reach his eyes. "You still got that light in you, Michelle, you know?"

"I don't know what you're talking about."

"That light in those go-to-hell eyes of yours that says I'm out of this dump, and damn the world."

"Sit down, Pelletier. We want to talk to you." Betancourt's voice cut through the tension with the finesse of a blowtorch.

Her brother's eyes narrowed on her. "Got yourself another cop, huh? I thought you would have learned your lesson with Blanchard."

Her blood stopped cold in her veins. "Shut up, Nicolas."

He looked down his nose at Betancourt. "Is this cop as good in bed as Blanchard was? Is he as good with a knife? I suppose a back is a pretty wide target. Doesn't take much skill."

Betancourt stood and yanked out a chair, his lips pulled back in a snarl. "Sit the hell down, Pelletier."

"I stopped taking orders from cops the day I walked out of Angola," the other man sneered. "Go screw yourself."

"Unless you want every cop in Lafourche Parish breathing down your neck, I suggest you put your ass in the chair."

Michelle watched the exchange, a combination of fascination and dread zinging through her. The last thing she wanted was an altercation between the two men. Betancourt could handle his own—he was both cunning and streetwise. But there was a recklessness about Nicolas she didn't want to test.

"Please. Nicolas. We need to talk to you about…a man's death back in New Orleans," she said.

Nicolas looked from Philip to Michelle. "I know the story."

"But how—"

"Even us swamp rats read the newspaper."

"That's not what I meant."

"That's exactly what you meant," he snarled. "But then that's you, little sister. Always trying to be something you're not. Always got that pretty little nose of yours up in the air. Look where it got you.''

Know your place. Her mother's words rang uncomfortably in her ears, even though Michelle hadn't listened to those words in years. She wondered if Nicolas still heard them.

''Please, sit down, Nicolas.''

Never taking his eyes from her, he lowered himself into the chair Betancourt had pulled out.

Michelle resisted the urge to scoot away, starkly aware of his size. He was still soaking wet; the hostility coming from him was so thick she nearly choked.

''You're all grown up, Michelle. Pretty. Smart, too, I can tell. But you still have those troubled eyes that always used to worry Mama so much.'' Turning, he motioned for the bartender to bring him his drink, then turned his attention to Michelle. ''I was wonderin' when you'd come back. We've been rooting for you down here in Bayou Lafourche. Our little Michelle up in the Big Easy taking on the world all by herself. I'll bet you didn't know that about all us lowly swamp rats, did you?''

Shame cut her. She felt Betancourt's gaze on her, but she couldn't meet it. She knew he would have questions. Questions she had absolutely no desire to answer. ''Nicolas, please, I'm in trouble. I need your help. Can you put…what happened aside long enough to answer some questions?''

Betancourt leaned forward, caught the other man's gaze. ''Do the names Honeycutt or Landsteiner ring a bell?''

Something flickered in her brother's eyes. She looked at Betancourt, realized he'd noticed the reaction as well.

The bartender brought three beers to the table, then hustled away. Nicolas popped the tab on his, took a long pull, then looked at Betancourt. ''I never met him, didn't even know Landsteiner was his name until I saw it in the newspaper a few days back.'' His gaze sliced to Michelle. ''I didn't find out till the day Mama died that he was the most miserable son of a bitch alive. Funny how people like that get their just rewards.''

Philip wanted to punch Nicolas. For having a smart mouth and a cocky attitude. But most of all for hurting Michelle. He knew the man harbored resentment toward her, but nothing she could have done excused the kind of cruelty he was doling out.

Michelle winced, hurt darkening her eyes.

With an oath, Philip reached for her, but she was too quick.

Sliding her chair back, she rose. "Go to hell, Nicolas. I don't need you." Her gaze flashed to Philip. "I've heard enough. I'm leaving."

Nicolas jumped to his feet. Grabbing her arm, he forced her to face him. "You come all this way, and now you don't want to hear the truth? That's the best part, little sister. I been waiting for this."

"I know better than to expect the truth from an ex-con," she spat.

"You prefer lies?" He shot a nasty look at Philip. "She's good at that, *non?*"

"You don't know how to tell the truth." Her voice shook, but her gaze never faltered. "I know what kind of a man Armon Landsteiner was. I also know what kind of a man you are. Let me tell you, there's no comparison."

"That's why you're here, no?" An unpleasant laugh bubbled out of Nicolas's chest. "You ain't gonna like what I got to say, little sister. But you better listen, 'cause I'm only going to say it once."

Philip should have seen it coming. He'd seen too many fights in his years as a cop not to recognize the signs. Nicolas had pushed her too far. Michelle reacted the only way she knew how. Drawing back, she splashed beer in her brother's face.

Nicolas recoiled, surprise and anger streaking across his

features. *"C'est dégoûtant."* He took a threatening step toward her.

She stood her ground, hands clenched at her sides.

Philip stepped between them. "Dammit, that's enough!" He didn't think Nicolas would strike her, but he didn't want to take any chances. Michelle had been hurt enough.

He reached for his pistol, cursed when he found his holster empty.

An instant later, a starburst of pain exploded at the back of his head. He saw color, then bright light. Michelle's voice rang out. The room dipped. Philip staggered, realizing someone had hit him from behind. He went down on one knee, looked behind him to see a fat man swing the cue stick a second time.

Philip ducked. Air whooshed. Nicolas moved like a bullet, taking the man with the cue stick down in a full body tackle. Philip heard the sound of flesh striking flesh and knew instinctively the man who'd clobbered him wouldn't be getting up under his own power.

"Philip!" Michelle's voice reached him over the roaring in his ears.

Shaking his head to clear it, he focused on her as she knelt at his side.

"My God. You're cut."

"Find my head, will you?" His own voice rang in his ears.

"You're bleeding."

Looking uneasily over his shoulder for the man with the stick, Philip struggled to his feet. Damn, he was getting too old for this. "Hell of a welcoming party you've got here."

Michelle steadied him. "We shouldn't have come. This is all my fault."

He looked up, saw Nicolas hauling the man toward the door, and felt his temper stir. "Not your fault. You didn't swing the cue stick."

"I'm sorry."

She was standing so close he could smell her—that woman-and-baby-powder combination that always made him a little dizzy. He looked into her bottomless brown eyes, felt something in his chest shift. The urge to touch her was strong, but he didn't. Once he touched her he wouldn't want to stop, and this was neither the time nor the place.

Philip probed the bump on his head, cursing when his fingers came away red. Out of the corner of his eye, he saw Nicolas shove the man who'd hit him out the door.

Standing on her tiptoes, Michelle inspected the cut. "You're lucky you don't need stitches."

"Yeah, it must be my lucky day."

Her fingers lingered at the back of his head, but every cell in his body was focused solely on her proximity. The scent of her shampoo wafted over him, clean and sweet. Her hair looked like silk, brown glinting with gold. He stomped down on a sudden urge to run his fingers through it.

A strand of hair had come loose from her ponytail. He reached out and tucked it behind her ear. "Worried about me?"

"I…it's just that…" The words stuttered out of her, then a tentative smile touched the corner of her mouth. "You went for your gun. You weren't going to shoot anyone, were you?"

Despite the pain in the back of his head, he grinned. "I just like to be in charge."

"You worry me, Betancourt."

"You okay?" Nicolas approached, eyeing Philip warily.

"I'm about an inch away from hauling you in just for the fun of it." Philip motioned toward the table. "Let's finish this."

"Some of the guys who come in here don't like cops much. You got big-city cop written all over you." Nicolas scratched the top of his head, then shot Philip an incredulous look. "You thought I was going to hit her, didn't you?"

"It crossed my mind."

"I don't hit women." He looked down at his sister. "Even if they deserve it."

"That would have been a fatal mistake on your part." Philip realized he'd underestimated Michelle's brother. He might be an ex-con, but beneath the layers of toughness was a decent man who'd seen more than his share of trouble. So much for first impressions.

"I'd appreciate it if you two wouldn't talk about me as if I'm not here." Passing between them, Michelle headed toward the table.

Philip hung back, shot Nicolas a hard look. "Are you going to talk to us or do I have to get the sheriff involved and make your life a living hell first?"

"I got somethin' to say."

Michelle reached the table first, turned and directed a killing look at her brother. "You're wrong about Armon."

Loyal to the end, Philip thought. The fierceness of that loyalty touched him. He studied her face, the stubborn set of her jaw, the unmistakable measure of fear in her eyes, and realized she was probably the most loyal person he'd ever met.

"Sit down, Michelle." Pulling out a chair, he eased her down into it, then took the chair beside her. He frowned at Nicolas. "Talk to us, Pelletier."

Nicolas uprighted his fallen chair, then sat across from them. His eyes flicked from Michelle to Philip. "In case you're wondering, I didn't figure out the truth until last week, when I saw the story on the news."

Philip thought he saw regret in the other man's eyes. "Figure out what?"

Nicolas looked at Michelle. "You remember what Mama used to call secrets when we were kids, *chère?*"

"Little keepers of midnight."

A smile touched the corners of his mouth, softening his hard features. "I was with her the night she died. You were at school, remember?"

"Yes." Michelle's voice was toneless.

Nicolas continued. "She knew she was dying, and she had some things to get off her chest. She didn't want to take her secrets to the grave. I was pretty broken up, didn't hear half of what she said, didn't believe the other half. She was delirious with pain and morphine and whatever the hell else the doctor had pumped into her."

He took a long pull of beer, then wiped his mouth on his sleeve. "I didn't believe her when she told me your daddy was some rich lawyer from New Orleans. I never told you because I didn't know it was true." His gaze bored into Michelle. "I didn't realize until last week that she'd been telling the truth when she told me Armon Landsteiner was your father."

The words tumbled over her like shards of ice, cutting her, freezing her, bruising her until she felt paralyzed by pain. Michelle stared at the brother she'd betrayed, disbelief and denial swirling through her in a violent vortex.

"You're lying." She rose abruptly.

"Think about it, little sister. Everything Landsteiner did for you. The scholarship. The job." A bitter smile whispered across his features. "Guilt can be a hell of a motivator."

It all made a sort of terrible sense, she realized. She didn't know whether to feel betrayed that Armon and her mother had lied to her for her entire life, or crushed that they had both died before she learned the truth.

"Why in God's name didn't Mama tell me?"

Nicolas laughed bitterly. *"For the love of money is the root of all evil."*

Blanche Pelletier had possessed undying faith in the Bible. Right or wrong, her own misguided interpretation of that book had ruled her life. For the first time ever, Michelle understood how far that faith had taken her.

"In her own twisted way, she was protecting you," Nicolas said. "Mama viewed the big city as an evil place filled with human weakness and sin. She saw money and wealth as the root of that evil.''

Michelle couldn't speak, couldn't breathe. Slowly, her knees gave way and she sank back into the chair. She felt Betancourt's gaze on her, but she couldn't look at him. Not when her whole world had just come apart at the seams.

"Easy.'' Betancourt's hand covered hers, squeezed.

His touch warmed her as no words could. She looked down at their hands and felt tears in the back of her throat. She didn't want to cry. Not now. Not in front of these two men who seemed determined to turn her world inside out.

She looked at her brother. "How did Armon and Mama... I mean, how did they...'' She couldn't say the words, couldn't imagine how her parents' paths had crossed.

Nicolas shrugged. "We're all sinners, little sister. Mama was human, just like the rest of us. We'll probably never know the whole story.''

Michelle felt shell-shocked. In an instant her entire world had shifted, slipped, exploded. She risked a glance at Betancourt, found him watching her through dark, cautious eyes.

"I'm not going to fall apart,'' she snapped.

"I didn't think you would.'' His gaze never faltered.

Betancourt was another problem she'd have to deal with. They'd crossed some lines in the last several days. Lines that could never be recrossed. He was getting too close, dangerously close, and threatening far more than merely her self control. For the first time Michelle realized her heart was in peril as well.

"Nicolas...'' She cleared her throat when her voice broke, knowing she was an inch away from falling to pieces.

"Shh. Don't say anything, *chère*. I'm here.'' Nicolas said. "I'm not going anywhere. You have a lot to deal with. We can talk about the other thing another time.''

Betancourt's gaze narrowed on Michelle.

He didn't miss a beat, she thought, hating it that she couldn't meet his gaze. He was too discerning a man not to have questions about some of the things Nicolas had said, particularly about Frank Blanchard.

From across the table, Nicolas contemplated them. "You two are…friends."

"No." Michelle said the word simultaneously with Philip's "yes."

Her brother looked amused. "Well, that's pretty clear."

"He's a cop," Michelle said. "Maybe he's here to take me back to New Orleans." She tried to ease her hand from Betancourt's, but he tightened his grip.

"Whether or not you go back is your decision, Michelle. I came here to talk some sense into that stubborn head of yours." He looked at Nicolas. "They issued a warrant for her today."

Outside, the tempo of the rain increased. Thunder rattled the windows.

"Le Bon Dieu mait la main." God help. Nicolas returned Betancourt's gaze. "I've got a cabin. That'll buy you some time."

"No." Taking a deep, shaky breath, Michelle looked at her brother. "You're on parole. I won't let you sacrifice your freedom for me." She turned to Betancourt. "I won't let him do it. I've got to go back." The words cut like shards of ice. She didn't want to go to jail, didn't want to go through the nightmare of having her dignity and freedom stripped away. If the experience that waited for her back in New Orleans was anything like what she'd gone through all those years ago in Bayou Lafourche, she didn't think she would survive it.

With an oath, Betancourt scrubbed his hands over his five o'clock shadow. "You're not going to jail," he growled.

"No one's gonna find my cabin, little sister, 'cept the gators maybe. Listen to the man. Jail ain't no kind of place for a woman like you. You don't want to be there."

A shiver rippled through her. Jail. A trial. Prison. Years torn from her life. She'd been so certain her memory would return, so certain Betancourt would find Armon's murderer that she hadn't considered any of it a possibility. But now the reality of spending the rest of her life behind bars for a crime she hadn't committed slashed through her like a straight razor.

"I can't hide out in Bayou Lafourche the rest of my life."

Betancourt frowned. "No, but we can formulate a plan, come up with some suspects. I've got my cell phone. Cory can help on the computer end of it."

Michelle didn't think she could stand the alternative. Jail time held about as much appeal as a firing squad. But even as she considered her options, she knew a bigger part of her—her heart—remained in peril if she stayed.

Michelle stood at the door of the cabin and watched Nicolas drive away. Her heart ached with the realization that she still loved him, had never stopped loving him. He'd put his freedom on the line by letting her stay at his cabin when there was a warrant for her arrest. He'd even agreed to drop off her rental car for her, and showed Philip where to park his own vehicle, so it would be out of sight. She wondered if he was trying to tell her he'd forgiven her for what she'd done all those years ago.

Rain still poured from a leaden sky, pinging against the tin roof. Spindly fingers of fog rose from the muddy ground. Behind her, she could hear Betancourt stacking wood in the fireplace.

The setting should have been perfect. The rain. An element of danger. Sharing a cabin with a man she was incredibly attracted to. But the situation couldn't have been more wrong. She was a fugitive from justice. He was a cop, a rogue with a reputation for always getting his man. His career lay in the balance. Something he would never give up for the likes of her.

Unhappy with the turn her thoughts had taken, Michelle sighed, hugging herself against the chill. The revelation that

Armon was her father had sent her entire world into a wild tailspin, shattering everything she'd ever known about herself, about the people she loved. She couldn't help but wonder why her mother had kept the truth from her all these years. Was Nicolas right? In her own misguided way, had Blanche Pelletier tried to protect her daughter from the evils of the world?

Michelle couldn't fathom the logic behind the ideology. The selfishness of it angered her. She hated poverty and the decaying effect it had on human dignity and spirit. Why had her mother chosen a life of poverty for her daughter over a life of opportunity? The questions overwhelmed her, exhausted her, zapped what little remaining strength she had. She felt physically and emotionally spent. And she had yet to deal with Betancourt.

Up until now, she'd refused to identify what was in that foolish heart of hers. She was attracted to him beyond reason, beyond logic. He wasn't a gentle man in any sense of the word, yet the way he touched her was so tender it brought tears to her eyes. Underneath the tough-guy facade lay a personal code of honor few men could match. Somewhere along the way, her heart had gotten so hopelessly tangled that she couldn't begin to sort out her feelings. She couldn't think of a worse fate for a woman who'd sworn never to make herself vulnerable again.

A man like Betancourt wouldn't think twice about doing the right thing. If the right thing included sending her to jail, the fact that her heart was involved wouldn't stop him.

"You're shaking."

Michelle started at the sound of his voice. Was she shaking? She felt so scattered she could no longer tell. Taking a calming breath, she turned to face him and felt that familiar tightening in her belly.

His eyes were the color of the sky outside. Dark. Stormy. With a hint of unpredictability that invariably unnerved her. He stood less than a foot away, staring at her intently. He'd taken off his jacket, and she recognized the woodsy cologne that had become familiar to her during the last days. The chambray shirt he wore accentuated the broad span of his shoulders. His jeans were faded and snug. She'd forgotten how good a man could look in a pair of jeans.

"It's cold." She tried to smile at him, but failed. "I need to see to that cut."

"It's not bad." He was watching her carefully. Too carefully. As if one wrong move on his part would cause her to break into a thousand pieces.

"You don't have to handle me with kid gloves, Betancourt."

He arched a brow. "Was I?"

"You have that look about you."

"It's called concern, Michelle." Though his tone was slightly sarcastic, his voice was soft.

She wondered what he made of all this, realized he knew more about her life than just about anyone she'd ever met. The thought made her stomach roll. "I saw a first aid kit in the bathroom."

Reaching out, he took her arm and guided her to the narrow cot in front of the fire. "You're white as a sheet. Sit down before you fall down. I'll get the damn kit."

She lowered herself onto the cot and watched him cross the room to the tiny, adjoining bath. He even moved like a cop; everything about him was cop. Another reason piled on top of about a dozen why nothing between them would ever work. It was a crazy thought to be having anyway, considering she'd be locked away in her own private cell in twenty-four hours.

She heard the medicine cabinet open, close, then he reappeared. Sitting down beside her, he opened the kit. "Cory told me Landsteiner's will has been turned over to probate. It was drawn up by a Metairie firm over five years ago. Cory's going to plug some data into the computer, see if he can find anything on the Landsteiners that might help us."

Michelle took the kit from him, dug out two aspirin, cotton and some antiseptic. She handed him the aspirin. "Are the police looking for me?"

"They put an APB out for you a couple of hours ago. You're not a high priority, but patrols are looking."

A shudder scooted through her. "You're risking a lot by being here. Your partner is risking—"

"We may have a break. Cory went to talk to Jacoby's paralegal. Turns out she and two other people in his office witnessed, actually signed a will Landsteiner had drawn up six months ago. The state of Louisiana requires three witnesses. Of course, the will is missing."

"Without the will, it doesn't matter if you have a dozen witnesses."

"There was a fireproof safe in Jacoby's office. The building was a complete loss, but the safe is intact. There were backup disks in the safe."

Michelle's heart bucked hard in her chest. Something vaguely resembling hope fluttered wildly.

One side of Philip's mouth quirked into a smile. "The disks are badly damaged from the heat, but may be readable. Cory has a computer guru trying to get information off them. It's going to take some time."

"Armon's will could be on the disk."

"The paralegal told me all legal documents drawn up by Jacoby are stored on the server. The server was destroyed but the backup disks were stored in the safe."

Michelle didn't want to get her hopes up. "That may not help me, Betancourt."

"No, but it could give us a motive, point us in the right direction."

"If Armon added me to his will, it could also work against me."

"True, but I think it's a chance we have to take."

Desperation licked at her. She felt as if she'd ventured into quicksand and was being sucked ever downward, the cold darkness smothering her. Every time she thought about the warrant, what she would be facing in the coming days, she had to fight down panic. And then there was Betancourt.

"Thank you," she said, realizing how glad she was that she didn't have to face this alone. A loner by nature, she found the realization startled her.

He looked at her sharply. "For what?"

"For being here with me."

"You didn't expect me to walk away, did you?"

His mouth drew her gaze. It wasn't exactly full, but his lips were well defined, chiseled. She knew from experience it was an accomplished mouth. Yes, he definitely knew how to kiss a woman. She remembered the way he'd teased her mouth into submission, trailing wet kisses down her neck until she thought she would explode with need....

Michelle gave herself a quick mental shake. What was she doing thinking of his kisses when her entire life was on a collision course with disaster? A man like Philip Betancourt, with his shiny badge and mistrust of the human race, wouldn't fall for a woman with a criminal record and a wrap sheet growing longer by the minute. He would move on after the case was closed whether she ended up in jail or not. He would go back to being a cop. If she allowed herself to get any more involved with this man, her heart would be ripped to shreds. She wouldn't put herself through that again.

Blinking back the sudden heat behind her eyes, Michelle wetted the cotton with antiseptic. "This is going to hurt." She pressed cotton against the cut.

Betancourt blew out a curse.

"Sorry," she said.

"Tell me about Frank Blanchard," he said between clenched teeth.

She nearly dropped the cotton. Her brain blanked, froze so solidly that she couldn't muster a reply.

He caught her wrist with his hand, lowered it. "No secrets, Michelle."

Her gaze snapped to his. Anger and another emotion she couldn't readily identify seethed in the gray depths of his eyes. "He's not important," she said.

"You went sheet white when Nicolas mentioned his name."

"Frank is a man I once knew...a long time ago."

"Don't patronize me. You damn well better not lie to me." None too gently, he pulled her down to the cot beside him. The cotton ball fell to the floor at their feet. "Nicolas said Blanchard was a cop. What the hell does that have to do with you?"

The urge to run was strong, but Michelle knew it was a crazy notion. She'd been running too long. Silently, she cursed her brother for dredging this up, for making her remember. "He was a deputy for Lafourche Parish. I...I had a relationship with him. A short one. That's all."

"That's why you're shaking." Philip said the words with biting sarcasm.

She started to rise, but he stopped her.

"I'm not stupid, Michelle. What the hell was Nicolas talking about when he said Blanchard stabbed you in the back?"

"I don't want to talk about it."

"This has something to do with your record, doesn't it?"

A shudder raced through her. The memories followed like floodwater, tearing down her defenses, slicing her open, bleeding her to her very soul. "He's the one who arrested me."

"You had a relationship with this man, yet he was the one who arrested you?"

She tried to wrench free, but he held her firm. "Yes, dammit, let go of me!" she cried.

"Did you care for him, Michelle?"

She wanted to lie; she wanted to tell him no. But she knew lies never helped anything. After a while, they just got all tangled up. "Yes, I cared for him! Let go of me."

He released his grip on her arm. "I'm not trying to crucify you."

"Just air my dirty laundry."

"You and I are the only ones here, Michelle." His voice gentled. "I'm trying to understand you. What you just told me explains a lot. Tell me the rest."

Everything inside her rebelled against it, but Michelle knew the time had come for her to get the truth out in the open, before some prosecutor twisted her past around and used it to destroy her, as happened to Nicolas.

"It's ugly," she said. "I don't like to talk about it."

"Whatever you're holding inside is eating you alive. Let it out. You know I care about you. You know I won't judge you."

She let out a deep, shuddering breath. "I met Frank Blanchard when I was seventeen. He was twenty-four, ambitious and from a wealthy family. He was the only man I'd ever known who didn't seem to care that I wore hand-me-down clothes or that I lived in a one-bedroom shanty on the wrong side of town. We began seeing each other, secretly because, he said, I was only seventeen." She laughed at the naïveté of the foolish teenager she'd been, but it was a hard sound that held no humor.

"The night after the explosion at the plant, Frank came to see me. At the time I didn't realize the police suspected Nicolas and me. Nor did I realize Frank was there for official reasons, rather than personal. Of course, he didn't bother to set me straight. It was the first time I'd seen him since Mama died and I…needed…to talk. I was hurting. He listened. He let me pour out my heart."

Michelle looked down at her hands, realized she'd clenched them into fists, and relaxed them. "I gave him my virginity that night. I was stupid enough to believe he cared." A sound erupted from her throat, but for the life of her she couldn't tell if it was a laugh or a sob. "After I told him Nicolas and I had been at the plant before the blast, that Nicolas had had that box with him, Frank arrested me.''

She steeled herself against the memories, the shame, but even now the betrayal cut. ''He handcuffed me. Read me my rights. At first I thought he was kidding. I couldn't believe this man I'd trusted would…betray me. I guess it didn't sink in until he forced me to his car. Then…I knew.

''He drove me to the police station. That was when—'' Her voice broke. She couldn't go on, couldn't tell that part. It was too ugly, so ugly she still couldn't bring herself to say the words. Even after all these years, she woke up with nightmares.

Philip's jaws were clamped so tight the muscles twitched. ''He used you to get to Nicolas.''

''Yes.''

''What happened at the station, Michelle?''

The question startled her. Her gaze snapped to his. The intensity burning in his eyes told her she'd already said too much. *He knows,* she thought. The realization made her want to curl into a ball and deny it. ''I was only seventeen years old, Betancourt. I didn't know about rights. I was scared. I didn't have a lawyer to tell me what to do.''

She jumped when he put his hand over hers.

''Whatever they did to you, it wasn't your fault,'' he said.

Pain slashed through the center of her. ''They made me feel like trash.''

His eyes were like coals, burning hot and bright with an emotion she'd never seen. ''Did they touch you?''

She couldn't speak, couldn't bring herself to say the words. All she could do was stare at him, while shame burned a path through her heart.

Closing his eyes, he scrubbed an unsteady hand over his jaw. ''Have you ever told anyone about this?''

''No.''

''Do you want to tell me?''

She did, she realized. The realization was like a boulder

being lifted from her shoulders. ''Frank and...another deputy...they said it was police procedure to...search a suspect.
They told me if I didn't submit to their rules, they'd force
me. So...I did as I was told.'' Humiliation seared her. She
closed her eyes, felt the tears on her cheeks. That was the
worst part, she thought, the fact that she'd obeyed those two
men without so much as a fight. ''They took me to a cell
away from the others. Frank ordered me to take my clothes
off. He said it was for my own safety, to make sure I didn't
have drugs or a weapon. They laughed at me when I cried;
they said I should get used to this kind of treatment.''

A breath shuddered out of her. ''And without the benefit
of counsel, those two men...touched me.... They...put their
hands on me. And I didn't stop them.''

Chapter 12

Philip lost the battle for emotional distance. He watched her come apart piece by piece. He saw the shame, the agony she'd carried around for so many years cut down her defenses, until she lay open and bleeding.

Raw fury twisted in his gut. Blood hammered in his ears until he could no longer hear her sobs. She hadn't deserved what had happened. The injustice outraged him. He wanted blood. Frank Blanchard's blood.

Philip didn't have an aversion to violence; he wasn't above using it to take out a piece of slime, had resorted to the darker tactics on more than one occasion over the years. As he watched the woman before him recount the incident that had nearly destroyed her, he silently vowed to bring down the cop responsible.

Emotion thickened his voice. "Michelle...I'm sorry."

"Don't you dare feel sorry for me. I'll never forgive you if you feel sorry for me."

She looked too fragile to touch, but he couldn't keep himself from reaching for her. She needed to be held. Even more, he needed to feel her against him.

"Come here." His arms went around her. He pulled her tightly against him. "I don't feel sorry for you, honey. I'm sorry it happened."

A shudder rippled the length of her. "They took my dignity, Betancourt. Then they laughed at me."

"Shh. Easy. It's over." Closing his eyes, he stroked the back of her head, marveling at the silky feel of her hair.

Her head dropped to his shoulder. "Nicolas was innocent."

"A jury convicted him, Michelle."

"He didn't do it." She pulled away and looked at him. "The prosecutor used what I told Blanchard that night against Nicolas in court. Frank twisted my words, made it sound like I told him Nicolas planted that bomb. I was so…upset, I didn't even remember what I'd said. That Nicolas and I drove to the plant that day. That he had a box for the stuff in his locker. In the end, it was Frank's word against mine. The word of an upstanding deputy against the word of a poor girl from the wrong side of town. The public defender was fresh out of law school and didn't have the experience to win. The judge let it stand."

"It wasn't your fault."

"How can you say that?" she choked out. "I sent my brother to prison, for God's sake."

"You were a kid. You told the truth."

"I panicked—"

He tightened his grip. "Stop it."

"They lied to suit their own agenda."

No wonder she didn't trust cops. No wonder she couldn't bring herself to trust him. "That's why you're hell-bent on becoming a lawyer."

She swiped at the tears on her cheeks. "It was the only thing I had left. The only way I could feel…empowered. That dream got me through two years of community college.

It got me through five years of working the vats at the Fortrex Plant.''

The respect he held for her solidified, deepened. Something else more profound stirred uncomfortably inside him. Leaning back, he put his fingers under her chin and forced her gaze to his. ''That's incredibly admirable. You know that, don't you?''

''Admirable isn't going to keep me out of jail.''

The thought twisted his gut. For the life of him he couldn't think of a way to avoid it. If she didn't go back, more charges would be levied against her, making her situation infinitely worse. ''I can promise you no one will hurt you.''

The life seemed to go out of her. It was the first time he'd seen resignation on her face, and he hated it. She was too proud for this, too strong.

He cared too damn much.

He didn't want to ask the question, but had to know. ''Did those men rape you?''

She dropped her gaze. ''No. Not…technically. But they demeaned me. They humiliated me.''

Fury rumbled through him, but he shook it off, knowing it wasn't what she needed at the moment.

''They did that to me because of who I was. Poor. Uneducated. My lack of status made me vulnerable.''

The need to protect rose up in him with such violence that for a moment he couldn't speak. When he finally did, his voice was low and dangerous. ''I'm going to make that son of a bitch pay. I'm going to make it my mission in life to ruin that—''

''No!'' Her eyes widened. ''I've put it behind me. I don't want it dredged up now. I've gone on with my life.''

Rage pumped through Philip with every beat of his heart. Struggling for control, he rose and stalked to the front window and stared out at the rain. ''What those men did to you is called sexual assault, Michelle. You were a minor—''

"I know what it's called, and I know how ugly it was. But I don't want to relive it."

He wanted to go to her, touch her, take away her pain, but he was too angry. "It goes against my grain to let something like that go unpunished."

"It happened ten years ago, Betancourt. I've moved on. I've put it behind me. Please, let it go."

He turned to her. The sight of her standing next to the cot with tears streaming down her cheeks and pain in her eyes struck him like a fist in the gut. Suddenly he knew why he was so furious. Why he wanted to take Frank Blanchard apart with his bare hands. Why he hadn't been able to get Michelle off his mind since the night Armon Landsteiner was murdered.

He was in love with her.

The realization stunned him. Terrified him. For an instant he had to stave off panic. He couldn't move. Couldn't stop staring at her. Couldn't keep his heart from breaking every time he thought of what she'd gone through.

Something had shifted inside him. Something profound and powerful he didn't want to confront.

He crossed the room to her. She backed up, but he didn't stop. He wanted to feel her against him. Need rose up inside him with an urgency that made him feel breathless and dizzy.

"Come here," he growled.

She halted her backward progression. Her eyes met his, and he saw uncertainty and fear in their soft brown depths. "I want to hold you," he said, reaching for her. "I need to hold you."

She stepped into his embrace, trembling and rigid. His arms went around her shoulders. She leaned into him. Soft. Warm. Her scent wrapped around his brain like an intoxicating drug. He'd known it would come to this. The inevitability of it tested his precarious hold on self-control. She'd been under his skin since the night he'd first laid eyes on her. He tried to tell himself he was giving in to long-ignored physical needs—he'd been celibate since his ex-wife had walked out on him over a year ago—but Philip knew better. It had never been like this with Whitney, or any other woman, for that matter. His feelings for Michelle went deeper than the flesh. The two of them had connected on a level that teetered somewhere between spirit and soul.

He wasn't sure exactly how he was going to handle that part of it. He hadn't counted on his heart getting involved. Hearts had a way of complicating even the simplest of relationships. He'd been burned too many times to partake in a relationship now.

But he wanted her with a desperation that left him quaking and weak. He had to have her. All of her. Heart, body and soul.

He lowered his mouth to the tender spot just below her ear and kissed her there. "You've been hurt," he whispered. "You trusted that guy and he hurt you."

"I'm okay. I've been okay for a long time." Tilting her head to one side, she gave him better access to her neck.

He opened his mouth, pressed it against her throat, tasted the sweetness of her flesh. "I'll never hurt you. I'll never let anyone hurt you. I'll never lie to you. You've got my word."

"You're in no position to make promises. I don't expect any."

"I keep my word, Michelle."

She went fluid in his arms. "You know, Betancourt, despite everything, I'd already figured that out about you."

Emotion punched through him. Pulling away slightly, he rested his forehead against hers. "I'm tangled up with you. More than you know. More than I want to be."

"We're both vulnerable right now."

"We've both got a lot at stake." His career. Her freedom. Their hearts. He didn't want to think about that. Not with desire pounding through him like a drum. "We can stop this

right now, before things between us get any more…
complicated…."

He could barely form a rational thought, let alone speak.
He wanted her so badly he was trembling. But the decision
of whether to continue had to be hers. She'd been hurt. If
they continued, their relationship, their futures, their very
lives, would be irrevocably altered.

"I like having your arms around me. Maybe we could
just play it by ear," she whispered.

"We're playing with fire."

Cocking her head, she looked at him from beneath her
long lashes. "Are you going to burn me, Betancourt?"

In a small corner of his mind, he noticed her pupils were
dilated. Her mouth was wet and trembling, her full lips
slightly parted. That space between her teeth was visible,
and he had the sudden urge to run his tongue over it.

"Never." Desire roughened his voice.

He was aware of her breasts against his chest. Even
through their shirts, the tight beads of her nipples tormented
him. Heat pooled in his groin. "There's more going on between us than either of us is seeing," he said.

"I usually try to take things at face value." Her hands
went to the front of his shirt, her fingers fumbling with the
buttons. "When you put your arms around me, something
clicks, and I know everything is going to be okay. Don't
you feel it?"

He caught her hands in his just as his shirt fell open. "I
don't want to hurt you."

"I know." Easing her hands from his, she parted his shirt
and brushed her fingertips over his nipples.

The rush of blood from his head made him dizzy. "Don't
do that unless you're prepared for the consequences," he
growled.

"I've always believed a person should take responsibility
for their actions." Leaning forward, she pressed a kiss to
his chest.

Philip groaned, and went down for the count.

Michelle loved him.

The realization shattered her. She felt overjoyed and devastated and panic-stricken at once. The vulnerability she'd opened herself to terrified her even as euphoria spread through her brain and desire hummed through every nerve ending in her body. The world had finally spun off its axis, and she was about to be flung into space.

Making herself vulnerable to Betancourt would destroy what little emotional balance she had left. She knew he would hurt her. But with her life careening toward disaster, she didn't care. She wanted tonight, wanted this precious moment so badly the need brought tears to her eyes.

The timing was wrong, and the situation between them couldn't have been worse, but Betancourt was definitely the right man. She'd known it from the start, just hadn't been able to see through the scars left on her heart.

His chest muscles were like steel beneath her palms. She ran her fingertips over the dusting of black hair, then brushed her knuckles against his hardened male nipples. His quick intake of breath told her he was sensitive there, and she felt a surge of feminine power.

Catching her hands in his, he lowered them to her sides. He looked at her, his eyes as black as a bayou night. "You sure about this?"

His mouth was inches from hers, so close she could smell the sweetness of his breath, the faint scent of his aftershave, the essence of male that surrounded him like a dark aura.

"I want this time with you, Betancourt. I don't want to think about tomorrow, or next week or next month. I don't want to think of the future at all. Just tonight. Just this once." Despite her efforts, her breath came shallow and fast.

His hands slipped to the sides of her face. "I'm going to see this mess through till the end, Michelle. I'll solve the case. I'll get the truth. You've got my word."

Oh, how she wanted to believe that. With her whole heart and soul she wanted to believe the charges against her would be dropped. That Betancourt would be free to love her. Tonight, when he'd put his arms around her and looked at her with those stormy gray eyes, even the impossible seemed within reach.

His breath warmed her cheek. Anticipation pulsed through her with every beat of her heart.

"Let me kiss you," he whispered.

She angled her face to his. He swooped down, his mouth claiming hers like a bird of prey. Her knees went weak. He kissed her hungrily, without gentleness, without finesse, letting her taste his frustration and urgency, and she reveled in it. When his tongue slipped between her lips, she opened to him, welcomed him.

His hands fell to the hem of her sweatshirt. In a single motion he tugged it over her head. Michelle shuddered when cold air washed over her bare breasts. Her sensitive nipples puckered impossibly tight. Her heart beat out a maniacal rhythm, the tempo of her blood deafening her.

"My God, you're beautiful."

Before she could respond, he reclaimed her mouth, kissing her deeply, possessively. A gasp escaped her when his hands closed over her breasts. He squeezed gently, molding her flesh, trapping her nipples between his thumb and forefinger. She arched into him, a moan bubbling up from her throat. Liquid heat speared her center, radiating to the point between her legs where her body clenched uncontrollably.

Tearing his mouth from hers, he whispered her name. Once. Twice. She closed her eyes, felt his hands work the ribbon from her hair. Her breasts swelled, ached with the need to be touched. She wanted his mouth there. Hot and wet against her.

"I wish I could give you silk sheets and music," he whispered. "You deserve that."

"Hmm. Johnny Mathis." She smiled, her hair tumbling over her shoulders. She felt like a queen.

"I was thinking more along the lines of Eric Clapton."

She opened one eye and they smiled stupidly at each other.

A chuckle rumbled out of his chest. "Maybe we could just settle for the sound of the rain."

"And the fire."

His fingers combed through her hair. Never taking his eyes from hers, he reached for the button of her jeans. Simultaneously, she worked the shirt from his shoulders and let it fall unnoticed to the floor.

Michelle had never seen such a magnificent chest. She knew he worked out; she'd seen the weights at his house. But even the knowledge that he was fit hadn't prepared her. His chest was rippled with muscle and covered with a layer of thick black hair that tapered to a flat belly, where lowrise jeans barely concealed the thick ridge of his arousal.

The sight of him brought a swarm of butterflies to her belly. "I'm a little new at this, Betancourt. I mean…I haven't actually done…this…since…that night…." Her voice trailed off at the stricken look on his face.

His hands froze where he'd worked her jeans down low on her hips. The white lace of her panties was visible. He blinked at her. "You haven't been with anyone…for ten years?"

The way he'd said it stung—as if she were some kind of anomaly—and Michelle took instant offense. "Maybe this isn't such a good idea." She tried to wrench free, but he was too quick and stopped her by tugging her to him.

"Don't turn away from me now," he said.

"Don't treat me like I'm some kind of…freak."

"I didn't mean anything by that. It's just that…ten years is a long time. I'm surprised…you've never been… Are you sure you're ready for this?"

How was she supposed to answer that? "This is a mutual thing, Betancourt—"

"Don't be angry." Raising his hand, he touched her cheek with his fingertips. "You're beautiful and kind and any man who let you slide through his hands was a blind fool."

Michelle wasn't sure if she wanted to cry or laugh. Since her disastrous first sexual experience with Frank Blanchard, she hadn't let herself feel anything for the men she'd known in the course of her career and law school. She'd dated occasionally, but she'd only been trying to do what other young women her age were doing. With Betancourt, all the suppressed emotions and denied physical longings had slowly boiled to the surface, culminating at this moment.

The next thing she knew, she was being swept off her feet into his arms. "What are you doing?"

"I'm going to show you what it means for a man to make love to you." He stared down at her, his eyes dark and glazed with something deeper than passion. "A man who cares for you. A man who admires and respects you as a human being."

She told herself she didn't expect him to confess his undying love for her. Denied that the anticipation of hearing those three words sent her heart into a free fall. Even so, a small part of her that still believed in happily-ever-after winced when the words didn't come.

"A man who thinks you're the most beautiful woman in the world."

"I'm not beautiful. I've got a space between my front teeth."

"You've got the sexiest mouth I've ever seen. I have erotic dreams about your mouth." He lowered her to the cot in a sitting position. Kneeling on the floor in front of her, he eased himself between her knees. "Your mouth drives me half-crazy with the need to kiss you."

Leaning forward, he kissed her slowly and deeply, then trailed kisses down her neck to the valley between her breasts. Michelle closed her eyes and drank in the sensations, the warm wetness of his mouth against her flesh, the cool air against her breasts. His tongue flicked over her nipple. The pleasure was so intense, so unexpected and erotic that she cried out. She arched, offering him full access. He suckled greedily, first one then the other, using his tongue and playful nips of his teeth. Exquisite sensation assaulted her. Her body clenched, relaxed. Need coiled inside her, and she knew there was no turning back.

Vaguely, she was aware of him tugging her jeans down her hips. She toed off her shoes, kicked once, and her jeans landed on the floor.

"You look really good in lace."

She opened her eyes to find him standing next to the cot, staring down at her appreciatively. He'd removed his jeans and was in the process of tugging down his boxers. She couldn't look away, couldn't speak. Her breath froze in her chest at the sight of him. She'd never seen a man up close and personal, not like this. The size of him startled her, sent a pang of lust through her belly.

Kneeling before her, he took her face between his hands and kissed her lightly on the mouth. "You're shaking." He kissed her nose, her brow, her temple, each kiss more gentle than the first, and more loving than she'd ever imagined a man like Betancourt could be. "Are you okay with this?"

"I'm terrified, Betancourt, but if you stop now I'm going to have to kill you."

One side of his mouth hiked into a grin. "I'm really glad you said that." He kissed her again, using his tongue. His hands skimmed down her sides, over the outside curves of her breasts, to the waistband of her panties.

"Raise up, honey, so I can take these off you."

She was still sitting on the cot and had to raise up slightly for him to work her panties down. He never stopped making love to her mouth, and she was lost to everything else. She kissed him back, putting everything she had into the intimate contact. The sensations coursing through her brought her body to new life, heightening every sense to painful sensitivity.

Grasping her hips, Philip pulled her to the edge of the cot. "Look at me. I want to see you when I touch you."

Michelle met his gaze, found him staring at her with an intensity that sent her heart knocking against her ribs. She wasn't sure when her breathing had become labored, but she couldn't seem to get enough air into her lungs.

"Open your legs for me."

The anticipation was almost too much. Emotion tangled with physical sensation until she thought she would explode. He hadn't even touched her yet, and already her control teetered on the edge of a steeply sloped precipice.

Never taking his eyes from hers, he parted her curls with his fingers, drew her apart, then gently stroked her most private area. The contact was like an electric current. Hot. Shocking. A tremor ripped through her, gripped her, shook her. She closed her eyes against the intensity. White light exploded behind her lids. A mewling sound escaped her as he stroked her more firmly, going deep. Shock waves built inside her, powerful and high. Her body convulsed. Once. Twice. She cried out his name, knowing this was somehow the most profound moment of her life. She loved this man. Wanted him no matter what the emotional cost.

"Make love to me, Betancourt. Please. Now." Her voice trembled with emotion as she lay back on the cot.

His jaw was set, his eyes dark with passion as he eased his body over hers. She stretched out and opened to him. She felt cold air against her heat, her heart hammering beneath her breast. Bracing his arms on either side of her, he leaned down and kissed her fiercely.

"It's never been like this for me," he said. "Never."

"I love you, Betancourt."

She felt him stiffen, then her mind went blank as he entered her. An instant of pain, then intense pleasure hit her as the length of him stretched her, filled her, until she thought she would die with the ecstasy of full, unrestrained penetration.

He moved inside her, setting a long, slow rhythm that scrambled her senses and sent her emotions tumbling. Her body reacted instinctively, and she met him stroke for stroke. The waves built inside her until she was mindless with pleasure. She couldn't breathe, couldn't think. Sweat slicked her body, but did nothing to cool the fire burning in her center. He pushed her higher, faster, moving her as no other human being ever had, taking her to heights no other man had ever matched, or ever would again. She responded in kind with everything she had in her heart, everything her body had to offer. She laid herself open, her body, her heart, her very soul, matching his strength with her own.

Completion crashed down on her, shattering the last of the control she'd held on to so fiercely. She writhed beneath him, taking him deeper, calling out his name, knowing in her heart she would never feel this way again.

He shuddered inside her, a low growl sounding in his throat and culminating with her name on his lips.

The intensity brought tears to her eyes. They streamed down her cheeks unnoticed as her spasms went on and on, shaking her with their power until she lay boneless and weak beneath him.

Philip listened to the rain against the roof and watched the hand of the clock above the fireplace sweep to midnight. He couldn't sleep. Guilt lay like a rock in the pit of his stomach.

I love you.

Her words echoed in his ears, haunting him. He tried to
tell himself she'd said them in the heat of the moment. That
their lovemaking had been so intense, she'd lost her head
and said something she hadn't meant. Only he knew better.

Michelle wasn't the kind of woman to open herself up
like that, no matter how mind-numbing the sex. Worse, he'd
seen the truth on her face, heard it in her every sigh, felt it
in every shudder, every tremor.

He hadn't the slightest idea what the hell he was going
to do about it.

How could he have let this happen, knowing she had a
murder charge and possible jail time hanging over her head?
She was vulnerable, for God's sake. More vulnerable than
he'd ever believed. He'd taken advantage of that vulnerability, knowing fully he had no intention of dealing with the
consequences.

Philip had known from the get-go he was in over his head;
he'd accepted it, figured he could handle it. Now he wasn't
so sure. The thought made him feel sick.

Restless, he stepped into his jeans, not bothering with the
button, and walked to the kitchen, found a bottle of beer in
the refrigerator and popped the lid. In the main room, he
tossed another log on the fire, then walked over to the cot
where Michelle slept.

The sight of her stole his breath. Firelight turned her hair
to spun gold, the delicate skin of her face to porcelain. Her
full mouth was slightly open, and he could just make out
the tiny space between her teeth. He smiled, remembering
what she'd said about her gorgeous, sexy mouth. In his eyes,
the tiny imperfection only made her more beautiful.

She was lying on her back, with her head cradled on her
arm. She hadn't dressed after their lovemaking, and he could
see the swell of her breasts and the curve of her hip beneath
the thin blanket. As he watched her sleep, a wave of affec-
tion engulfed him. He wanted to go to her, open her, bury

himself inside her heat and forget about everything except the moment.

Blowing out a sigh, Philip scrubbed his hands over his face. Despite the situation, making love to her in this tiny cabin with the rain pounding outside was the most erotic experience he'd ever had. Her passion had touched the deepest reaches of his heart. The moment he'd sheathed himself inside her heat, his control had toppled, and he'd been mindless with the need to fill her with his seed. The sight of her writhing beneath him with tears in her eyes and her body clamped tightly around his had devastated him, moved him as nothing else ever had.

How the hell was he going to handle this?

She stirred, rolling onto her side. Philip watched as the blanket slipped lower, exposing her breast. He'd never seen such beauty. His body stirred undeniably, but he didn't touch her. He wouldn't give in to his own selfish needs again. He cared about Michelle too much to hurt her. Worse, he didn't want to risk his own heart.

Steeling himself against the rush of blood to his groin, Philip leaned down and tugged the blanket over her satin shoulders. Her eyes fluttered open, settled on him. Her full mouth lifted into a smile.

His chest constricted unexpectedly. He'd never seen such a beautiful smile. "Hi," he said.

"Can't sleep, Betancourt?" Rolling onto her back, she propped her head on a lumpy pillow and regarded him thoughtfully. "I don't kick in my sleep, do I? Steal the covers?"

"You were snoring."

She landed a playful punch on his stomach, hard enough to make him grunt. "I was not."

He took her hand, wished he hadn't as her baby-powder scent teased his brain. He stared at her, realizing with some surprise he was once again fully aroused and aching to be inside her.

She licked her lips, and he sensed she was aware of the same sexual tug.

"We need to talk," he said.

"I don't want to talk about the case. Not tonight."

"That's not what I mean."

Wariness entered her eyes. "You mean...us."

He nodded.

She stared at him, and he could see she was mentally bracing, as if expecting him to fling something hurtful and unexpected her way.

"What happened between us..." His voice was low and rough, not at all the way he'd intended. "We're going to make...things more difficult for each other, Michelle."

Her gaze hardened. "You know, Betancourt, you can always come visit me in prison." Clenching the blanket against her, she tried to sit up.

Grasping her shoulders, he pressed her down firmly. "You know that's not what I meant."

"What exactly *did* you mean?"

Couldn't she see what this would do to them? Couldn't she see that if they got any closer, their inevitable parting would only be that much more difficult? "You know damn good and well what the situation is between us. I'm a cop and I live for my job. I'm not good at relationships, Michelle. I destroy them. I destroy the women who love me. I don't want us to end up hating each other. Dammit, I don't want to hurt you."

"You think I need protecting from you?"

"I think you need protecting from yourself."

"Don't do me any favors, cop." She said the word with loathing.

His temper stirred. "Is that what I am to you?"

"Look, Betancourt, we slept together. I'm a big girl. I can

handle it. I know what I'm doing, and I can take care of myself. How many times do I have to prove that to you?'' Clenching the blanket to her chest, she shook off his hands and sat up. ''I sure as hell don't need you to do it.''

Philip gaped at her. She'd dismissed him. He should have been relieved, considering his reservations about getting involved. But he wasn't. Not by a long shot. ''The coming days are going to be tough for both of us, Michelle. I'm no longer thinking clearly when it comes to you—''

''You're going to bail, aren't you?''

He didn't miss the bitterness behind her words. ''No. I'm going to see this case—''

''It's who I am, isn't it? Where I come from?'' Incredulity laced her voice. ''I should have known—''

He moved before he even realized he was going to, grasping her biceps in his hands and shaking her. ''Stop it, dammit! Just stop with the tough-guy act! I know you're not. And I sure as hell am not going to sit here and let you belittle yourself.''

''No, that's your job.''

''I've never treated you like that.''

''You're doing it right now.''

''The hell I am.''

''And the correct term, if you're wondering, is swamp trash. Some diehards prefer swamp rat, or you could just go with the old standby white trash—''

He shook her again, none too gently this time. ''I'm involved with you, Michelle! I care about you! But I'm a cop! You're a suspect, for God's sake! Where does that leave us?''

She was breathing hard, her nostrils flaring with each breath. ''Why don't you just say it, Betancourt? You don't think I'm good enough for you.''

He ground his teeth. ''You're *too* good for me!'' His shout was like a gunshot in the silence of the cabin.

Her surprised gaze snapped to his.

"I don't know how to handle what's happened between us," he admitted.

The fight went out of her, like air out of a balloon. "I can't change what happened."

"I don't want to change it." That wasn't exactly true—he didn't like it that their relationship had become so infinitely complex—but he didn't say it. "We have to deal with this. We've got to deal with tomorrow. With next week. Next month. We've got to deal with what we're facing in New Orleans. We've got to be prepared for the outcome."

A breath shuddered out of her. "I'm afraid, Betancourt."

His heart wrenched like a wounded animal in his chest. The pain that followed took his breath. With an oath, he reached for her, pulled her to him. He tried to tell himself it was because she needed to be held. But a wretched little voice in the back of his mind called him a liar.

"I'm sorry I said those things." She wrapped her arms around him and laid her head on his shoulder.

"Maybe I needed to hear them."

"No. You're right. This is getting really complicated."

"I knew it would." He closed his eyes. "I'm taking you back to New Orleans tomorrow."

She stiffened in his arms. "I don't want to go to jail."

"I'll take you to my place. Or a hotel—"

"I won't let you risk your job."

"That's not why I'm—"

"Then why?"

"Michelle, you can't become a fugitive from the law."

A tremor rippled through her and he held her tightly against him. But no matter how hard he tried, he couldn't erase the feeling that she was slipping through his fingers, into a dangerous place he didn't want her to be.

The blanket had fallen at some point, and suddenly Philip was aware of her naked breasts against his chest. Her hardened nipples brushed against his flesh, tormenting him with sweet temptation. He called himself a fool a dozen ways. He knew better than to give in to the lust burning through him, knew he would live to regret it. Dammit, he already had enough regrets. His career was about to go down the proverbial drain, and all he could think of was this proud, frightened woman going to jail. The thought tormented him. Her spirit was too precious to be crushed. How could he let that happen? How could he live with himself, knowing he would play a role?

The weight of the questions devastated him, sent a choppy wave of panic through him. He wanted her, suddenly couldn't bear the thought of her slipping away. "I've never wanted anyone the way I want you. You make me desperate. Insane. But I've got to have you. Now."

Her startled gaze met his. "I'm not going to fall apart when you walk away. I've got my own life—"

"I'm not going to walk away."

"Don't make promises you can't keep!" she repeated.

He didn't bother with kissing her. The needs inside him were too urgent, churning, hot, violent. Using the muscles in his arms, he lowered her to the cot, then stepped out of his jeans. She tried to cover herself with the blanket, but he jerked it from her and tossed it aside.

"I want to see you." He knelt. His mouth met hers so hard their teeth clicked together. He feasted on her for an instant, his tongue battling hers, then going deep. He couldn't get enough of her and, in a moment of insight, knew he never would. Knew she was slipping from his grasp, and he felt that surge of panic again. Stronger. Shaking him to his core.

His mouth trailed to her breasts, where he used his teeth on her nipples. She arced into him. Need and fear and pain churned in his gut, his mind, until he was shaking from head to toe. He cupped the softness of her mound, and she opened to him. A groan rumbled out of his chest when his finger found her wet and hot. He kissed her belly, then the crisp curls below. She tensed, but he didn't stop. He was mindless with the need to taste her, to devour the sweetness he knew lay there.

She cried out his name when his mouth found her. He kissed her deeply, greedily, drinking in her scent until her hips rose up to meet him and her muscles jerked with every flick of his tongue.

And Philip knew he was lost to her forever.

Michelle thought she would die of pleasure. No man had ever touched her intimate places with his mouth, and she'd never dreamed it would be like this. She crested twice before he stopped. Her body was still in spasms when he eased himself between her legs, entered her in a single, long stroke and went deep.

The world simply ceased to exist. Her senses shut down until there was nothing except the moment between them, the pleasure pounding through her, the exquisite pain of two hearts beating as one. She knew he was fighting it. She could tell by the tautness of his muscles, the determined set of his mouth; she knew he wouldn't give up his heart easily. Not this man with his cynical view of the world and hardened facade. But Michelle knew he felt the connection. Perhaps not love, as she'd hoped, but something profound and beautiful. No man could look at her the way Betancourt did and not feel something. He just didn't realize it yet.

Sweat beaded on his forehead as he gazed down at her, moving within her. She felt the waves beginning, wondered if they would drown her this time, if she would survive. They were coming so quickly she couldn't catch her breath.

"We're going to ride this one out together." His voice was low with tension. His jaws were clamped tight, his arms trembling with strain. His eyes were so intense, she thought he could see right through her to that part of her heart that belonged to him now.

She couldn't breathe, couldn't form a single rational thought. Her body took over, and she met his strokes with the same desperate ferocity. Darkness washed over her vision. Her body clenched. He shuddered. She heard her name, felt his breath on her cheek, and she knew as surely as she felt his seed spilling into the deepest reaches of her that, somehow, everything would work out. Philip would be there for her. Stand by her. Never betray her.

Chapter 13

Philip should have been relieved driving back to New Orleans, where he could salvage what was left of his career, resume his quest for Armon Landsteiner's murderer and, ultimately, save Michelle's life. Only he wasn't relieved. Instead, he felt as if he were leading a lamb to slaughter.

He couldn't hide her in a hotel. He couldn't take her back to his house. The notion was worse than stupid; it was insane. Running from the law would only result in more charges being levied against her. He'd already laid his career on the line. Was he prepared to do the same with his freedom?

He loved her. He told himself he could deal with it. He even thought he could walk away when the time came. After all, that's what he did best. That was the kind of man he was. Only he couldn't quiet the little voice that kept calling him a liar.

His cell phone chirped. Out of the corner of his eye, he saw Michelle stiffen, then lean back in the passenger seat and close her eyes. He couldn't blame her for being jumpy. He was getting that way himself.

Philip answered with a curt utterance of his name.

Cory's curse burned through the line. "Where the hell have you been?"

Had the situation not been so dire, Philip would have smiled at his partner's tone. "Bayou Lafourche. Why?"

"You could have answered your damn phone."

"I was out of range."

"You with Michelle?"

"Who wants to know?"

"I figured you were. Well, brace yourself, my man, because that bastard Montgomery just put out a warrant for you, too."

The words hit Philip like a kick in the solar plexus. He nearly dropped the phone. He saw Michelle watching him, and swallowed the outrage that had risen like bile in his throat. "What the hell for?"

"The strongest charge is aiding and abetting a fugitive from justice. A couple of others won't stick."

Disbelief swamped him. "Somebody's pulling Montgomery's strings, Cory."

"I figured that. The question is who."

"Someone with a lot at stake."

"Sounds like they want you out of the way pretty badly."

"You can bet on it." Philip's gut clenched as the repercussions of what his partner was telling him hit home.

"You've got to bring her in, Betancourt."

He cursed, knowing Cory was right. God, he hated this. Hated it that Michelle had been caught up in someone's ugly game. "Call Jane Bevins, will you? Fill her in on the situation."

"For you?"

"No, for Michelle." Philip's chest tightened. Jane Bevins was a feminist attorney who thrived on high profile cases, and he knew she'd stick by Michelle like a terrier to a bone.

"She's expensive."

"I'll cover it." He didn't know how, but somehow, he would. "I'll see you at the station in about an hour." He disconnected, then glanced over at Michelle.

Her eyes were large and dark against her pale complexion. "You're turning me in, aren't you?"

The sadness in her voice struck a chord, but the resignation there sliced him clean through the middle. "If I don't take you back, we'll both be fugitives from justice."

"Better I go to jail than both of us, huh, Betancourt?"

"Don't say it. Don't even think it," he warned.

"Who's Jane Bevins?"

Michelle was too cool, too calm. He wondered what was really going on behind that tough facade. "An attorney I know. She won't let you out of her sight."

"Oh, you mean so the guards don't get to put their hands all over me like they did when I was seventeen?"

Fury cut through him with such force that for a moment he was blinded. Philip mashed his foot against the brake and brought the car to a screeching halt, throwing both of them against their shoulder harnesses. "I don't have a choice in the matter! I have to do this!"

"Feeling guilty?" she asked nastily.

"Hell yes, I feel guilty! What do you think? I care about you, dammit! I don't want to do this!"

"Then don't do it!" A sob tore from her throat.

He slammed his fist against the dash. Plastic shattered. Pain zinged up to his elbow, but he welcomed the diversion from the agony ripping through his heart. "What would you have me do?"

"Take me back to Bayou Lafourche."

"That's how much faith you have in the criminal justice system? And you're a year away from taking the bar?"

"Ask my brother about faith in the criminal justice system, cop!"

His hands were shaking. Blood oozed from his knuckles.

Realizing he'd damaged the dash, he wrapped his fingers around the steering wheel and looked straight again. "I can't take you back to Bayou Lafourche."

A hard laugh broke from her mouth. "I didn't think so."

"That would only make things worse."

"For me or for you?"

She said the words with a flippancy that set his teeth on edge. He looked down, realized the engine had died. "I'll take care of your bail. Jane will see you through processing. You'll be out in a few hours."

"Unless, of course, the judge deems me a flight risk."

"You're not a flight risk." Philip couldn't look at her, couldn't bring himself to look into the soft depths of her eyes, knowing what he did about her past. And do this to her. The realization made him feel as if he were dying inside.

"I hate you for this, Betancourt. I'll never forgive you."

The rancor in her voice made him wince. Without looking at her, he reached down and turned the key. "You're not the only one," he said, and pulled onto the highway.

Michelle knew Betancourt didn't have a choice. She knew she was being unreasonable, but she was furious, with him, with fate, with the person who'd destroyed so many lives the night he'd murdered Armon.

Betancourt hadn't spoken to her since the angry exchange on the highway, and she didn't know how to breach the tense silence that had fallen between them. She tried to tell herself it didn't matter. That her heart wasn't shattering. That it didn't hurt her to her soul that he wasn't willing to put his career on the line to keep her out of jail. But the pain was so sharp, so intense it was physical. The logical side of her brain knew she'd be out in a few hours. But if Betancourt was right, and someone in high places was calling the shots, who was to say that same individual hadn't also convinced the judge to deny bail?

Michelle's stomach rolled when they pulled into the rear

lot of the Broad Street Police Station. She told herself she was prepared for the coming hours. Prepared to have her dignity, her very humanity stripped away. Only she knew better. Dread congealed in her chest as she spotted Cory walking toward them with long, purposeful strides, his face grim.

She started when Betancourt opened his door. She watched him get out of the car, then approach Cory. The two men spoke briefly, then Betancourt returned to the car and opened her door. Rather than let her get out, he leaned down and met her gaze.

"I swear I'll have you out as soon as you're processed. Jane Bevins will be here shortly. She got held up in court. She'll make sure—"

Michelle raised her hands. "Don't say it."

He sighed, looked down at the ground. "Cory's going to take you inside. I've got to go see Montgomery."

Her heart skittered wildly, then beat out of control. Her breathing was short and choppy. Her face heated and for an instant she thought she might faint. "I don't want handcuffs," she said.

"No handcuffs. Cory will be with you as much as he can. You'll be fingerprinted, then processed, and probably put into a holding cell. You'll be out in no time. You've got my word."

His eyes were darker and more solemn than she'd ever seen them. He reached for her hand, squeezed. "If it's the last thing I do, I'm going to find who killed Landsteiner. I swear I won't let you burn for this."

Michelle believed him. The realization stunned her, gave her the strength she needed to get through the next hours. "I know."

He stepped back.

Her legs trembled as she got out of the car.

Without warning, he pulled her to him, crushing her

against his chest. "I'm sorry it came to this, honey. I wish there was another way."

"I'm glad I've got you on my side, Betancourt." Tears stung her eyes, but for the first time in her life, she didn't care. She let them fall unheeded, and held on to him for dear life. He kissed her deeply, possessively, stirring her undeniably in spite of the fact that she was sore from their lovemaking the night before.

When her heart couldn't take any more, she eased away from him and looked at Cory. "I'm ready," she said.

Her courage faltered, but she knew it was too late to change her mind. Without looking back, she started toward the building, praying she could get through this without falling apart.

Five hours, and still no Betancourt.

He wasn't going to show.

As she watched the clock on the wall outside her cell sweep to five o'clock, Michelle knew in her heart that he'd betrayed her. Five hours had passed since she'd walked away from him in the parking lot.

He wasn't coming for her.

She looked down at the ink imbedded in her fingertips. Processing had been a nightmare, but not nearly as demeaning as what she'd endured all those years ago in Bayou Lafourche. Cory had stayed with her during the fingerprinting, then Jane Bevins had taken over as Michelle had checked in her possessions.

Betancourt hadn't cared enough to show up.

Every time the doors clanged somewhere in the jail, her heart lurched with the anticipation of seeing him. Every hour he didn't show, she'd come up with a new excuse for him. Only now, alone with her thoughts, did she realize how foolish she'd been.

He wasn't coming.

He was a career cop. A detective who always got his man

no matter what the cost, no matter who got hurt. She'd known all along he wouldn't fall for a woman like her. Just because they'd shared a night of mind-numbing sex didn't mean he loved her. Damn her heart for getting in the way and blinding her to the truth.

Turning away from the cold, steel bars, Michelle began to pace. Claustrophobia closed in on her like a pair of crushing hands. Panic rose in her throat, but she choked it down. She had to stay calm, had to think. Had to formulate a plan. She couldn't spend the night here; she'd be stark, raving insane in another hour. Was there someone else she could call? Oh, God, how could she have been so stupid to have believed Betancourt cared for her? He'd betrayed her, just as Frank Blanchard had all those years ago. Only this was worse because she'd known better and jumped in feetfirst anyway.

She'd gone against everything she believed in by falling for Betancourt. She'd given him her body. Her heart. Her very soul. In return, he'd used her, lied to her, betrayed her. Now her heart was breaking and there wasn't a thing she could do about it.

I swear I won't let you burn for this.

His words rang in her ears with such clarity that tears sprang into her eyes. Furiously, she brushed them away. No, she wouldn't cry; she wouldn't break down now. Not when she would need every ounce of strength to get through the coming days. She couldn't imagine spending the night here. She was cold and exhausted and felt dirty all the way to her bones.

Despair settled over her like a black cloak. She was alone. On her own. The reality hit her so hard she barely made it to the bunk before her legs gave out. She felt helpless, more vulnerable than she'd ever felt in her life.

I swear I won't let you burn for this.

Liar, she thought.

Lowering her face into her hands, she wept.

* * *

Philip looked at the clock and squashed down anger for the dozenth time. He'd been locked up in Hardin Montgomery's office for nearly five hours without respite. He'd lost count of the charges against him. Oddly, he couldn't seem to muster enough interest to care.

"Betancourt? Are you listening to me?"

Philip glared at his superior. "I'm listening." Damn, he'd been thinking about Michelle again. How could he not, knowing she was sitting in some dank cell waiting for him to bail her out?

He glanced at his watch.

"You got somewhere to go, Betancourt?" Ken Burns sneered.

"I'm just counting the minutes until I lose control and turn you inside out with my bare hands."

Burns's face reddened.

Philip smiled, but he felt as if he were going to explode. He was in trouble. Big trouble. From the looks of things, he'd be lucky to walk away without criminal charges being filed against him.

"Turn off the recorder, Ken," Montgomery said.

Burns shot the superintendent a surprised look, then jumped forward to obey, punching the off button of the recorder.

Montgomery looked first at Ken, then at Philip. "We've been beating around the bush in here for five hours, gentlemen. I'm hungry, and I want to go home."

The hairs on the back of Philip's neck rose.

Montgomery's gaze narrowed on Philip. "You're facing some very serious charges, Lieutenant."

"I'm aware of that."

"Charges that could ruin an outstanding career if you make the wrong decision today."

Philip met his gaze. "I'm not sure I follow you."

"I spoke with the D.A. this morning. He wants the Land-steiner case closed. We've got our suspect. All he wants from you is your final report detailing the evidence that compelled you to bring Michelle Pelletier into custody. Let the courts take it from here. If you have the report on his desk by nine o'clock tomorrow morning, he's willing to reconsider the charges our Public Integrity Division has levied against you.''

In an instant, the situation crystallized. Philip felt it all the way down to his belly. He nearly choked on the ensuing fury. ''I can't do that.''

''Why not?''

''There is no report. Michelle Pelletier is not a suspect, and she hasn't been for quite some time.''

One of Montgomery's jowls lifted in a snarl. ''I'll destroy you, Lieutenant. If you don't submit that report and close this case, I'll bring charges against you starting with aiding and abetting a suspected felon and obstruction of justice, all the way down to sexual misconduct. You'll do time. You sure as hell won't ever work as a cop again.''

''You know she didn't do it, don't you, Hardin?''

''You'll be in a cell by day's end if you don't cooperate with me. I'll make it tough for you.''

The thought of jail sent a quiver through his gut, but Philip didn't react. He knew how cops were regarded by the inmates. He also knew that Montgomery wasn't above that kind of blackmail.

''Go to hell,'' he said.

''I'll publish those photos if it's the last thing I do. You won't be able to get a job as a security guard. Not in New Orleans or any other city, for that matter. I'll make damn sure you get a felony conviction on your record.''

Raw fury swept through Philip. He felt like a time bomb about to go off. Only the rage pumping through him with every beat of his heart wasn't due to the loss of his career. The realization surprised him.

I love you.

Her words rang clearly in his ears, and for the first time

he understood fully their meaning. The outrage burning inside him erupted from the knowledge that someone wanted to use him as a pawn to ruin an innocent woman's life. A kind woman who'd already had more than her share of trouble.

A woman he loved.

A woman he wanted to spend the rest of his life with.

Rising, Philip pulled the miniature tape recorder from his trouser pocket and hit the off button with his thumb.

Montgomery's piggish eyes widened.

Burns gasped and scooted his chair back as if expecting violence.

Planting both hands on the desk, Philip leaned forward until his face was inches from Montgomery's. "Is this off the record, Chief?"

The fat man jerked his head once.

Philip smiled. "If any harm comes to Michelle Pelletier before I get down there to bail her out, I'm going to kill you with my bare hands."

Montgomery choked. "You're in no position to threaten me!"

"I'm in the perfect position to threaten you." Philip had suspected for years Montgomery was dirty. Like most of the other detectives, he'd overlooked it. But no more. Not when Michelle's life hung in the balance.

Beside him, Burns picked up the phone. "He's a loose cannon, Mr. Montgomery. I'm calling in a patrol. A few hours in a cell ought to cool him off."

Philip didn't even look at him. "Put the phone down or I'll break your arm, Burns."

"Put it down," Montgomery echoed.

The phone dropped back into place.

"That tape will never hold up in court, Betancourt," Montgomery said. "You know that."

"Maybe not, but the *Times Picayune* will have a freaking field day with it." He started for the door.

"You walk out of here and you're finished, Lieutenant!" Philip never looked back.

Chapter 14

"Pelletier! You made bail."

Michelle was on her feet before her eyes were fully open. Somehow she'd managed to fall asleep on the lumpy mattress. Bewildered, she blinked at the matronly guard and shoved a lock of hair from her eyes. "Someone's bailing me out?"

"That's right." The woman's keys jingled as she twisted the lock and opened the door. "I'll take you to get your things."

Michelle's heart swelled as she stepped into the hall. Had Betancourt finally come for her? "Who bailed me?" she asked.

"Nobody's waiting for you, if that's what you mean." The woman motioned toward the end of the hall. "Let's go."

Michelle fell in beside her, her mind running through the possibilities. Betancourt was the most logical candidate. But if he had, why wasn't he waiting for her?

She stopped short of making excuses for him. No, she

told herself firmly, she wouldn't do that to herself. No matter how much she loved him, she had to accept the fact that Betancourt didn't love her.

After picking up the few items she'd checked in, Michelle left the police station through the front door. Even in her exhausted state, an incredible sense of freedom engulfed her the moment she stepped outside. The night was so cold she could see her breath. The wind smelled of rain.

"Michelle."

She started at the sound of her name, then spotted Derek Landsteiner standing beside his Volvo a few yards down the street. Surprise rippled through her when he motioned for her to approach.

"Derek?" Quickly, she descended the concrete steps and walked to his car. "What are you doing here?"

"I drove straight down when I heard. I couldn't stand the thought of you locked up like an animal. I arranged bail."

She tried to ignore the sharp pang of disappointment. She'd hoped Betancourt cared enough to make her bail. The realization that he hadn't only confirmed what she already knew in her heart. He didn't love her. She had to accept it. She had to go on. The cold reality of it sent tears to her eyes.

"Hey, we'll get you a lawyer. You won't go back."

Derek mistook the cause of her tears, and Michelle didn't bother correcting him. Disgusted with herself, she used the sleeve of her denim jacket to wipe her cheeks. "Thanks for coming through for me. It means a lot to me. Whatever the cost of my bail, I'll repay you."

He looked from left to right as if anxious about someone noticing them together. "I don't want Danielle or Baldwin to know I did this. Hop in and I'll take you home."

Forcing a smile, she got in the car. The interior was warm. Michelle huddled in her jacket, trying not to think of everything that had happened in the last week, or how drastically her life had changed. She had lost not only her career and the only opportunity she would ever have for an education, but her very freedom.

The loss of her heart hurt infinitely worse. Every time she closed her eyes, she saw Betancourt, the way his eyes had darkened when he'd made love to her, the way he'd looked at her when she'd walked away from him for the last time.

I swear I won't let you burn for this.

Tears threatened again. *Oh, Philip.* She closed her eyes against the rush of pain. Why did she have to go and fall in love with him? After what had happened with Frank Blanchard, how could she have given her heart so foolishly?

"You okay?"

She started at the sound of Derek's voice, realized she hadn't said a word since she'd gotten in the car. "Yes, I'm just…shaken up."

"I know a good defense lawyer, Michelle. I'll give him a call, if you like."

Her first impulse was to refute the fact that she needed an attorney, but after spending more than five hours in jail, she knew better. She couldn't afford Jane Bevins. She obviously couldn't count on any help from Betancourt. "Yes, I'd appreciate that."

"I tried to call you yesterday, but I couldn't reach you."

For the first time it dawned on her that Derek didn't know about Armon's past, or that she was his half-sister. "I went to Bayou Lafourche yesterday."

He shot her a questioning look. "Why did you do that?"

"I went to see my brother, Nicolas." She pondered the best way to break the news. Should she wait until Danielle and Baldwin were present and tell all three of them together? No, she thought, the truth had been buried too long already. Derek had cared enough to risk his siblings' wrath by bailing her out. She'd tell him everything now, then they could figure out together how best to break the news to Danielle and Baldwin.

"Detective Betancourt had dug up some information on Armon," she began.

"Betancourt's off the case." Derek grimaced. "In fact, I think he's off the force for…taking advantage of you."

Heat rose in her cheeks at the memory of everything she and Betancourt had shared. She tried to tell herself it didn't matter what Derek or anyone else thought. But it did matter, she realized. Part of her wanted the world to know that her relationship with Betancourt had been beautiful and magical and rare.

Shoving the memories aside, Michelle looked over at her half brother, wondering how he would feel knowing she shared his blood. "This is complicated, Derek, so I'm just going to tell you what I know."

The words drew a puzzled gaze from him. "What are you talking about?"

"Betancourt told me Armon hired a private detective to find me a year before I moved to New Orleans. He also has evidence linking Armon to my scholarship at Tulane."

A laugh broke from his throat. "That's absurd."

"I thought so, too, at first. Yesterday I went back to Bayou Lafourche. I met with Nicolas, who proceeded to take my world apart by telling me Armon and my mother had an affair."

"My God."

"Armon was my father."

Derek's hands tightened on the wheel. "Who else knows about this?"

Something in his voice chilled her. "Betancourt," she said slowly. "His partner. I think Betancourt was meeting with his superior this afternoon, so the commander may know as well."

"Montgomery won't be a problem." Derek's gaze swept to hers. The iciness of it sent a shiver up her spine.

"What do you mean?"

Though he didn't look away from his driving again, a smile twisted his mouth. "That makes you my half sister."

"After everything that's happened, I wasn't sure how you'd feel about that."

"Do you want me to tell you how I feel?" His voice was cold and flat.

Uneasiness crept over her. For the first time, she realized they weren't heading in the direction of her apartment. "Where are we going?"

"I left my briefcase at the office." His gaze met hers once more. "You don't mind if we make a quick stop, do you?"

"Gone? What do you mean, gone? How the hell did she make bail?" Philip glared at the female officer, worry working its way into the pit of his stomach.

Sighing, she looked down at the notebook on the counter. "Someone bailed her out about twenty minutes ago."

"Who?"

"Bail bondsman down on Poydras."

"Give me the number."

"Look it up in the phone book, hotshot," she snapped.

Reaching across the counter, he snatched the notebook from her and ripped out the page in question. "I'm in a hurry."

"You can't do that!"

"I just did." Philip didn't stop until he reached his desk. He felt the stares of his fellow cops, but no one dared stop him. He had to find Michelle. The need to see her, to touch her, pounded through him like a drum.

He'd just picked up the phone to dial the bondsman's number when he heard Cory's voice.

"What are you doing here, Betancourt?"

"Looking for Michelle."

"I thought she was in custody."

"She's not. I was just down there."

Cory sat down across from him and leaned forward, a

sober look on his face. "You sure this is the best place for you to be calling her?"

"She's in trouble, Cory."

His partner's eyes narrowed. "You're in deep with her, aren't you, Betancourt?"

Philip snarled into the phone when he was put on hold, then raked a trembling hand over a day's worth of stubble. "God, Cory, I love her."

Cory's jaw dropped. "I'll be damned. Coming from you, my man, that's about a ten on the Richter scale."

"Tell me about it."

"Well, here's a news flash. While you were cozied up with Montgomery and Burns, we got a break in the case."

Hope spiraled through Philip. "Talk to me."

Looking pleased with himself, Cory grinned. "You remember the cuff link you found at the scene?"

He nodded, remembering Michelle had gripped it so tightly, the post had pierced her palm. God, what she must have been going through that night.

"I went to see Derek Landsteiner last night. Just to bug him, see if I could get some reaction out of him. The dude's one cool cookie. When I was using his john, I looked down and this cuff link was just staring right up at me."

A twinge went through Philip's chest. "Did the lab match it with the one at the scene?"

"Not yet, but how many diamond cuff links like that do you think exist in this city?"

"Probably just those two."

"That puts him at the scene. I figure he stepped on it, and the post went into his shoe. Then he carried it back to his penthouse."

"There wasn't any sign of a struggle at the scene," Philip said. "How do you suppose both cuff links came off?"

"Maybe the old man was trying to leave some kind of clue."

"If that's the case, looks like it worked."

The bail bondsman came on the line, and Philip's attention snapped to the phone. "This is Detective Betancourt with the NOPD. I need to know who bailed Michelle Pelletier from the Broad Street city jail."

"Usually we don't give out this kind of information, but since you're a cop…" Papers rustled on the other end of the line. "Bill Smith signed the form. He said he was an attorney and paid cash—"

The seed of worry augmented, shifted into something dark and terrible. "Describe him."

"Uh…well, he was blond. About six feet tall. Expensive suit. Green eyes and little round glasses."

With an oath, Philip slammed down the phone. Panic gripped him with such force he couldn't draw a breath. "Derek Landsteiner bailed Michelle."

Cory reached for his coat. "I'm on it."

"Go to Landsteiner's penthouse. Put out an APB—"

"We don't have a positive match—"

"Do it!" Philip struggled for control when he realized Cory was staring at him.

"Betancourt, you're a civilian—"

"Just do it. I owe her, Cory." His chest felt as if it were caving in, and he choked down panic. "I'm going to her apartment. I've got my cell. Keep me posted."

Derek opened the office door and motioned for Michelle to precede him. She hadn't wanted to come inside. In fact, she'd tried to convince Derek to let her wait in the car while he retrieved his briefcase, but he'd insisted she accompany him, saying it wasn't safe for a woman alone in the parking garage after hours.

The reception area was dark and deserted. Michelle started when Derek closed the door behind them.

"You're jumpy tonight, Michelle."

"I…I guess I'm still tense about everything that happened today." It was a lie. She didn't know what made her so uneasy—something subtle she couldn't put her finger on. But Derek was definitely the source. "I'll just turn on the lights—"

"No."

Her stomach went into a slow roll. "Why not? It's dark in here."

"We don't need the lights."

She couldn't seem to get enough oxygen into her lungs, and realized belatedly she was afraid. She told herself she had nothing to fear from Derek. He didn't hate her the way Danielle and Baldwin did. He'd always been the quiet, calm one of the three Landsteiner siblings. But something was different about him tonight. Something dark and menacing she'd never seen before.

For a moment the only sound came from her shallow breathing. "Are you angry with me, Derek? Is that why you're trying to frighten me?"

A ribbon of light bled in through the window of Baldwin's office across the hall, just enough for her to make out Derek's features. What she saw made her blood run cold. She'd never seen such detached, blank eyes. It was as if every emotion had been sucked out of him. Every emotion except hatred. In that instant, Michelle knew Derek wanted to hurt her.

"I didn't want it to come to this," he said.

Adrenaline burst into her muscles. Quickly, she gauged the distance to the door, realized she'd have to pass close to him to reach it. "Take me home, Derek. Please. We can forget this ever happened."

"I'm sorry, sis, but I can't do that."

Michelle bolted to the door. Her fingers closed over the knob, twisted. In her peripheral vision she saw Derek reach for her. His fingers bit into her shoulders, spun her around. Michelle screamed, lashed out with her fists. He slammed her against the wall so hard the impact took her breath. Pain streaked up her spine. Stars exploded before her eyes. She couldn't breathe, couldn't move. Her knees buckled, but he caught her beneath her arms and kept her from falling.

"Come on, Michelle. You're tougher than that. You can keep your feet under you, can't you?"

She'd never thought of Derek as being physically strong—he was a slightly built man—but the ease with which he'd overpowered her stunned and amazed her. She knew if he chose to hurt her—or worse—he could manage with nothing more than his bare hands.

Wrenching free of his grasp, she staggered to the hall. Her old office was off to the left. If she could reach the phone…

"Don't even think about it, Michelle."

Her head felt fuzzy, her thoughts disoriented. She couldn't remember if there was a lock on her office door. "Why are you doing this?"

"Don't tell me you haven't figured it out yet."

Understanding struck her like a club. Slowly, she turned to face him. "Oh, God. Oh, no. Derek, no."

He smiled. "I always knew you were smart."

"You killed Armon, didn't you?"

"He didn't leave me a choice."

Pain congealed deep in her belly. "Your own father? Why in God's name did you do it?"

"The crazy old fool changed his will. He didn't like the direction Baldwin wanted to take the firm. I wasn't strong enough. Danielle didn't care enough. So he willed a controlling portion of the firm to you."

Bile rose in her throat with the knowledge that the only father she'd ever known had been killed because of greed. The truth sickened her. "You destroyed the new will. Then you murdered Armon. You murdered Dennis Jacoby to cover it up."

"I had to make sure no one got that will."

Outrage burned through her. "There was a disk in Jacoby's fireproof safe. Betancourt has someone looking at it.''

Derek made a sound of annoyance. ''Do you have any idea how many cops I've got in my pocket, Michelle? The big PR campaign the NOPD has been putting on is all a line of bull. They're corrupt. Just like the rest of us.''

She cringed when he came up beside her and laid his hand on her shoulder. ''Not Betancourt.''

''Ah, loyal to the very end. I'm sure he'll appreciate that when reading your obituary.''

The thought cut her, but she refused to give him the satisfaction of a reaction. ''You've already murdered two people, Derek. Am I going to be your third? Your own sister?''

''Half sister. And I really don't have a choice, do I, sis? I mean, put yourself in my shoes. Hell of a thing, my old man getting a conscience after twenty years. I was pretty annoyed when I found out about you.''

''How long have you known?''

''He told me the night I killed him. I needed to protect my interests.''

Michelle wanted to hurt him, wanted to take him apart with her bare hands until he lay on the floor helpless and bleeding.

''It was you that night in the cemetery, wasn't it?''

''I didn't want you getting any closer to that cop. If I'd succeeded, this would have been all over by now. If I didn't know better, I'd think you had nine lives, Michelle.''

''You won't get away with this.''

''You were the perfect candidate to frame. Poor girl from the wrong side of the tracks. Rich older widower with money to blow. It almost worked. Everyone thought you were sleeping with him. Everyone thought you killed him for that neat little life insurance policy. The amnesia thing threw me for a while, but in the long run it worked to my advantage. The cops thought you were lying. Well, everyone except Betancourt. But he wasn't hard to do away with. The fact that he fell for you was the icing on the cake.''

Her chest constricted. If she died tonight, Betancourt would never know the truth. She wondered if he'd keep digging. If he'd try to solve her murder…

''People are going to get suspicious if there's another murder. Betancourt already suspects Armon's murder had something to do with the will. You're already a suspect.''

A cruel smile twisted the corners of Derek's mouth. ''The irony of the whole thing is that you're going to solve the case, Michelle. Guilt over murdering Armon combined with the knowledge that you'll be spending the rest of your life in prison sent you over the edge. You're going to commit suicide tonight. I thought it would be a nice twist to bring you here to do it. After all, we've got the privacy of the penthouse. I thought eight stories would do nicely.''

He withdrew a folded note from his pocket.

Nerves jumping, Michelle stepped back.

''I'm not going to hurt you. Yet. This is just your suicide note and confession.'' Grabbing her hand, he pressed her fingertips against it. ''Now we have fingerprints.''

She repressed a shiver as he tucked the note into the breast pocket of her jacket. ''No one's going to believe I committed suicide.''

''You have nothing to live for. Why wouldn't you? Your career is gone. Your education. Your freedom. Even your cop spurned you.''

She winced, and swallowed the pain that welled up in her throat. ''You don't know anything.''

''Tough to the end, too. I really like that.''

''You won't get away with this.''

''I'm tired of talking, Michelle.'' Reaching into the waistband of his slacks, he withdrew a shiny chrome pistol. ''Let's go up to the roof.''

Philip stood on the porch of the old Victorian and felt his world shatter around him. He'd been praying she'd be home.

That she wasn't told him his worst fears were correct. The need to feel her safe in his arms was like a living thing inside him, hammering away at his very sanity.

I love you.

Her words haunted him, taunted everything inside him until he thought he would explode with desperation. He had to find her. If anything happened to her, if Landsteiner harmed her in any way, Philip would never be able to live with himself. Why had it taken something like this for him to realize he loved her?

Back in the car, he pulled onto the street and sped toward the central business district, disregarding traffic signals and the speed limit. He punched the number of Cory's cell phone.

Cory picked up on the first ring.

"Is Landsteiner at his apartment?" Philip asked.

"No sign of him. His car's not there."

Desperation cut him a little more deeply. Where the hell could he have taken her? "I'm going to the Whitney Building to see if he took her there."

"I'll contact Baldwin and Danielle, then meet you there."

Philip disconnected and pressed the accelerator to the floor.

Michelle couldn't believe her life was going to end like this—in a final act of violence that would wipe out everything she'd ever loved or wanted or believed in. Wipe out the dreams she'd clutched desperately for so many years, the love she held in her heart for Betancourt.

Everything that made her human cried out with the injustice of it.

Wind and rain lashed her when she opened the door to the roof. She paused, stunned by the cold, frozen by the terror slithering through her.

The muzzle of the gun pressed into her spine. "Keep moving."

Her legs were shaking so badly she could barely make herself walk onto the open roof. "It doesn't have to end this way, Derek. I'll sign the firm over to you." Her voice trembled with each word.

"You know, Michelle, I've always admired the fact that you're smart. That's the one reason I wasn't ashamed to have you as a sister. Unfortunately, this problem has moved beyond mere control of the firm."

"No one has to know."

"The police need to close the case. To do that, they need to catch the murderer. I'll be lucky as it is to pull this off."

From where she stood, she could see the yellow lights of the building across Royal Street to the north.

Derek motioned with the gun. "Walk over to the edge."

Rain soaked through her jacket, but Michelle was oblivious to the cold. She couldn't even hear the rain over the jackhammer rhythm of her heart. She tried to imagine what it would be like to fall eight stories, and shuddered. She didn't want to die.

Oh, Philip, where are you?

On numb legs she started for the ledge.

"That's far enough."

She stopped four feet from the edge. Adrenaline stabbed through her, burning like acid in her gut when she risked a glance down at the street.

"Turn around and face me, Michelle. I want to see your face when you realize you're going to die."

Slowly, she turned to face him. "I'm not going to let you get away with this."

Amusement flashed across his features. "Really?"

In that instant, Michelle made a decision. An eerie calm washed over her. "If you want to kill me, Derek, you're going to have to pull the trigger. I won't jump. I'm not going to make this easy for you."

"Don't be stupid, Michelle. I'll do it."

"The police will know it's murder. And your plan will fail. You'll spend the rest of your miserable life behind bars."

"I own the police department."

"You don't own Philip Betancourt."

Rage contorted his face. Without warning, he charged. Terror jolted through her. Oh, God, he was going to push her. He drew back to strike her, but Michelle sidestepped. Air whooshed as his fist grazed her shoulder. Light glinted off the gun in his other hand. She kicked, aiming high, and felt her foot connect solidly with his hand. The gun arced away from him.

"Police! Halt or I'll fire!"

Betancourt's voice cut through the wind and rain like a blast. Hope exploded in Michelle's chest. Out of the corner of her eye, she spotted Derek's gun near the ledge. He dived for it. Behind her, Betancourt cursed. She heard movement, then rough hands shoved her aside. She stumbled, went down on her hands and knees. Betancourt sprinted toward Derek.

The gunshot deafened her.

Betancourt's body jerked.

Not Philip! Not like this. A scream tore from her throat. Then she was running to him, oblivious of the danger, and the fact that Derek had control of the gun.

The two men rolled toward the roof's edge. The rain and darkness blinded her. She could barely distinguish one man from the other. Quickly, she scanned the area for a weapon she could use to incapacitate Derek.

Derek lurched to his feet.

Philip lay supine at his feet.

Derek's gaze sought hers.

Even in the darkness she saw the insanity in the hollow depths of his eyes. "Run, Derek. There's still time for you to escape," she said in a strangled voice.

He leveled the gun at her chest. "I'm not going to die alone. I'm taking you with me, Michelle."

Philip's legs lashed out, slamming into Derek, driving him backward. He stumbled, lost his balance when his foot found only air. His mouth opened in a silent scream. His eyes widened. Arms flailing wildly, he went over the ledge.

Sickened, Michelle turned away.

In an instant Betancourt was beside her, solid and strong, pulling her into his arms. "It's over, sweetheart. It's over."

A sob wrenched out of her. "Oh, Philip. Oh, God, I thought you were…" She couldn't say the words. "You've been shot."

"Shh. I'm okay. I'm here."

She couldn't stop crying, didn't care about the tears. All she cared about was that the man she loved was holding her and nothing had ever felt so right in her life. "He murdered Armon."

"I know. I'm sorry, honey."

Closing her eyes, she wrapped her arms around his waist. "He did it for the will. Because of the firm. He was going to kill us both."

"Everything's going to be okay. Just let me hold you for a minute, okay?" He reached up to stroke the back of her head, and winced.

A low moan followed, and she felt him wobble. Gently, she extracted herself from his arms. Shock vibrated through her when she saw the blood on the front of his trench coat. "Oh, my God. You're bleeding."

"It's just a scratch."

"Scratches don't bleed like that."

"It always sounds good when they say that in the movies."

Michelle pulled away just enough to get a look at his face. Despite the grin, he was sheet white. A new kind of fear quivered in her belly. "Give me your phone so I can call an ambulance."

Another moan escaped him as he fished his cellular from his coat pocket. "Cory's on his way," he said.

Quickly, she dialed 911 and requested an ambulance.

"I think I'd better sit down awhile," he whispered.

Gently, she eased him down on the wet concrete. Working her jacket from her shoulders, she covered him with it. "Don't pass out on me, Betancourt."

"Wouldn't dream of it." His gaze met hers. "I was desperate to find you, Michelle. I'm glad you're okay. I would never have forgiven myself if something had happened to you."

Her heart quivered at the sight of those stormy gray eyes. She'd never forget the way he was looking at her. Oh, how she'd wanted him to love her.... "Shut up, Betancourt. You're obviously delirious with pain."

"My mind is more clear at this moment than it's ever been in my life." His voice was rough. He touched her cheek, but his fingertips were cold. "I've been trying to find you—"

"Don't waste your strength trying to woo me, Betancourt."

The rooftop door burst open and Cory Sanderson rushed out with his service revolver drawn. "Betancourt!" Holstering his gun, he rushed over and fell to his knees beside Philip. "How bad is he?" he demanded.

"Shoulder wound," Michelle said. "He's lost some blood."

She started to rise, but Betancourt stopped her. "Don't go. Please. Stay with me."

Cory sent her a silent message with his eyes, telling her to stay.

Michelle was still at Betancourt's side when the paramedics lifted him onto the gurney and transported him to Charity Hospital.

Chapter 15

Using his good arm, Philip knocked on the door, wondering if he should have left the flowers in the car. He wasn't sure what made him angrier, the incessant pain in his shoulder or the fact that Michelle hadn't come to the hospital in the three days it had taken him to recover from his gunshot wound and surgery. What the hell was he doing, bringing flowers to a woman who hadn't even bothered to call?

But Cory had told him that Michelle was there the first night. All night, in fact. Cory had also told him that when she'd finally left, she'd told him she wouldn't be back.

Philip figured he was an intelligent enough man to figure out why.

She didn't have the slightest idea that he was head over heels in love with her. Hell, he still couldn't quite believe it.

The door opened. Philip's chest compressed when he found himself looking into the gentle brown eyes he'd dreamed of too many times to count in the last three days. Her hair was pulled into an unruly ponytail and strands of damp hair clung to her face. A Tulane sweatshirt and cut-off denim shorts swept over curves he knew intimately now, but would never get enough of.

"You're out of the hospital."

It wasn't the response he'd hoped for, but it was a start. At least she hadn't slammed the door in his face. Definitely a step in the right direction.

"They let me out for good behavior." Not exactly sure of the protocol when a man brought a woman flowers, Philip shoved them forward. "These are for you. Uh…a house-warming gift."

She blinked at the mass of colorful blooms, then accepted the small vase. "They're beautiful. Thank you."

"I hope you like them."

"I love wildflowers."

An awkward silence descended. Not a good sign that she hadn't invited him inside. Damn.

She didn't meet his gaze. "How's your shoulder?"

"Broken clavicle. Should be like new in about eight weeks." He wanted to ask her why she hadn't come to see him in the hospital, but the words wouldn't come. He gazed through the open door at the boxes littering the small living room. "I see you're just about moved in. This neighborhood's a little better. I won't worry about you so much."

She fidgeted with the flowers. "How did you find me?"

"Cory plugged you into the computer for me." Philip's chest felt tight. He couldn't stop looking at her. Why couldn't she meet his gaze? Why hadn't she invited him in? "Can I come in?"

Stepping aside, she motioned him into the living room. "The place is a mess. I've been unpacking most of the day. I need to paint. The landlord's going to give me a break on rent if I spruce up the place for him."

Philip took in the details of the room, realizing the tiny apartment with its dusty lace curtains and worn cypress floors seemed more like a home than his empty house, and she wasn't even moved in yet. Michelle had a way of filling a place, of turning an empty shell into a home. Not with furniture or things, he realized, but with her presence. Her essence.

"I understand you got your memory back." He sat on the sofa.

Placing the vase of flowers on the coffee table, she took the wing chair across from him. "Yeah. Dr. Witt took me through another hypnosis session. I remembered everything about that night." She shivered, then looked down at her hands.

Philip saw that she was trembling, and wanted to go to her. Hold her. Tell her everything that was bursting to get out. "Are you all right?"

Her smile came too quickly. "I'm good. Really. I just landed a job with another firm. I resumed classes at Tulane." Her gaze met his. "What about you?"

I'm dying inside because I miss you. "Couldn't be better."

"When do you go back to work?"

After what had happened with Hardin Montgomery, Philip had given that very question a lot of thought. "I've decided not to go back. I thought it might be more interesting to go into the private sector. Open my own private investigation firm."

She smiled a thousand-watt smile. "You mean like *Magnum, P.I.?*"

The smile warmed him from the inside out. "Without the Ferrari."

Tense silence hung between them. When Philip could no longer stand it, he asked the question he hadn't been able to get out of his head since he'd come to after surgery. "Why didn't you come see me in the hospital, Michelle?"

Her shoulders went rigid. "I think you know the answer to that. I'm trying to be smart about this, Betancourt. Things are too impossible between us. They always have been."

"I don't know what's so impossible about two people who love each other."

Her jaw dropped, a small sound escaping her.

He almost smiled, but realized the moment wasn't right. Not yet.

"Those must be some painkillers they've got you on, Betancourt. Are you sure you should be driving?"

Rising from the sofa, he crossed to her and knelt before her. When she didn't look at him, he placed his fingers under her chin. A tremor went through her when he forced her gaze to his. "I love you, Michelle. I've loved you since the moment I first laid eyes on you. I love everything about you, inside and out, only I was too pigheaded to realize it. That's pretty cut-and-dried. Nothing complicated about it."

Michelle had known he would come to her eventually. Only she hadn't expected it to turn out like this. Just like Betancourt to throw a monkey wrench into the mix. She'd spent the last three days trying to exorcise this man from her heart, and here he was making her fall in love with him all over again.

"When I was sitting in that jail cell and you didn't come, I realized whatever was happening between us wasn't going to work." Swallowing the lump in her throat, she squared her shoulders and met his gaze. "It's okay. If I've learned anything in my life, it's that things don't always work out the way we want them to."

Something dark flashed in the gray depths of his gaze. "What's happening between us is called love, Michelle. It's not perfect. I'm sure as hell not perfect. I didn't mean to hurt you."

"You tried to tell me, Betancourt. You don't do relationships. You're married to your job…." Her voice trailed off when it dawned on her that he'd given up the career he'd devoted his life to.

"That was before I realized I'm crazy in love with you."

For an insane instant, she believed him. Her world tilted, shifted, began a slow, rolling tumble down a steep hill. Her heart beat so fast she felt as if it might pound its way right out of her chest. "Don't do this to me now."

"Don't what? Tell you how I feel? That I haven't been able to get you off my mind since the first time I saw you? That I can't sleep nights because I want you beside me and you're not there?"

"Don't lie to me."

"You know me better than that," he growled.

"I've got an arrest record, Betancourt. I've got an ex-con for a brother. I'm from the wrong side of the tracks in a very big way. I don't think I'm the kind of woman you want to spend the rest of your life with."

Grimacing, he raked an unsteady hand through his hair. "I don't give a damn about any of it, Michelle. None of it matters. It never did. I'm not going to walk away from this. I'm not going to walk away from you. I love you. God, I love you. All of you. Past. Present. And future. If anybody can make this work, we can."

Tears sprang into her eyes, and she blinked furiously. Not wanting him to see her cry, she rose. Couldn't he see that he was tearing her heart out by prolonging this?

Betancourt rose in turn, snagging her hand with his good arm. "I love you because of who you are, Michelle. I don't care about where you came from. What you've been through has made you exactly the kind of woman I want to spend my life with. Dammit, I'm not Frank Blanchard."

The words hit her with such force that she winced. "I know that."

"Look at me."

Choking back the tears, Michelle raised her chin, then faced him. "You're making this difficult."

"I'm sorry it hurts, but you've got to hear this. I won't let you go. I won't walk away without a fight." He wiped a tear from her cheek with his thumb. "I knew I couldn't live without you the day I let you walk away, the day I let you go into that cell. Part of me died that day. But at the same time, something else was born. Something powerful and good, and by God, I'm not going to let it slip away.

"It took almost losing you for me to realize how blind I've been. My heart stopped when I saw Derek try to push you from that building. That's when I knew I couldn't live the rest of my life without you." He paused, his gaze intense, jaws working. "I love you, and I think you know me well enough to know I'll never hurt you. I'll never lie to you. I'll never betray your trust. Maybe you don't want to hear this right now. Maybe you're not ready..."

Michelle didn't hear the rest of the sentence. Her resolve to protect her heart collapsed. Her defenses crumpled like dry earth. Her love for him burst free of its shackles. Suddenly she needed to feel his arms around her. Feel his heart beating against hers. With a sob, she reached out to him. "I've been trying to convince myself for three days that I'm not in love with you."

"Hell of a way to spend your time." His good arm wrapped around her. Pulling her against him, he rested his cheek against the top of her head. "You didn't succeed, did you?"

"No." Despite the tears, she smiled. "Why do you always have to be so difficult?"

"I thought that was what you loved about me," he said.

Happiness bubbled up inside her, making her feel giddy. "I love you, Betancourt. I love you so much I ache with it."

"But it's a good ache, right?"

"Best ache I ever had."

"I ache, too, Michelle. I ache for you day and night. I never want that to change. Maybe we should make it permanent."

Her heart stopped for two full beats, long enough for the blood to leave her head. "Betancourt, you're just full of surprises today. First flowers, then a proposal. What's a girl to do?''

Easing her to arm's length, he gazed steadily at her. ''Is that a yes or a no?''

''That's a definite yes.''

''You're smiling.''

''So are you. I love it when you smile.''

''Me, too.'' Again he brushed tears from her cheeks. ''You know, Michelle, I think I've got just the cure for that peculiar ache that's been ailing you.''

She laughed, marveling at the sheer joy loving this man brought her. ''I'll just bet you do.''

Grinning, he kissed her forehead, then the tip of her nose. ''Interested?''

''Think you can manage with that cast, Betancourt?''

''Might be fun trying.'' Another kiss landed on her temple. ''I don't think the cast will be a problem. We're pretty creative.''

Happiness burst through her, stunning her with the promise of a future as breathtaking and brilliant as a bayou sunrise.

''How long does it take to get married?'' he whispered.

''Well, I'd have to get dressed, get my sneakers on, brush my hair…. About an hour.'' Smiling, she nipped his earlobe.

''I'm not sure I can wait that long.'' His voice was low and dangerous.

''A judge or a priest?'' she asked.

''Whoever has an open schedule.'' Cupping her face in his hands, he pulled away, his stormy gaze boring into her. ''I'm going to spend the rest of my life showing you how a man loves a woman.''

''You've got my undivided attention.''

''And kids,'' he murmured. ''I've always wanted kids. Three of them. Two boys and a girl.''

''Two girls and a boy, and you've got a deal.''

He grinned and nipped her bottom lip. ''We can get married again in June. I mean, do it right. I know of this great little church in bayou country—"

"I'll be there, Betancourt."

"Promise me." He kissed her then, deeply, possessively. "Promise me, my love."

"I promise," Michelle said, and went down for the count.

*   *   *   *   *

THOSE MARRYING McBRIDES!:

The four *single* McBride siblings have always been unlucky in love. But it looks as if their luck is about to change....

Rancher Joe McBride was a man who'd sworn off big-city women. But his vow was about to be sorely tested when he met Angel Wiley. Don't miss A RANCHING MAN (IM #992), Linda Turner's next installment in her *Those Marrying McBrides!* miniseries— on sale in March 2000

And coming in June 2000, *Those Marrying McBrides!* continues with Merry's story in THE BEST MAN (IM #1010). *Available at your favorite retail outlet.*

Where love comes alive™

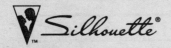

Look Who's Celebrating Our 20th Anniversary:

Celebrate 20 YEARS

"Working with Silhouette has always been a privilege—I've known the nicest people, and I've been delighted by the way the books have grown and changed with time. I've had the opportunity to take chances...and I'm grateful for the books I've done with the company. Bravo! And onward, Silhouette, to the new millennium."

—*New York Times* bestselling author
Heather Graham Pozzessere

"Twenty years of laughter and love... It's not hard to imagine Silhouette Books celebrating twenty years of quality publishing, but it is hard to imagine a publishing world without it. Congratulations..."

—International bestselling author
Emilie Richards

INTIMATE MOMENTS®
Silhouette®

presents a riveting 12-book continuity series:

A YEAR OF LOVING DANGEROUSLY

When dishonor threatens a top-secret agency, twelve
of the best agents in the world are determined to
uncover a deadly traitor in their midst. These brave
men and women are prepared to risk it all as they
put their lives—and their hearts—on the line. But
will justice…and true love…prevail?

**You won't want to miss a moment of the
heart-pounding adventure when the year
of loving dangerously begins in July 2000:**

*Available only from Silhouette Intimate Moments
at your favorite retail outlet.*

Where love comes alive™

SILHOUETTE'S 20TH ANNIVERSARY CONTEST
OFFICIAL RULES
NO PURCHASE NECESSARY TO ENTER

1. To enter, follow directions published in the offer to which you are responding. Contest begins 1/1/00 and ends on 8/24/00 (the "Promotion Period"). Method of entry may vary. Mailed entries must be postmarked by 8/24/00, and received by 8/31/00.

2. During the Promotion Period, the Contest may be presented via the Internet. Entry via the Internet may be restricted to residents of certain geographic areas that are disclosed on the Web site. To enter via the Internet, if you are a resident of a geographic area in which Internet entry is permissible, follow the directions displayed on-line, including typing your essay of 100 words or fewer telling us "Where In The World Your Love Will Come Alive." On-line entries must be received by 11:59 p.m. Eastern Standard time on 8/24/00. Limit one e-mail entry per person, household and e-mail address per day, per presentation. If you are a resident of a geographic area in which entry via the Internet is permissible, you may, in lieu of submitting an entry on-line, enter by mail, by hand-printing your name, address, telephone number and contest number/name on an 8"x 11" plain piece of paper and telling us in 100 words or fewer "Where In The World Your Love Will Come Alive," and mailing via first-class mail to: Silhouette 20th Anniversary Contest, (in the U.S.) P.O. Box 9069, Buffalo, NY 14269-9069; (In Canada) P.O. Box 637, Fort Erie, Ontario, Canada L2A 5X3. Limit one 8"x 11" mailed entry per person, household and e-mail address per day. On-line and/or 8"x 11" mailed entries received from persons residing in geographic areas in which Internet entry is not permissible will be disqualified. No liability is assumed for lost, late, incomplete, inaccurate, nondelivered or misdirected mail, or misdirected e-mail, for technical, hardware or software failures of any kind, lost or unavailable network connection, or failed, incomplete, garbled or delayed computer transmission or any human error which may occur in the receipt or processing of the entries in the contest.

3. Essays will be judged by a panel of members of the Silhouette editorial and marketing staff based on the following criteria:

   > Sincerity (believability, credibility)—50%
   >
   > Originality (freshness, creativity)—30%
   >
   > Aptness (appropriateness to contest ideas)—20%

   Purchase or acceptance of a product offer does not improve your chances of winning. In the event of a tie, duplicate prizes will be awarded.

4. All entries become the property of Harlequin Enterprises Ltd., and will not be returned. Winner will be determined no later than 10/31/00 and will be notified by mail. Grand Prize winner will be required to sign and return Affidavit of Eligibility within 15 days of receipt of notification. Noncompliance within the time period may result in disqualification and an alternative winner may be selected. All municipal, provincial, federal, state and local laws and regulations apply. Contest open only to residents of the U.S. and Canada who are 18 years of age or older, and is void wherever prohibited by law. Internet entry is restricted solely to residents of those geographical areas in which Internet entry is permissible. Employees of Torstar Corp., their affiliates, agents and members of their immediate families are not eligible. Taxes on the prizes are the sole responsibility of winners. Entry and acceptance of any prize offered constitutes permission to use winner's name, photograph or other likeness for the purposes of advertising, trade and promotion on behalf of Torstar Corp. without further compensation to the winner, unless prohibited by law. Torstar Corp and D.L. Blair, Inc., their parents, affiliates and subsidiaries, are not responsible for errors in printing or electronic presentation of contest or entries. In the event of printing or other errors which may result in unintended prize values or duplication of prizes, all affected contest materials or entries shall be null and void. If for any reason the Internet portion of the contest is not capable of running as planned, including infection by computer virus, bugs, tampering, unauthorized intervention, fraud, technical failures, or any other causes beyond the control of Torstar Corp. which corrupt or affect the administration, secrecy, fairness, integrity or proper conduct of the contest, Torstar Corp. reserves the right, at its sole discretion, to disqualify any individual who tampers with the entry process and to cancel, terminate, modify or suspend the contest or the Internet portion thereof. In the event of a dispute regarding an on-line entry, the entry will be deemed submitted by the authorized holder of the e-mail account submitted at the time of entry. Authorized account holder is defined as the natural person who is assigned to an e-mail address by an Internet access provider, on-line service provider or other organization that is responsible for arranging e-mail address for the domain associated with the submitted e-mail address.

5. Prizes: Grand Prize—a $10,000 vacation to anywhere in the world. Travelers (at least one must be 18 years of age or older) or parent or guardian if one traveler is a minor, must sign and return a Release of Liability prior to departure. Travel must be completed by December 31, 2001, and is subject to space and accommodations availability. Two hundred (200) Second Prizes—a two-book limited edition autographed collector set from one of the Silhouette Anniversary authors: Nora Roberts, Diana Palmer, Linda Howard or Annette Broadrick (value $10.00 each set). All prizes are valued in U.S. dollars.

6. For a list of winners (available after 10/31/00), send a self-addressed, stamped envelope to: Harlequin Silhouette 20th Anniversary Winners, P.O. Box 4200, Blair, NE 68009-4200.

Contest sponsored by Torstar Corp., P.O. Box 9042, Buffalo, NY 14269-9042.

ENTER FOR
A CHANCE TO WIN*

Silhouette's 20th Anniversary Contest

Tell Us Where in the World
You Would Like *Your* Love To Come Alive...
And We'll Send the Lucky Winner There!

Silhouette wants to take you wherever
your happy ending can come true.

Here's how to enter: Tell us, in 100 words or less,
where you want to go to make your love come alive!

In addition to the grand prize, there will be 200
runner-up prizes, collector's-edition book sets
autographed by one of the Silhouette anniversary
authors: **Nora Roberts, Diana Palmer,
Linda Howard** or **Annette Broadrick**.

DON'T MISS YOUR CHANCE TO WIN!
ENTER NOW! No Purchase Necessary

Silhouette ®

Where love comes alive™

Visit Silhouette at www.eHarlequin.com to enter, starting this summer.

Name:

Address:

City: State/Province:

Zip/Postal Code:

Mail to Harlequin Books: **In the U.S.**: P.O. Box 9069, Buffalo, NY
14269-9069; **In Canada**: P.O. Box 637, Fort Erie, Ontario, L4A 5X3

*No purchase necessary—for contest details send a self-addressed stamped envelope to:
Silhouette's 20th Anniversary Contest, P.O. Box 9069, Buffalo, NY, 14269-9069 (include
contest name on self-addressed envelope). Residents of Washington and Vermont may
omit postage. Open to Cdn. (excluding Quebec) and U.S. residents who are 18 or over.
Void where prohibited. Contest ends August 31, 2000.   PS20CON_R2